Delicious Zombie

WOL-VRIEY

Burning Bulb
PUBLISHING

Other Books By Wol-vriey:

The Bizarro Story of I
Meat Suitcase
Chainsaw Cop Corpse
Vegan Zombie Apocalypse
Boston Posh (Bud Malone #1)
Vegan Vampire Vaginas
Vagina Mundi
Melanie Nemesis Catchpole
Bizarro 101: A Basic Primer
Boston Corpse (Bud Malone #2)
Dr. Orgasm
Boston Lust (Bud Malone #3)
Pussy Transmission
Hell Dancer
Girls Are Not Smiling
Brainchew
Brainchew 2: Out of Their Heads
Blue Nightmares
Daria (An Erotic Nightmare)
Wet Bones
Mr. Ugly
Brutal
Evil
666
The Cleaverman
Perverse
The Virgin
The Book of Atrocities
The Final Girl
Women
Ratio of Brookes to Ashleys

Novellas and Short Stories By Wol-vriey

Big Trouble in Little Ass
Forever Ago Sunshine

Delicious Zombie

WOL-VRIEY

Burning Bulb
PUBLISHING

Delicious Zombie
By **Wol-vriey**

Burning Bulb Publishing
P.O. Box 4721
Bridgeport, WV 26330-4721
United States of America
www.BurningBulbPublishing.com

Cover artwork by Anton Rosovsky.

First Edition.

Paperback Edition ISBN: 978-1-948278-48-5

Printed in the United States of America.

CHAPTER 1

The Beginning

The current destroyed state of the world existed because porno actress Jessie Jizz was late for her anal bleaching.

The way the story went, Jessie drove to the beauty salon that afternoon and left her car, which had bad brakes, parked at the head of the salon's driveway. But the driveway happened to end at the top of a slight hill, and so once Jessie was out of the car—she was also too stoned to remember to apply the hand brake—the car rolled back downhill again and out through the front gates and into the street.

And then . . . Jessie's car rammed into an unmarked gray van that was transporting top secret biological materials.

The van cracked open . . . there was a fire . . . and the van's deadly contents spilled . . . boiled/bubbled off into the air.

The rest . . . was modern history.

***

Seated over by the front passenger side window of one of a convoy of trucks making their way southward through the deserted town of Johnstown, Pennsylvania, Ethan Hackman smiled to himself as he stared at the landscape of blackened ruins.

His girlfriend Zoe, who was seated between him and their driver Paula, nudged him in the ribs with her elbow. "Hey, baby, what you thinking about?"

Still smiling, Ethan turned to stare at her. "Huh?" The three of them rode alone in the black pickup truck, which carried crates of scientific equipment in both its backseat and carriage bed.

"You've a goofy grin on your face like something is amusing you about all this damage around here," Zoe explained.

Ethan scratched in his dark hair and shook his head. "No, I'm just remembering that Jessie Jizz bullshit AFI initially sold everyone about how the world got into its present mess."

Zoe nodded. "Well, they had to blame someone, and who better than someone both dead and sleazy. I couldn't stand her myself—tits were too big."

Remembering the late Jessica Jizz's humongous chest, Ethan laughed. "Honey, that must have been half the reason why they went with that story as the primary one back then. Less-endowed women like yourself would all take one look at Jessie and conclude that with boobs that size she had to be guilty of whatever she was being accused of; while the men would hope she was guilty and dream they were the ones legally assigned to discipline her."

Zoe elbowed him in the ribs and Ethan winced.

Paula tapped the steering wheel, took her eyes off the road ahead, and nodded. "Guys, personally I preferred that other rumor they spread."

"Which of them?" Zoe asked. "Back then there were at least six different fables circulating."

"Yeah," Ethan agreed. When the zombie apocalypse happened two years ago, new, supposedly true stories about its origins had emerged each week. "I remember there was even a completely ridiculous one about the space station malfunctioning and blowing up a radioactive plankton shipment."

Paula, her eyes once more on the road and the AFI vehicles ahead of them, shook her head. "I mean the one about Osama Bin Laden's son spilling a biological warfare agent into the sea."

Zoe giggled and then covered her mouth as if embarrassed. "Oh, that one. But that was the lamest rumor ever. I don't think anyone bought that version of events."

"And therein lay the genius of it," Paula said, licking her lips to moisten them as the air seemed dry out here. "Thing is—most of the other rumors spread about how things got the way they were put the blame solidly on us Americans . . ."

Zoe shook her head. "No, you're wrong, Paula. It varied by country."

"And you're exaggerating too," Ethan added. "They weren't *blaming* us, everyone was *grateful* to us. That's the damn problem."

Paula waved a dismissive hand. "Whatever, guys. My point is, that the Bin Laden story shifted responsibility for the zombie virus onto an exterior threat. It's always best to blame your enemy for shit caused by your own misdoings—ask any propagandist."

Zoe seemed to consider this argument seriously, but Ethan wasn't buying it.

"Whatever you say, girl," Zoe said finally, relaxing back on the seat as Paula stepped on their truck's brakes, because the grey AFI pickup truck ahead of theirs had just slowed at an intersection. "The way I see it, the government's evil aim was accomplished, which was what really mattered. No one ever suspected what had actually happened."

"Which was a whole lot worse than the final 'official' version of events," Paula said and then burst out laughing. She was a tall, full-figured woman with short black hair. Paula really fit the stolen religious robe that she wore. The Church of Zombie liked its ministers well-fed and jolly. ChoZo didn't go for the old time asceticism of Christianity and the other religions. Zombianity wasn't a religion of denying the flesh.

Ethan wasn't paying attention to the road ahead of them. ChoZo creeped him out big time. Church of Zombie . . . Zombianity . . . Zombook . . . the doctrine of the new flesh . . . His eyes, normally as bright and blue as the sky, now seemed full of gray storm clouds.

He glanced left at both Zoe and Paula, both young and in radiant good health, and then shifted his gaze outside of the vehicle and looked at the town they were passing through. Blackened by fire and totally abandoned by the apocalypse survivors, Johnstown was deader than a graveyard in the old days.

***

Yesterday, after making a late start from the AFI administrative offices in Springfield, Massachusetts, the convoy had spent the night in Saddle Brook, New Jersey.

Today too, the convoy had made another late start, leaving Saddle Brook after noon because they'd been waiting for a team of medical researchers from Rhode Island to join their traveling party. Once they set out, they had mostly been motoring along I-80, but a major pileup of crashed tankers on the interstate a short while ago had detoured them south through Johnstown.

Here in Johnstown, except for the noise of their small convoy—four trucks of scientific and research equipment, four trucks of supplies, three military trucks, and the obligatory AFI meat wagon at the rear—there was no indication of any life.

Of course there were rats everywhere, their eternally despised presence a marker for death. The rats were sleek and well-fed, their gorged state most likely resulting from feasting on the corpse flesh in the makeshift graveyards that now dotted the town. The rodents sat on the sidewalks and lounged fat and easy on glassless window ledges and watched the convoy pass as they licked their paws. They clearly weren't afraid of the convoy; their fear of man had passed with man's passing.

No men, no women, no children; definitely no pets of any kind. No birds in the sky or nearby trees. No zombies even, though occasionally they passed part of a skeleton—a human skull or maybe a dog's or a cat's ribcage. The facades of the buildings they passed were marked by fire, the sidewalks marked by dark patches that may or may not have been dried blood. Lawns, flowerbeds, and hedges had grown up in bounteous profusion, the unmown and uncropped vegetation rising and expanding to levels possibly unknown here since the sixteenth century. Both the walls of the houses and the stationary dust-covered vehicles that lined both sides of the roads they traversed were pocked with gunfire. Shattered glass was the rule where house windows and storefronts were concerned—souvenirs of when the cleanup crews began driving through and flushing the zombies out of those towns closest to the surviving centers of human civilization. The deadness seemed absolute. Like most towns, Johnstown was now merely a mausoleum to humanity's most recent fall from grace.

We sure have fallen far this time, Ethan thought. *It's not just our numbers that have plummeted to an all-time low, but our humanity has reduced as well and yet no one seems to care either way. The tradeoff is worth it, they all say. But . . . no, it isn't!*

The thought depressed him greatly and to take his mind off of things, he once more began retreating into his reverie about the much maligned porno star Jesse Jizz.

But then Paula hit the brakes again, bumping their vehicle a little, and Ethan found himself snapped back to full alertness. He pitched forward and just stopped short of ramming into the dashboard. He shoved himself back into the seat.

4

Zoe pushed strands of brown hair out of her eyes. "What're we stopping for, Paula? Zombies?"

At that suggestion, Ethan looked cautiously out of the window.

They'd stopped at a road junction. The convoy was headed north-to-south through the town and this turnoff came from the east. From Johnstown they intended to journey further south and connect to the I-76 and then the I-70 interstates, which (avoiding another unnavigable road obstruction like the one that had forced this detour), should see them reaching Athens, Ohio by early evening.

Ethan glanced at the GPS. The unit gave the connecting road as Prospect Street. Their current road was William Penn Avenue.

Zoe was also staring out of the pickup truck, trying to see around the military transport ahead of them. "I don't see any zombies out there."

"No, it isn't zombies," Paula explained after a glance at the GPS herself. "Security are just checking out the highway ahead because it curves. It's standard procedure on these trips. We don't wanna pass the intersection and discover we've been ambushed." With a blue index fingernail she traced the curved line on the GPS, which duplicated how the highway itself bent out of sight along the Conemaugh River. "Random zombie stragglers along the roadside aren't so much a problem as running into a herd of them in the middle of the highway, maybe even in the middle of the bridge that's coming up. Once that happens we'll be in deep shit."

Ethan nodded and dropped his hand to the holster at his waist. Beside him, Zoe did the same. For both of them this was an unconscious move. Paula, however, kept both of her hands on the steering wheel. Church of Zombie priests didn't carry weapons, just vials of holy oil extracted from the undead.

Ethan realized he was gripping his revolver and let go of it. At the moment, there seemed to be little danger, although the guards in the truck ahead of theirs were already spilling out into the street and taking up positions.

The heavily armed guards looked warily from side to side. Just like in the movies, zombies weren't either smart or fast, but they had the numbers advantage and except you got them in the head were ridiculously hard to kill. And the undead were hungry with a capital 'H.'

"I don't see why we go to all this trouble each time we reach a turnoff," Ethan grumbled, gesturing to the deserted woods and the few houses nearby. "There are no damn zombies anywhere here. The frigging roads are empty of them; we've not seen even so much as a sparrow since our arrival in this town." He frowned. "Yeah sure, I know this convoy is a scientific expedition and not equipped for dealing with any large zomb attack, but if we get into any major scrape with the undead we can simply radio for backup."

Zoe shook her head. "Too dicey. You're forgetting that in small towns like this, all the telecoms towers are dead. We can only call Massachusetts by sat phone and those calls are queued. First come, first served. AFI may run the world, but even we don't get phone priorities."

Paula nodded grimly as the black-uniformed men and women walked to and fro and conversed with each other via walkie-talkie. "Zoe's right, Ethan. If we hit trouble we could radio for military backup, but that might take hours to arrive and all those rescuers might find on their arrival here might be our corpses."

"So, the long wait keeps us alive, baby," Zoe said, squeezing Ethan's arm encouragingly. "Try to grin and bear it."

Ethan tried to smile. "Oh, I'm trying, but I'm so damned impatient to get this over with. I'm impatient to put an end to this craziness we call modern life."

"We are too," Paula said.

"We sure as hell are, baby," Zoe agreed with a grim look on her face.

***

Paula Neyman was a stone-cold killer. An ex CIA assassin and an expert with deadly weapons. Zoe had hinted to Ethan that beneath Paula's smiling exterior beat the heart of a serial killer, someone on a par with Ed Gein, but so far Ethan wasn't buying it; except for the one burst of violence he'd seen from Paula (which had revealed that she was more than up to the task ahead of them) their companion's behavior seemed average enough. Ethan easily pictured her as a business executive or a school principal if life hadn't turned belly-up.

"Fine, be fooled if you like, but I'm not buying that sweetness and cream act she's putting on," Zoe had told Ethan two nights ago. "I can't help but think she's liable to snap at any minute. Post-combat traumatic stress or something."

Zoe and Ethan had just finished making love and she was sitting up in their bed with the sheet pulled up over her breasts to fend off a late-spring chill that had blown into the bedroom.

"All I'm suggesting," she'd then gone on earnestly, "is that we watch our backs around her. It'll be the easiest thing in the world for her to turn traitor on us and sell us out to AFI. Exposing something as serious as what we've got planned is a sure-fire way to rapid promotion through the ranks of government."

Ethan had nodded sleepily. "Okay, noted. But, baby, she's Mickey's niece. And even if she wasn't, I'd still trust Mickey's judgment. He's certain to have run extensive background checks on anyone who'd be traveling with us."

"I'm just saying," Zoe had said, kissing him. "Hey, but no worries—if you won't watch your back I'll watch it for you. I can't have anyone killing the love of my life." Then she'd lain down again, snuggled close to him and pulled the sheet over them both.

***

Now Ethan stole a glance over at Paula. The woman was smiling and her concentration was on the road ahead, her full lips slightly parted. Ethan followed Paula's gaze and saw that the guards were hauling a pair of zombies towards the convoy.

One of the captured undead was a woman in a tattered red dress. The other zombie was a little kid of maybe six or seven years of age, who might or might not have been her son. The zombie kid was wearing filthy underpants and nothing else. Even from this distance the pair's bright green eyes were obvious, as was the greenish-purple skin veining that marked them both as infected.

The snarling pair had been expertly restrained by the guards, who were keeping well out of the way of their snapping teeth; one bite and you became a zombie too.

"I guess they don't want my blessing on those two," Paula said as two more guards approached the zombie pair, one rolling a portable guillotine ahead of him, the other pulling a body cart after him.

The zombie woman's head was shoved into the guillotine and its blade activated. Her head fell forward into the body cart and her body fell to the ground. There was some bleeding, but not much. Ethan flinched at the sound of her decapitation.

The kid was next for the same treatment, after which both headless zombie corpses were heaved into the body cart and it was rolled back into the meat wagon.

"And dinner for the world is served," Zoe commented without a touch of humor in her voice.

Ethan was silent, as was Paula. The three of them waited quietly until, having satisfied themselves that the highway ahead was safe for transit, the guards got back into their vehicles and the convoy set off again.

CHAPTER 2

First Contact. . .

Ethan had met Zoe Patterson a year ago.

Despite his moderately high standing in the AFI hierarchy, he hadn't met her at any of the social functions he was regularly invited to.

Ironically, he'd met her in a Boston supermarket. Specifically in the Meat Department of Cashstretch, where she'd been loudly complaining about something to the butchers while they attended to the other customers.

Behind the meat counter a large butcher chart hung on the wall. The chart showed a zombie body partitioned by dotted lines, with arrows leading from each section to info balloons that gave their names. 'Neck,' 'Chuck,' 'Brisket,' 'Shank,' 'Sirloin,' 'Flank,' and so on. At the counter's far end stood a life-sized plywood Church of Zombie cutout of a smiling young man projecting a speech balloon that read: "Digestion is Salvation."

This was a 'live service' counter. A headless zombie—in this case a skinned woman—was laid out for the shoppers, who, after studying the chart on the wall, pointed to which part of her corpse they wanted to purchase. Along with the other bodies scheduled for sale today, the zombie's innards had already been removed and separated into trays according to type—'Liver,' 'Kidney,' 'Stomach,' 'Meatballs,' and so on. Then there was the 'Head' area of the counter, where 'Brains,' 'Cheek,' 'Tongue,' 'Eyes,' and 'Nose' were also laid out. This section of the counter was manned by a different butcher, whose job was to scoop up what the customer wanted, weigh it and bag it.

Whatever wasn't sold today would either be minced and frozen or reprocessed into zombie spam.

This is undeniably wrong, Ethan often protested to himself. *This is so, so, so wrong.*

He found this part of the sales process both grisly and chilling. Watching a 'human' corpse being chopped up and bit by bit become nothing more than chunks that would soon be roasted or stewed . . .

He ate zombie meat too. There was no escaping it; if he didn't eat it, he would age, and if he began aging, both his religious beliefs and his dedication to AFI would be questioned; and he would lose his job. In addition AFI staff regularly received presents of 'specially butchered flesh.' Most of this 'specially butchered flesh' came from zombies that had suffered extensive physical trauma before their capture for processing, and whose bodies therefore wouldn't look nice and appetizing in butcher displays.

When he'd noticed Zoe, Ethan hadn't recognized her as a fellow AFI executive. His initial interest in the attractive and expensively dressed young woman near the counter had been entirely professional. He'd walked over to her and asked: "What's the problem, miss?"

The trio of butchers behind the counter were all attending to others and Zoe had turned to make some acid comment to him, but then she had recognized him.

"Hey, aren't you Ethan Hackman?"

He forced a smile. "Guilty as accused." Ethan was used to being recognized in public now. Along with the other Athens, Ohio research institute scientists who'd survived the zombie apocalypse, people viewed him as a 'founding father of modern society'; one of the daring modern Prometheuses who had stolen the 'fire of eternal life' from the gods. It was a notoriety he really hated, but he was learning to grin and bear it as best he could.

Ethan still hadn't figured out how himself, Mickey Sanderson, and the other scientists hadn't all wound up on death row, been summarily executed or lynched, or even just been thrown to the zombies without the benefit of a trial.

Instead, everyone regards us as heroes to emulate.

Beside Ethan and Zoe, a woman was telling the butchers. "I'd like some brisket please. As much as she has—my three teenaged sons eat so much nowadays, it's incredible."

In the wake of the customer's order a moment of silence passed between Ethan and his female companion. To Ethan it felt as if they were both mourning the past. He stole a quick look at the speaker. She looked like most of the other queuing women: blonde hair, firm young flesh, and a mid-twentyish youthful face though she was most likely in her middle forties or even her fifties.

And the teenagers she's concerned about will age up to look exactly like her. In ten years tops, it will be impossible to tell who's older between she and her offspring. Such is the miracle of the modern age.

A short distance away, totally unconcerned about this most basic and drastic of changes to the foundation of their world, shoppers walked back and forth and purchased cornflakes, ear pods and cellphones, bottles of wine, stationary supplies and computer accessories, bed sheets and batteries, televisions, soya milk (seeing as the world was mostly out of cows now), and packs of the egg substitute Albumen Plus.

And then Zoe asked Ethan, "But . . . but what are *you* doing here?"

"Just a routine quality control check." He pointed to the zombie on the counter. One of the butchers was handling the customer's order, expertly slicing the zombie woman's breasts off of her chest to expose the muscle beneath. The man dropped the severed breasts into a tray. The fat globules in the breasts had a prominently green color.

Zoe's eyebrows lifted. "Ah yeah, I remember now—you're with AFI's quality control division." She gestured at the zombie being butchered, the butcher now slicing off her pectoral muscles. "But don't your subordinates handle that for you?"

Ethan nodded. "Sure they do. At least I hope they do. But every two months or so, I drive around town to have a look-see for myself." He gestured at the lines of women the butchers were attending to. "We don't want anyone getting food poisoning." He then pointed to the life-sized Church of Zombie cutout at the far end of the counter and said in a raised voice, "Since digestion is salvation, I think indigestion qualifies as damnation and going to hell? At least that's my take on it."

Zoe laughed at that, as did the butchers and some of the other shoppers at the counter.

In Ethan's mind his companion's pretty face had begun resolving itself into that of someone he knew. He'd met her before, he was certain of it. Nowadays he met lots of attractive women at parties, but the hurt of losing his family still stabbed at his heart and extinguished his desire for new female companionship.

The world is so insecure nowadays, he often told himself. *I don't want to gain another dose of happiness just to lose it too.*

Other than laughing at it, Zoe had not responded to his last statement and he had the uncomfortable impression that she was sizing him up.

"So, what's the problem you're having here?" he asked her.

She shrugged and whispered to him, "Oh, nothing major. I don't know if it's me or the meat, but my beef-flavor additive don't seem to cut it anymore. Same goes for chicken flavor. I'm almost wishing I had real beef to eat again."

"Well, zombie meat tastes better than just about everything else." He realized he was whispering back, and then realized why: in this most public of places, her own whispers had unconsciously drawn him into a private conspiracy. He also realized that he was enjoying this feeling of sharing something with her. She wasn't saying anything illegal—mild public complaints weren't frowned on, but he liked the feeling that she seemed to be confiding in him.

"Oh, don't give me that crap, Ethan," she replied. "You know exactly what I mean."

"No, I don't," he joked. "You'll have to explain louder. Or better still, how about you do it over dinner tonight?"

She frowned and at first he'd thought he'd offended her and she would turn him down. Then she said: "Aw, I was supposed to attend a cocktail party with dad tonight. But I'll cancel. The party is certain to be boring as hell anyway."

Then raising her voice to a normal level again, she'd smiled at him. "So, okay, it's a date then. Oh, and by the way, I'm Zoe Patterson."

That was when Ethan realized that he'd just asked Senator Patterson's daughter out on a date.

Unaware that an alliance had just been formed that would have major implications for the modern world, the customers at the butcher's counter continued making their purchases. The woman who'd ordered briskets collected her bag of meat, and next up, as if the shoppers had made a silent conspiracy to strip the dead woman (or 'thing') on the counter, the next woman in line said, "I'll have the zombie's breasts, please. Oh, and also ribs—lots of ribs."

Normally, Ethan would have cringed at what she'd said. But at the moment, he was captivated by Zoe Patterson and was busy taking down her phone number.

***

That night's dinner had led to another date and another, and in a fortnight the pair of them were lovers.

It didn't take long for Ethan to realize that his new girlfriend was very unconventional. Most importantly, she didn't share her father's political convictions about zombies.

"I'm not religious," Zoe protested, "But I'd rather grow old gracefully and die that extend my life by cannibalism. Oh, sure I've got rights; but what about the rights of all those poor others?"

The 'rights' she was referring to was the UN's recent addition of the 'Right to live forever' to humanity's list of human rights.

Zoe's father, Senator Trevor Patterson was a favorite of the Church of Zombie, and was constantly pushing for stricter legislation concerning the zombies. The most recent (back then) being plans to corral the undead in 'zombie reservations.'

"Because I for one see no reason why good American farmland should go to waste just because some herd animals are running wild now," Senator Patterson (Missouri) had said during a TV interview. "Personally, and I believe I speak for most Americans when I say this, I feel we need to recolonize our country, just like the original settlers did. We owe it to ourselves and we owe it to our children's futures. Remember this is real life, folks, not some dystopian teen movie!"

"Dad's got his eye on the presidency," Zoe had said disgustedly. "I've tried to tell him to forget it, but he won't have it. He thinks he's got a fair shot at being elected and his flunkies keep egging him on."

She and Ethan had just moved in together and had watched the interview in their apartment.

Ethan disagreed with her point of view. "Recent opinion polls give your dad a good chance. Him championing AFI's plan to start rebreeding household pets from the surviving cats and dogs is pure political genius. We've still two years to go before people vote, so—"

"Dad hasn't got a snowflake-in-hell chance of winning," Zoe interrupted. "President Harper is going to be reelected. I'm just waiting for daddy to fall flat on his face, so I can tell him 'I told you so.'"

Zoe's father was single, her mother having succumbed to breast cancer the year before the zombie outbreak. In Zoe's mind, boredom and loneliness were her father's reasons for wanting to rule America.

"I disagree," Ethan had said. "The pet reintroduction scheme is brilliant and is certain to endear him to the public. Also, your dad's making the right moves by aligning himself with ChoZo."

Zoe 'hmmphed,' reached for the remote, and switched off the TV.

"Honey, in this case you're so dead wrong it's a wonder you've got a shlong," she said while unbuttoning her top.

"What makes you say that?" Ethan asked as Zoe's cute little breasts popped out of her pink blouse. She clearly had only one thing on her mind now, and he wanted to either win or lose their political argument before he too only had one thing on his own mind (which judging by the sudden tight feeling in the crotch of his shorts would soon be the case). "If things continue as they are, I see a good chance of your dad becoming our next president. VASL are already demonizing President Harper, likening him to the biblical Devil. That is certainly going to hurt our current prez, particularly down in the Bible Belt—well, what remains of it anyway."

Zoe giggled, got up from the couch they were sharing, and began rolling down her black leotards. "Baby, you're overlooking the fact that most of the Christians in the south have abandoned the faith and are now hardcore Zombelievers." She twirled her panties, their crotch wet, on her fingers, then pulled back the waistband and snapped them at Ethan. "True or not, Prez Josh Harper takes credit for giving the human race the eternal life that they once all believed they had to die to achieve. There are enough people who think he's God or at least God's best friend, to completely negate any proof the Vegan and Seafood Lobby may present to the contrary that he's the Devil. Now mankind know for sure that they will live forever, even if it is at the expense of eating their one-time friends, lovers, work colleagues, and families. What more do you want from a leader?"

"Honey, your dad also—"

He hadn't finished making his argument, because Zoe had stuck her panties in his mouth so he couldn't speak. He tasted her juices on his tongue and the musk of her lust drifted from his mouth to his nostrils and brain.

"Oh, forget my father's doomed presidential ambitions," she'd said. "Dad's got less chance in the next presidential race than if he was riding a dead horse." She winked at Ethan, bent over and slapped her ass. "And you, baby, come on into the bedroom and ride this very much alive filly. I assure you that tonight you'll be riding a sure-fire winner."

Ethan had leapt to his feet and followed her. His penis seriously motivated him. It felt hard enough to snap in two.

CHAPTER 3

Mr. Tricks at the Hog Compound

Even from a distance one could smell the corpses.

The air out here in the Springfield, MA southern neighborhood of Sixteen Acres should have been just as sweet smelling as elsewhere in the city, but as one reached the Hog Family compound, it took on a taint of decay and rot; and, down deep at a more psychic level, a reek of intense evil.

As if one was approaching one of Satan's residences on earth.

Seated in the rear of his black limousine, AFI (or Ambrosia Flesh Incorporated) executive Mr. Tricks grimaced as his chauffeur Vernon steered the car towards the gore-splattered front gate at the end of the street. "Looks like the Hog's have been redecorating," he said.

The black chauffeur didn't reply, but his eyes widened in fright. What his employer was referring to was the new 'writing' affixed to either side of the front entrance. 'HOG FAMILY' the writing merely said, with one word on either side of the entrance, but the letters were made from human body parts, human arms and legs that had been broken and bent into the shape of letters. The grisly human letters were rotting and in some places, where birds and rats had gotten to them, stripped to the bones.

Mr. Tricks shook his head as Vernon drove into the compound, the gate having been left open in anticipation of their arrival. *Something really has to be done about this lot*, he thought.

Mr. Tricks of course wasn't actually named 'Mr. Tricks.' However, everyone he worked with—superiors and inferiors—called him this because as boss of AFI Intelligence, he had consistently proved himself expert at handling and defusing tricky situations. Even some of his superiors had forgotten his real name.

The Hog Family compound was a depressing place. The entire yard was dotted with human bones. Like someone had unearthed an ancient ossuary.

Vernon drove up to the compound's main building and parked.

"Here we are, boss," the black chauffeur said respectfully. Mr. Tricks could hear the fear in his voice.

He looked out of the car window. As on their previous trips to this place, Vernon had parked about twenty yards from the compound's quartet of buildings. Mr. Tricks didn't blame him; he too had no real desire to witness what went on inside there.

Vernon's lucky. In my case, I have no choice. I'm here on serious AFI business. Possibly the most serious AFI business ever.

In the meantime, the chauffeur had gotten out of the driver's seat to open the rear door for him. Mr. Tricks got out and nodded to the man. "I'll be back in about thirty minutes, Vernon." Then, unable to resist making a morbid joke, he added, "But if you suspect the Hogs have eaten me, radio for backup."

"Yeah, boss." Vernon nodded nervously, but he wasn't looking at his employer while doing so, and his dark skin also seemed to have grown several shades lighter in the short period he'd been standing outside of the limousine, which made Mr. Tricks turn to follow the black man's gaze, which at the moment was directed past his right shoulder.

"Oh . . . shit!" Mr. Tricks said and felt like vomiting. About twenty feet away from them, affixed to a wide upright wooden board which was itself secured to the wall of the next building, hung a corpse. The dead man had been stripped naked and had apparently been used for target practice. Large chunks of his body had been blown away by shotgun fire; his torso was a mess of holes and his guts had all plopped out of him and now lay in a fly-covered pile on the floor between his legs.

After regaining control of his emotions, Mr. Tricks carefully scrutinized what remained of the dead man's face. But no, he didn't recognize him. Had to be just another unfortunate who'd pissed either Hogwash or Gorehound off. Though just as evil as their menfolk, the Hog girls were more likely to use knives on their victims. Jenni and Scary would either have skinned this guy or castrated him, and the dead man still had all his family jewels intact. So it had definitely been the guys who'd had their fun with him.

Sighing, Mr. Tricks set off for the porch of the main house. He was only halfway there when the front door opened and Scary stepped out.

"Hey there, we've been expecting you!" she greeted brightly. Then she looked down at her watch for a moment. "It's two p.m. now. You said you'd be here two hours ago."

"Work delays," he explained as he climbed the porch steps. "And the phone wouldn't connect."

Scary Hog was a petite woman. Mid-twenties, with long black hair and large gray eyes. Her denim clothes were bloodstained and the blood was wet, which Mr. Tricks took to be a bad sign indeed. She had fresh blood on her hands too.

Scary noticed his gaze on her clothes. "Oh, we're just having a little fun—you know, to kill the boredom till you got here." She turned to reenter the house and waved him on. "Come on in, the others are waiting."

***

The rest of the Hog Family—Jenni, Hogwash, and Gorehound, were gathered around a low table in their living room on the top of which another man had been bound and gagged. Though this man was still alive, Hogwash was busy sawing off his right arm at the elbow, while his sister and her husband watched, and while their captive's eyes seemed about to pop out of his face from the sheer agony he was in. Full and empty bottle of wines littered the floor and spoke of much drinking happening in here.

Mr. Tricks grimaced at the sight. The bound man had been tightly, expertly restrained and could only gape helplessly and mumble as Hogwash worked on him. Blood spilled from his arm, but the Hogs had applied a tourniquet above his elbow, so he wasn't about bleeding to death on them. Not yet anyway.

"Hey, finish up with that," Scary said as she and their guest walked over to them. "The boss is here."

The other three looked up from their grisly doings.

"Hey, boss," Jenni greeted.

Jenni was Scary's physical opposite, a tall and ungainly blonde.

"Hey, Mr. Tricks, how's tricks?" Hogwash joked. "Just hold on a minute while we get this jerk's arm off." That said, he and Gorehound—two large muscular men, with identical dark buzz cuts and both covered with tattoos—grabbed hold of the almost severed forearm and wrenched it, so that the bone cracked and the flesh and skin shredded and the forearm detached completely from its owner, who immediately fainted from the agony.

"What did he do?" Mr. Tricks asked them, simply out of the need to say something. He felt sick watching this. He wished he was outside in the car with Vernon and already speeding far away from here.

But I work for Ambrosia Flesh Incorporated and they need this group of sociopathic bounty hunters to help fix their latest crisis. So now here I am watching them a tear a guy's arm off.

Hogwash handed the severed forearm to his sister and then pointed to his girlfriend who still stood beside Mr. Tricks. "We were at a bar drinkin' last night and he pinched Scary's ass."

Mr. Tricks looked down at the petite Scary, who nodded back up at him. "We figured if he didn't have any hands, he'd be unable to grope any more women."

Gorehound laughed at the grimace on their visitor's face. "Brothers and sisters, we need to remember that the boss here don't like violence . . ."

"No, he leaves that dirty part of his dirty business to us to handle," Jenni agreed with a cold smirk. "He thinks we're psychos, but he don't dare tell us."

Hogwash walked over to Mr. Tricks, and laughing, slapped him on the back with one bloody hand while gesturing at their fainted victim with the other one. "Don't worry, boss. We ain't gonna kill the sleazy sonofabitch. We'll let him go after we cut his other arm off."

"Listen, guys," Mr. Tricks said. "Jokes aside, you know I'm not your real boss. Like you all, I'm just another employee of Ambrosia Flesh Incorporated. And you know the higher-ups have reservations about how you conduct your business."

Hogwash pondered on that for a moment. "Then . . . why you here again?" he asked with genuine puzzlement in his voice.

"Yeah, I don't think you drove out all this way just to inform us that we're fired," Jenni agreed, dropping the severed forearm on the floor and wiping her bloody hands clean on her sky-blue Church of Zombie tee shirt. Hers was about the only religious statement in the room, but there was a tattered copy of Zombook—the Church of Zombie bible—lying on one of the end tables. Mr. Tricks assumed the Zombook had been the property of one of the Hogs' victims; as had also most likely been Jenni's tee shirt.

"We got a big problem," Mr. Tricks told the four of them. "At least we think we do. But we're not a hundred percent sure of it." Then, seeing that the hapless groper on the table was coming to again, and not willing to witness him losing his left forearm, he quickly suggested: "Look, can we talk someplace else? I won't be able to concentrate on what I've got to say if I have to keep staring at that piece of shit you've got tied to your table."

Hogwash nodded. "Sure, come on outside, we'll sit under the canopy out back."

***

Out back was worse that in the living room. There were three armless corpses lying beside the wall, one of them with no eyes. A group of buzzards that had been busily pecking away at the bodies took to the air at Tricks' and the Hogs' approach.

A short distance from the corpses lay a severed human head—not a skull yet, still in 'wet and stinking and festering-with-maggots' condition. The arms belonging to the corpses were most likely amongst those used to write the HOG FAMILY on the wall outside the compound.

At this rate, looks like everyone in Springfield will soon be guilty of groping Scary's almost nonexistent ass. And the guy with no eyes, was he ogling her or what?

Mr. Tricks hid a shrug. It came with the territory. The Hog Family were an insane bunch but they got the job done. These were violent times and the Hogs didn't shy away from doing whatever was necessary. They charged high but were more than worth it.

The men sat around the table beneath the brown garden umbrella, while the women fetched beer and sandwiches from the kitchen. Mr. Tricks made certain to position himself facing the house and not the corpses.

"So, what's this problem of yours, Tricks?" Hogwash asked when all three men were seated. "On the phone you sounded like someone had shoved a stick of dynamite up your butt." Hogwash was the Hog Family's accepted leader. He had the best brains and the others all deferred to his judgment.

For a moment before speaking, Mr. Tricks considered the faces of the two men sitting opposite him. Both looked young and in the prime of life—late twenties or early thirties at most. But he knew for a fact that Hogwash was actually forty-nine years old, and Gorehound fifty-two. Same went for their womenfolk: Jenni was forty-seven but looked twenty-five, while Scary, who was actually forty-five, also looked like she was in her mid-twenties. And all these age-reversal changes had occurred in the past year-and-a-half.

Same goes for me too, Mr. Tricks thought. *The rejuvenating properties of zombie meat really are something. I'm sixty years old now, but look and feel thirty, and my brain and libido and everything else has regressed in time to put me back in my prime, just like it has everyone else. And it's the same thing all around the world.*

Vernon, his chauffeur, was seventy-two, but looked twenty.

Mr. Tricks smiled at the thought of the modern miracle that AFI had wrought, and then asked his two companions: "You guys familiar with the name Mickey Sanderson?"

"Rings a bell but I can't clearly place it," Hogwash replied. He looked at Gorehound. "Name mean anything to ya?"

Gorehound was about shaking his head, but then he said, "Hey, ain't he that Zombie Research guy?"

The pair looked at Mr. Tricks who nodded back at them. "Yeah, that's him. Mickey Sanderson, head of the Zombie Research Institute in Agawam."

Hogwash and Gorehound both looked puzzled. "But Dr. Sanderson's a national hero," Gorehound said. "So what's your problem with him, boss?"

Mr. Tricks considered waiting till the women joined them beneath the parasol, but then decided that the men could fill them in later, or they could play catch-up when they arrived from the kitchen.

"Okay," he explained, "recently Sanderson's been acting shady. Thing is, we don't know what he's up to. But he's been inquiring into stuff he isn't supposed to be interested in, and there have been several hacks into the AFI database which, while not directly traceable to him, bear a similarity to his own inquiries."

"What sort of inquiries is he making?" Gorehound asked.

"*That* is the problem," Mr. Tricks replied. "On the surface, it's nothing serious. Sanderson is merely asking about AFI expansion plans into the interior—into Ohio, Kentucky, Indiana and Illinois, all four states of which were abandoned to the zombies two years ago, but which are currently being reclaimed." He paused at an abrupt noise from the house, then, looking up and seeing that it was just the screen door slamming behind Scary and Jenni as they emerged onto the back porch with trays of food and beer, he relaxed again.

"But I'm suspicious," he went on. "AFI pays me to be suspicious. Sanderson's interest in our expansion might be innocent, but it's none of his concern—his job is food processing, so why is he suddenly so interested in our attempts to reclaim zombie-occupied territory?"

Hogwash moved his chair slightly so Scary could place her tray on the table and then sit beside him. "But doesn't AFI's expansion involve creating new supply lines for zombie flesh? That's certain to concern him."

Mr. Tricks mouthed his silent thanks to Jenni as she placed a sandwich and a cold beer in front of him, and then replied, "No, I've already considered that explanation. If it was just that that Dr. Sanderson wanted to know, he could simply ask directly. He's an important enough figure that the information would have been made available to him. Indeed, he'd be consulted—I think he actually was consulted."

"What's the matter?" Jenni asked, sitting down in the final empty chair beneath the parasol.

"The boss thinks Doc Sanderson is about to betray AFI."

Jenni looked surprised. "Dr. Sanderson of Zombie Research? Now why the hell would he do that?"

Scary nodded around a mouthful of sandwich. "You know, even after all this while of eating 'em, I still can't get around how delicious zombie meat tastes. It's like I could eat them forever and—"

"You *are* gonna be eatin' them forever, woman," Gorehound said with a laugh. "But let's let the boss Mr. Tricks get through with his explanation of what he wants to do about the bad doctor."

Mr. Tricks had begun eating his own sandwich, a thick slab of spiced meat, pickles, and tomatoes between thin slices of dark bread. He had to agree with Scary. Zombie meat really did taste delicious. It wasn't anything like beef or chicken, or even like pork, which human flesh was supposed to taste like. No, zombie meat was in a class all of its own; its taste addictive in a different way from narcotics. And then there were all its health benefits to consider.

He paused to drink some beer. "Sorry, guys, but you're gonna have to wait till I'm through eating this. Tastes too damn good to interrupt with biznezz." Then he remembered Vernon. "Oops, I don't think my driver had any lunch yet."

Scary waved a hand at him. "No problem—we already fed Vernon." She laughed. "He seemed very scared of Jenni and I."

"But I like people being scared of me," Jenni added, her eyes flashing dangerously. "I like it a lot." She smiled coldly at her husband Gorehound, who was chewing away at his own zombie sandwich. "Honey, you never see men grabbing my butt the way they do to Scary."

Gorehound paused in mid-chew. "Yeah, that's right."

"They grab my ass 'cos I'm little and they think they can get away with it," Scary retorted.

Mr. Tricks nodded at the surreal conversation and finished eating his sandwich.

Jenni scared him too. Tall, slovenly and verging on fat, she nonetheless gave off the aura of a shark. All of the Hog family gave off that same vibe of constantly needing someone to hurt. He resisted the urge to turn and look at the armless corpses behind him. (However, he didn't need a visual reminder, their stink of death filled the backyard.) Instead he picked up his beer and took a long gulp from the can while Jenni placed another aromatic and tantalizing zombie sandwich on his plate.

The sudden noise of flapping wings behind Mr. Tricks made him turn around. He instantly regretted doing so—one of the vultures was just pulling a corpse's eye from its socket, extending it out on its decaying nerve cord. The grisly sight coincided with a breeze blowing the stink over their way.

Feeling like he was going to throw up, Mr. Tricks quickly returned his attentions to his hosts. "What's really got me so suspicious about Sanderson's inquiries is the fact that the old AFI research facility where the zombie virus was accidentally created is situated out that way—in Athens, Ohio to be exact. Sanderson was head researcher at the facility."

Hogwash gestured with his beer can, his eyes cold. "Yeah, so we heard." His brow creased thoughtfully. "So, boss, . . . you think Doc wants something he forgot there, something dangerous?"

Scary giggled. "You think maybe he's in league with those Vegan and Seafood Lobby idiots?"

"I don't know," Mr. Tricks admitted. "And that's what bothers me. But Mickey Sanderson is a genius, a very brilliant man, and his work at the Zombie Research Institute makes me think he might be after some kind of a poison . . ."

"A poison?" It was Gorehound who'd asked the question. "What the hell would Doc want a poison for?"

Mr. Tricks shrugged. "There is one possibility; and of course, I don't mean a real poison in the sense of something that will kill. Assuming Sanderson's ideology *has* been corrupted by the Vegan and Seafood Lobby, he might be after something like a chemical that permanently alters the taste of zombie flesh, something that renders it too bitter for human consumption."

Hearing this didn't please Mr. Tricks' listeners.

Hogwash opened his mouth to ask a question, but Mr. Tricks preempted the query by saying, "Obviously, if we can't eat the zombies . . . anyway, Sanderson's actions have the AFI's board of executive directors worried."

"What's our part in this?" Jenni asked.

"We want to know exactly what Sanderson is up to, and fast at that. A convoy of AFI vehicles departed for Athens, Ohio yesterday morning. It's a previously scheduled scientific trip—not something Sanderson had any hand in planning. But, like I just mentioned, Athens, Ohio is exactly where the abandoned AFI research facility is situated." He frowned and now found it impossible to keep his unease from revealing itself in the tone of his voice: "Needless to say, if Sanderson does have something traitorous planned, this is the perfect time for him to spring his surprise on us. He'll never have a better opportunity to betray us."

Hogwash nodded. Crumpling his empty beer can in a huge and hairy fist, he leaned forward over the table. "Boss, how far can we go with Sanderson?"

Mr. Tricks sighed. "As far as you need to, to find out what he's up to. AFI has deemed Sanderson expendable. There are lots of other national heroes we can replace him with. And if we can't find anyone suitable, we'll make ourselves some." He raised a finger to make a point. "But . . . if you have to get rough and bloody, make certain you don't leave any witnesses. AFI don't need the hassle of explaining to the public why Mickey Sanderson was executed."

Mr. Tricks hated the sadistic gleams that now entered the Hog Family members' eyes on hearing that they'd have free rein to hurt Sanderson. Gorehound and Jenni both grinned, while Scary actually licked her lips.

Mr. Tricks personally liked Mickey Sanderson, but the security and safety of the world always came first.

And you definitely can't make eggnog without breaking eggs.

Dr. Mickey Sanderson was disposable. Sanderson had brought this on himself. The reports of the man's actions didn't just have the top AFI executives worried; Nervousness at the top was at an all-time high; like someone had pushed the global corporation's panic button.

Everyone's concerned and I need to confirm if there really is cause for concern, Mr. Tricks mused to himself as he reached down for his fresh zombie sandwich. The delicious odor of its pale, veined meat managed to cut through the backyard's corpse stink. He even found it possible to ignore the noise of the buzzards' feeding on the nearby corpses.

With the basic job spelled out, everyone now concentrated on finishing their meal. Mr. Tricks ate his sandwich in large bites, savoring the chicken-flavored flesh while chewing reflectively, and washing it down with gulps of beer.

Then, when lunch was over, everyone hunched over the table to discuss the finer details of the job:

"So . . . how soon do you want us to visit Doc?"

"Best you go see Sanderson today. Tomorrow he's leaving for a conference in Washington. But he's home today—resting in his house, not working in the office. I confirmed that before coming here."

"We'll go see him right away then . . ."

CHAPTER 4

Athens

The city of Athens, Ohio was located in a river valley, surrounded by hills covered with trees up to their peaks. On all sides of its buildings trees rose skyward on gentle slopes.

"Welcome to the birthplace of the death of mankind," Paula said, her lips tightening into a grimace.

"Oh, don't be so damn gloomy," Zoe immediately countered, an irritated look on her face. "I'd prefer to think of this place as 'humanity's last hope.'"

But Ethan agreed with Paula. This city they'd just driven into screamed to him of the death of mankind.

To him, death was represented even by the lush spring landscape. Because zombies had green eyes, the color green no longer symbolized life to Ethan.

***

The AFI convoy had turned off the I-70 at Zanesville and headed south. And then, on being informed by the advance team who'd arrived here a fortnight ago that the I-33/I-50 interstate that skirted the city of Athens on its east side was blocked off, the convoy had decided to drive directly through Athens instead. (The advance team was mainly comprised of security men, whose job was to secure and barricade the camp and prepare it for the arriving scientists)

Their destination was the OHIO Museum Complex and Kennedy Museum of Art in the south part of the city, down across the Hocking River, but still merely a figurative stone's throw from the Ohio University campus in the north part of Athens, where Ethan and the other scientists expected to find sufficient infrastructural equipment to work with.

Assuming they could clear the zombies out of the place, of course. Otherwise, they'd be stuck with breaking into the university laboratories and carrying the required equipment back to their OHIO Museum base.

***

"It's amazing how much the world has changed in just two years," Zoe said while gesturing around them as the convoy of vehicles rolled down a central highway.

"It really is," Ethan agreed. Prior to the zombie holocaust, he'd lived and worked here in Athens and returning now was a bittersweet experience.

No AFI cleanup had occurred here in Athens and the reasons for the city's abandonment were evident—stripped human skeletons lay all over the streets and on the sidewalks; desiccated corpses filled cars that had crashed in their efforts to flee.

The convoy rolled forward over a carpet of human bones. Behind the vehicles, zombies shambled into sight through open doorways.

"And so it was that the zombie holocaust turned domestic animals into endangered species," Zoe said.

Animal skeletons lay everywhere—mostly those of household pets—cats and dogs that hadn't realized their owners now loved them in an entirely different way from before—as food. The bleached pet bones were scattered all over the place; skeletons pecked clean by the ubiquitous rats and crows and vultures.

Even now, Paula drove past a lone crow on the sidewalk pecking in the eye sockets of a dog's skull, vainly looking for meat; or maybe the bird was sharpening its teeth in anticipation of a feast now that the convoy had arrived in town? The expression in its brown eyes as it looked the passing vehicles over certainly gave Ethan that impression.

Ethan winced at the sights. He felt tears coming to his eyes and blinked them away.

"Are you okay?" Zoe asked him on noticing his facial expression.

He nodded. "Sort of. I'm just remembering . . ."

She nodded sympathetically. He was clearly remembering his wife Holly and their daughter Jennifer. Holly and Jenny Hackman had been traveling back home from visiting Holly's parents in Connecticut when the plague had struck. Their car had been found a week later, turned over, and with its windows shattered and its interior stained with blood. Four-year-old Jenny's gnawed left hand had been wedged under the front seat.

Ethan hadn't been the same since that day. The only reason insanity hadn't claimed him after his wife's and daughter's deaths was because by the next day the entire world had seemed to be going insane. Everyone seemed to be dying, so much so that his family's passing was merely another unfortunate statistic in a sea of many.

As the convoy accelerated, Zoe leaned over and kissed him. "Baby, you can rest assured that Holly and Jenny are in a better place now," she whispered. "And I don't mean that lightly. Whatever the afterlife is like, it has to be better than this messed-up world we have now."

Ethan nodded his gratitude. Meeting and falling in love with Zoe Patterson a year ago was the other reason he'd kept his sanity after the loss of his family. He knew Zoe understood how he felt; she'd told him that the zombies had eaten her teenaged brother while she'd looked on, powerless to save him. They'd been safe in hiding, but then her brother had run out of the house to rescue a dog, and the zombies had eaten both he and the dog.

Ethan's guilty conscience over Holly and Jenny's deaths was something he'd never escape from or come to terms with, but Zoe helped him manage the past.

Here in Athens the undead were everywhere. They shambled into sight at the noise of the convoy's approach and attempted to reach the vehicles, but they weren't fast enough. They were like a New Orleans jazz funeral procession, if they—rotted clothes and all—were the ones being buried. Men and women of all shapes and sizes, and kids of all ages; even toddlers with the same striped skin and those glowing tell-tale green eyes. Undead babies crawled in the rearguard; they were naturally slower.

"Judging from the number of zomb out in the streets today, it seems like the entire townsfolk are still living here," Zoe mused.

"And they all look so damn healthy too," Paula said, tapping blue fingernails on the steering wheel. "I wonder what they eat to keep them looking so well-fed without us humans about."

"They're getting energy from sunlight," Ethan told her. "The process is similar to the way we humans synthesize Vitamin D when sunlight touches our skin. It's more advanced in the zombies though—almost photosynthetic in its efficiency. They also absorb

28

some moisture directly from the air. It keeps them in a sort of 'standby status' until humans turn up for them to eat."

Paula whistled. "Wow, I never heard it explained that way before."

"That's the scientific theory anyway," Zoe said, then she reached over and tugged the sleeve of the other woman's sky-blue robe, exposing the red and black patch over her right breast—a red 'Z' over a black cross. "Of course, your temporary bosses the Church want everyone to believe there's partly a supernatural element to it too."

"Yeah," Ethan agreed angrily. "Those bastards have no consciences—they'll do anything to make the sheeple feel good about eating zombie meat."

"Ah yes, 'Digestion is Salvation,' " Paula quoted mockingly, then added, "Well, what'd you expect? ChoZo is a part of AFI, and AFI runs the government. President Harper is just a mannequin."

Ethan was about saying something acid in support of that, but then thought better of it.

The zombies' clothes might have been ragged, but they themselves were all remarkably well-preserved, except for those who had suffered damage of some other kind, either from gunfire, knife wounds, or personal misadventure; like the zombie they were driving past now, who seemed to have fallen down the stairs somewhere and broken her neck: her head lay flat at a ninety-degree angle to her body as though using her shoulder as a pillow.

The sights here reminded Ethan that these 'zombies' weren't dead people. Which was the reason they were called 'undead'—because they weren't actually dead. This situation wasn't like in those films where a virus killed everyone and then reanimated their corpses.

The zombies that nowadays stalked the streets of the world were really *brain-dead*.

The plague virus had completely consumed their intelligence and reverted them back to an evolutionary place where they weren't even as smart as cats or dogs. All that mattered to them now was the hunger evident in their wet and shiny green eyes and visibly expressed by their loud growls and the gnashing of their teeth.

So no, they weren't exactly alive either—in the sense that the normal human being is alive—zombies existed in a mental/psychic limbo, one where their intelligence had itself been consumed by the ravaging hunger consuming them.

Distressingly, the infected developed longer and sharper teeth than the average person. They couldn't properly close their lips anymore because their teeth were now too long. Other than that they looked normal enough (meaning their bodies didn't automatically start decaying), if one discounted the green and purple veins that now webbed their skins. This veining showed up regardless of if the zombie was Negro or Caucasian or any of the skin tones in between.

The ethics of the matter was very complicated; a point everyone agreed on.

So now the five-hundred-or-so million humans who had survived the plague (the so-called 'living') were being terrorized (and *eaten*—it was important not to forget the 'eaten' part of the zombie terror) by billions of sort-of-dead people.

But this cloud definitely had a silver lining. Or as the Church of Zombie loved to say: 'Turnaround *is* fair play.'

***

The convoy's route through Athens had so far been a smooth passage, with the vehicles simply driving up over the sidewalk or through a route of adjoining front yards when the streets were blocked by stalled vehicles. But suddenly the lead trucks were forced to stop moving.

"Oops, I don't like the looks of this," Paula said, on seeing the AFI guards dismounting from the vehicle ahead.

"We must've hit a bottleneck," Zoe said easily. "We're driving through a commercial district, so some crashed or burnt cars have blocked the street between the shops or something." She gestured at the armed men taking up positions to keep the undead at bay, and beyond them at the expanse of shattered storefronts, their glass either exploded out onto the sidewalk or imploded into the buildings themselves. "Seeing as we've no lawns here to drive over, they'll either clear the street or make us reverse."

Paula laughed and tapped the GPS display, then she hit the button to shut the windows in case the zombies made it past the convoy defenders. "Reverse? Another detour? This trip seems to keep getting longer."

"I'd like for it to be over already," Ethan grumbled. "Hanging out in public with the undead isn't my idea of entertainment. Way too much can go wrong in a really short period of time."

Zoe leaned over and kissed him on the cheek. "Don't sweat it, baby—you worry too much." She pointed forward. "Hey look, the nasty zombies are coming out to play. Time for some fireworks."

Fireworks? Sometimes my girlfriend seems to enjoy this madness a little too much. Ethan grimaced as the guards began firing at the approaching undead. He was repulsed by the carnage, but was fascinated the zombie's strange metabolism. When wounded, green-tinted blood dribbled from their bodies, and if you didn't kill them, it clotted much quicker than human blood.

Groups of undead people walked towards the convoy, their arms outstretched towards the vehicles, their fingers clutching, their eyes mirrors of the most intense hunger imaginable; a soulless desire to eat others.

Ethan felt a strong horror as the guards mowed the zombies down with machine gun fire.

Don't, don't, don't! Those are people you're shooting! he felt like yelling. But of course, no one believed that anymore. At least no one in this convoy, except he and his two companions. To the most of the world, zombies were simply food, exactly like cows and chickens had once been.

All the convoy vehicles were armored, but still, if they got swamped by zombie numbers they would be facing a crisis. The shattered windscreens of the surrounding civilian vehicles were morbid testament to that fact.

"Ouch! That definitely had to hurt," Paula joked when a shotgun blast took off the head of a zombie right in front of them.

The headless man slumped down into the road, but another three zombies immediately took his place, each of them lurching forward with outstretched arms and yawning jaws, though comically, the rearmost of the three had no hands. They all drooled with hunger as they advanced, as if they had been waiting all of their undead lives for the convoy to turn up so they could feast on the travelers.

The guards efficiently put the trio down, but more zombies instantly took their places.

And this skirmish was just beside Ethan's truck. Up and down the street fighting and shooting was going on to protect the convoy.

31

Then a mob of undead emerged from an alley and swamped the convoy and the guards couldn't handle the number of zombies anymore.

"What the hell is holding us up now?" Zoe growled testily as the guards nearest to them succumbed to the teeth of the undead. "At this rate we're all gonna be eaten by our food."

"Time to fight for our lives," Paula said grimly. Then she looked at Ethan. "Give me your gun."

Ethan shook his head at her. "Remember your cover; you're supposed to be a priest. After we get out of this, how are you going to explain your proficiency with firearms?"

"Shit!" Paula scowled. "So what do we do now? Sit here and wait to be eaten?"

Her point was made by a zombie banging up against the driver's side window. The woman pressed her lips tightly against the glass and in a puddle of slobber seemed to be trying to bite through it. The woman's eyes looked like giant olives stuck into her face—there was no color distinction to either sclera, pupil or iris; all were a universal green.

Zoe laughed and shook her head and handed Paula her own firearm. "Here, use mine." She shook her head in anticipation of Ethan's protests. "Don't worry, we're in such a mess now that no one's going to remember they saw her shooting." She leaned over Ethan and slipped his revolver from its holster. "And if they do, we'll just lie and claim they imagined it; we'll say they mistook me for her."

Ethan didn't protest. While slipping the gun out she'd also squeezed his penis through his pants. This wasn't the first time Zoe had shown evidence of being sexually aroused by violence.

Paula already had her window down again and had put a bullet through the head of the woman who had been attempting to bite through the glass. Her head blew apart like a pumpkin—her brains had a greenish tint to them as they exited it. Another shot from Paula, equally expert, blew the head off of a large male zombie who'd been locked arm-in-arm with a female guard, trying to eat her face. The pair went down together, but the woman stood up a moment later unharmed. She looked their way to see who'd saved her, and couldn't conceal her surprise on seeing it was the lady priest.

"Well, that's one pretty secret admirer you're gonna have from now on," Zoe said, as the woman waved her thanks.

"She looks good enough to eat," Paula said, licking her lips appreciatively.

"Oh, shit no! I think the zombies heard you," Zoe said next, when two previously unnoticed pairs of green-and-purple veined arms grabbed the relieved guard and jerked her sideways out of view behind a crashed truck. The woman's screaming reached them a moment later. A moment after that, a bright red splash of her blood painted the sidewalk; and a few moments later her head followed, shooting across the sidewalk like a ball and ending up somewhere inside the nearest storefront.

The zombies who had killed the guard dragged her headless body back into view. Their mouths dripped crimson and their eyes lacked even the faintest hint of humanity. An ape looked more human than these feeding things.

Leaning out through the window, Paula took aim and dropped both zombies with headshots. "Jerks!"

Ethan looked away. The guard's death left him cold. It did however rule out any possibility of her later raising difficult questions as to Paula's real identity, particularly if Paula, who was bi, had taken the woman to bed.

On his side of the conflict, the zombies had the upper hand; the guards they'd swamped over were on the ground bleeding and the undead were ripping massive chunks of flesh from their bodies. One man's face had been bitten off. Ethan watched another prone and twitching man lose a bloody chunk of his buttocks to a toddler's teeth. This was the first time since the zombie outbreak that he'd been this close to an undead attack and it was a completely unnerving sight.

With a string of human guts dangling from her lips, and both her face and bare torso splattered with blood, a female zombie looked directly at him. The inhuman hunger expressed in her face filled Ethan with a sudden inexplicable panic. He felt like leaping down from the black pickup truck and running away; running away as fast and as far as his legs would convey him, to the end of the world if possible.

And I'm partially responsible for this terrible mess, he thought in disbelief. *A large amount of this is my fault. But I had no idea. None of us had the slightest idea of what we were creating; or that it would turn out this way.*

"Hey, move aside," Zoe told him.

She was indicating that he switch places with her. He slipped inward, while she scooted over him until their positions were reversed and she was sitting by the door and he between she and Paula, who was refilling Zoe's Glock from a box of bullets.

Zoe lowered the window and began shooting too. Ironically, her first target was the zombie woman who'd been looking at Ethan. Ethan had no idea if this was motivated by jealousy or not. Zoe wasn't as good a shot as Paula. Her first shot hit the woman in the breast, flinging her back into another zombie and then toppling her out of sight. Zoe's next shot did better, shearing off the top of an obese male zombie's head, just before he could clamp his teeth on the arm of an AFI guard who'd gotten separated from the other convoy defenders.

Ethan watched the saved guard detach himself from the falling zombie and then run through a gauntlet of flailing zombie arms to finally fling himself over the side and into the bed of the AFI pickup truck ahead of theirs, which had just kicked into motion.

"Thank heaven we're moving again," Paula spat. She hit the controls to put up the windows again, and twisted the key in the ignition.

"Hey, baby, we made it!" Zoe told Ethan, dropping her hand to his lap and giving his thigh a meaningful squeeze.

"Yeah, we did," he agreed, nodding dully back at her. Her face was flushed with excitement and she seemed oblivious to his personal discomfort at the deaths.

Honey, working an AFI admin desk was clearly the wrong choice of career for you, he thought. *But of course Daddy insisted you climb the corporate ladder instead of going into the armed forces, and Daddy is rich and powerful, and so what Daddy wants Daddy gets.*

Zoe was clearly primed for lovemaking now. As their truck followed the others through the cleared bottleneck and out of the street, she kissed him and he managed to respond, although his mind was really occupied by the mess of human and zombie wreckage they were leaving behind them . . .

. . . And how it had all begun . . .

CHAPTER 5

Rise of the Zombies

Approximately two years ago, on the fifth of May, about a quarter of the world's population simultaneously went 'crazy' and began trying to eat everyone else.

It was later discovered that the disease responsible for this had been incubating in the infected for weeks, possibly months.

The outbreak was short and brutal. Within two weeks, fifteen percent of the world's population had been massacred and eaten by the zombies.

The world's governments reacted quickly but there was little they could do. The zombie virus—'Intro-Z' it was called after a while—had infiltrated them too. Politicians and soldiers, captains of industry and factory drones, the rich and the poor; all were equally affected.

Despite the world leaders' most valiant efforts to fight it and curb its spread, the zombie pandemic raged on and on and on. A single bite was all it took to turn anyone into one of them, as the then US President Kendra Harris unfortunately discovered on a visit to a Washington D.C. facility where the undead were being studied. Once bitten, she was instantly detained at the facility and her vice-president Josh Harper sworn into office instead.

One of the most iconic images still remembered around the world was the day the undead broke into the United Nations building in Geneva and ate all the delegates at a conference that had been convened specifically to discuss how to defeat them.

And who could ever forget the terrifying and bloodcurdling TV images of zombie cardinals eating the Pope . . . or those of the undead horde ripping apart the devout Muslim worshippers who were celebrating Ramadan by praying at the Kaaba in Mecca.

***

It took three months before conditions around the world reached a sort of stability again. An impasse. By then thirty percent of the world's population were dead and rotting in the streets, sixty-two percent were walking those same streets as zombies, and the remaining eight percent who hadn't either succumbed to the zombie virus or been eaten by the infected were barricaded away and desperately trying not to starve to death.

But then . . . the US-based corporation Assured Future Innovations—AFI for short—had explained to everyone that their laboratory research had proved that not only was zombie meat very good to eat, but that it was also the long sought after 'fountain of youth.'

AFI's lab tests had proved conclusively that consuming zombie meat drastically slowed down the human aging process.

Of course in normal times, no one would have taken these research findings seriously, and the researchers would have found themselves facing murder and cannibalism charges.

But these were the most unusual of times. There was the worldwide meat-shortage crisis to consider.

The zombie virus didn't affect animals. The world's animals hadn't died from the plague.

No, the zombies had *eaten* the animals.

Household pets that had been owned by zombies were the first to go. Then the undead had gotten into farms and eaten all the livestock—cows, sheep, goats, pigs, fowls—whatever they could catch. And then the zombies had shambled on into the woods and consumed whatever wildlife they found there—deer, antelopes, moose, giraffes, raccoons, chipmunks, snakes, rabbits, zebras—even hippos and elephants.

Snakes, giant pythons and anacondas included, all suffered the same fate; with the Asian cobra failing to realize that now it wasn't just the mongoose it needed to be wary of.

The undead ate whatever they could swarm over and subdue. Even natural predators like lions and tigers had their numbers drastically reduced by the hungry hordes.

The USA's surviving bears, wolves, and mountain lions had all learnt by experience not to attack the undead. Across the globe zoo animals had survived at first, but then had all died of starvation.

By the time the world stabilized again, there was almost no meat left to eat. Just like pets, cows had by then become an almost extinct species.

Yes, there was fish, but in addition to a worldwide shortage of fishermen and lack of access to the rivers and seaports because of the zombies, eating fish didn't make one live longer.

Plant protein, another viable substitute, was similarly unavailable, because the zombies had overrun the world's farmlands.

And now AFI, which had just changed its name to Ambrosia Flesh Incorporated, let out a further bombshell about the dietary benefits of zombie meat.

"Not only does zombie flesh slow down the aging process," they announced on their online news page, "but we have now also conclusively proved that eating it also reverses one's age to a biologically optimized version of oneself. Folks, you'll not only live forever, you'll be young, strong—and for you wrinkled ladies out there—beautiful forever!"

That 'beautiful forever' was what swung the argument in their favor. Just like in the Garden of Eden, the world's women ate the bait. The men followed shortly after, lying that their women had coerced them into compliance.

The zombies were dangerous, however, and since no one wished to hunt them, for fear of either being eaten by them or turning into one of them—AFI gladly offered to do the catching and processing for everyone.

And this was how practically overnight, Ambrosia Flesh Incorporated became the world's most prosperous business conglomerate.

And so it was that eating zombies became the new order of the day. Relevant legislation that dehumanized infected human to food-animal status was quickly passed worldwide and the slaughter was on. And seeing as zombies outnumbered humans eight-to-one, there was more than enough zombie meat to last for a very long time.

It didn't hurt that zombie meat tasted delicious. Prepared right, this juicy green-and-purple-marbled meat was literally the best thing anyone had ever eaten in their lives.

Of course, things didn't go smoothly. Every religion on the planet (except for Satanism and a few primitive tribal ones in the Third World) forbade eating people; and the surviving adherents of these religions held out for as long as possible. Even the atheists protested that eating people went against their principles, claiming it was something an 'evil god' would demand of his followers. But AFI (which was fast becoming the most powerful political lobby around the world) had a counter for conscientious objections:

The Church of Zombie was launched. 'ChoZo' as it quickly became known.

And Zombianity became Earth's new premier religion.

***

Fast-forward a year-and-a-half, and today the Christian church was almost completely forgotten. Now the Church of Zombie ruled both the televangelist airwaves and the hearts and minds of the American populace and the surviving millions worldwide. Almost everyone was a Zombeliever now.

It wasn't just Christianity that ChoZo had swept aside. Every other religion had suffered a similar fate, though Hinduism was still proving stubborn. But even reincarnation's resistance to the idea of eating meat was becoming obsolete when the benefits of carnivorism (and stylized cannibalism) were considered.

There were no more sacred cows in India—the zombies had eaten them all. That fact in itself had served as motivation for a good part of the surviving Hindu population to convert to Zombianity—the idea that by in turn eating the zombies they would be exacting a form of revenge on them for their sacrilege against cowdom.

The Church of Zombie's message was a simple one: that rather than an afterlife that had been promised by religions for thousands of years, or being recycled though succeeding lives till one was considered suitable to achieve personal divinity, eternal life could be had now by everyone. By eating the sacred and long forbidden 'ambrosia flesh,' every man and woman could and would live forever here on Earth.

As was written in Zombook: 3:16—*Some people say God gave man a predetermined life span of seventy or eighty years. But that is nonsense. We are God now and we have determined that man will live forever. The Christian God can keep his Heaven, there is enough space here on Earth for immortal, eternal man.*

38

Everything about the Church of Zombie was carefully calculated. Even their logo, a red 'Z' superimposed on a black cross, was designed to *almost* offend those who had been Christians; and yet at the same time to also offer them a sort of comfort in the form of that most familiar and universal of religious symbols.

ChoZo hadn't dared put a zombie on their cross. It was rumored that some of their archbishops had suggested doing so, but that the AFI executive board of directors had vetoed the idea. Several of these exalted men and women had been devout Catholics who even now weren't sure God Almighty wasn't playing some divine game by letting humanity feed upon themselves.

***

AFI's claims about zombie meat—now technically referred to as 'ambrosia flesh'—were all true. Ambrosia flesh did both halt and reverse the human aging process. The wonder-working compounds and enzymes in zombie meat stimulated perfect cell regeneration and replacement, even in the brain.

So now the survivors were all younger (most people went back in age to their twenties), were stronger and were guaranteed to live longer—possibly forever—which was sufficient justification for their hunger and the zombie slaughter.

The age of the Delicious Zombie had come to stay.

Mankind had become his own cow.

AFI had initially wanted to sell mostly 'processed' and prepackaged zombie meat, but ChoZo had resisted this, claiming that to maximize the spiritual benefits of the 'holy ingestion,' the meat should be eaten directly 'off the bone.' And then there were those shoppers who wanted 'organic' unprocessed zombie meat to buy at their local butcher anyway.

With no beef anywhere, McDonald's sold Big Zack burgers, with lettuce and extra (synthetic) cheese.

And at another worldwide franchise, Kentucky Fried Zombie— KFZ—was the order of the day.

CHAPTER 6

In Transit Again

Once the AFI convoy had broken through the bottleneck, it found itself faced with a fresh mob of undead. Alerted by the shooting a short distance away, the zombies were out in force in the districts bordering the Hocking River and had blocked the highway.

The convoy made a right turn to avoid them, and for a while Ethan found himself headed back the way they'd come. This street had a long-abandoned McDonald's restaurant.

Zoe sighed as they drove past the eatery's dust-covered windows. "Whoever said real life imitates art must have been crazy. I can't recall ever seeing even one zombie flick in which the undead ate up the world's animals. Even the gators. How the hell did that happen? I saw a documentary of zombies ripping a giant gator to bits. It was eating one of them and they were eating it . . . but of course the zombies carried the day—weight of numbers prevailed . . . they ate open its stomach and all its guts spilled out—including the zombie it had just eaten. From what I hear, the Mississippi River Delta is completely out of gators now."

"Even chickens," Paula mournfully agreed. "Guys, I used to love fried chicken buckets . . . and now the only place to see chickens is in the zoo? Colonel Sanders must be turning over ceaselessly in his grave."

"Zombie-chicken-flavor just isn't the same thing," Zoe said. "I'm glad we'll soon be putting an end to all of that nonsense. I wanna eat the real thing again."

"Chickens breed super-fast," Ethan said. "Give them a year or two and they'll have overrun the planet again."

"But if that's the case, why haven't they done so yet?" Paula asked.

"Two reasons," Zoe said sharply. "First of all, because the zombies keep eating the chicks that do hatch out—just like they do with other bird species that can't fly—turkeys especially . . . but I also think the

African ostrich is more extinct that the Dodo now, except if the South African zoos have some in captivity . . . and secondly, because,"—she tapped the ChoZo patch on Paula's right breast—"our bosses don't want competition with zombie flesh."

"It isn't much competition," Ethan interjected into the conversation. "Chicken has no magical qualities—it's just food."

The convoy was leveling out now. The pickup truck's GPS indicated that a southern turn was coming up.

"It's still competition," Zoe argued. "Once there's an alternative to eat, people will find a reason—logical or otherwise—to eat it. It doesn't matter that chicken won't make you live forever—there are enough people who still hold on to our previous ethical and religious value systems who'll eat it anyway, even if doing so means they'll age and die."

"Amen to that, honey," Paula said in a voice tinged with irony. "I'm one of those people. Waking up in a world without fried chicken used to be my biggest nightmare and now it's come to pass."

While speaking, Paula drove up into the woods to avoid a giant pothole that extended across the road. Doing so brought two zombies out from the trees ahead of them, one of them a giant black man missing his right arm, the other a blond lumberjack-looking guy with half of his face gone.

The zombies lurched at their truck. The one missing half his face was in the front and the sight of his bony skull without a left eye was unnerving.

Zoe pulled out her gun and fired at the zombie. She missed and instead hit the one behind him in the chest, which jerked the big negro back a few paces but didn't stop him.

"Gotcha," she enthused nonetheless.

Ethan sighed with relief when Paula got them back down on the road again and they'd left the zombies to harass the vehicles behind them. Thankfully those in the rear vehicles were better shots than Zoe. Hearing a couple of gunshots behind them, Ethan looked past Zoe into the side-view mirror and saw both now-headless zombies staggering and toppling over.

Keeping her pistol in her lap, Zoe went on with her previous argument: "Look, this is just like with eating fish," she explained with a flush on her pretty face. "The Vegan and Seafood Lobby claim we don't need to subsist entirely on zombie meat. They say eating just a little bit a day has exactly the same effect of preventing aging and restoring youth."

"Dunno how true it is, but I've heard rumors that it's possible to make pills of the zombie essence," Paula said, tapping the steering wheel. "Which would mean we wouldn't have to eat them at all."

"Exactly," Zoe said. "While I agree with AFI that the VASL are mostly a bunch of cranks, they do raise some interesting points. Like I agree in principle with Hailey Farmer that . . ."

Three of us on the way to save the world. Ethan found his thoughts straying away from his girlfriend and their driver. *The world is insane and we're the doctors with the cure. Or are we?*

In this case the cure seemed almost as bad as the illness. Billions had already died, and if he, Zoe, and Paula were successful on their quest now, hundreds of millions more—maybe even up to a billion more people—might die as well.

But zombies aren't considered people anymore. We think of them as food. I'm certain death is better than waiting to be eaten. If you're going to die either way, it's much better to die with dignity.

Ethan's constant guilt over his share of the blame for the world's current state hit him like a bullet to the conscience, and he grimaced.

I have to try and fix things. Even if it kills me.

CHAPTER 7

Genesis - The Plot

Three weeks ago Ethan and Zoe had driven over to the Zombie Research Institute in Agawam to meet with Mickey Sanderson.

"Bring your girlfriend too," Mickey had said on the phone. "What I've got to say is certain to interest her."

"What time should we get there?" Ethan had asked.

"Midnight or later. I'm working late tonight. But make sure you make it—this is serious shit."

Despite the urgent tone of Mickey's voice and the late hour of their requested meeting, the summons out to the ZRI complex hadn't surprised Ethan that much. Mickey Sanderson had been his boss at the now defunct AFI lab in Athens (this was back when AFI still meant Assured Future Innovations), and the pair of them were still smarting about how their innocent research into prolonging human life had ruined the world.

Not that the world cared about that though—to everyone except themselves Mickey and Ethan were heroes, part of the pioneering group who'd built the railroad of human immortality.

Ethan and Mickey drank together occasionally to bitch about how great a social and societal fuckup they'd both helped bioengineer.

The Zombie Research Institute's name was a misnomer; the only research that went on there involved making new seasonings for zombie meat. Delicious as zombie meat undoubtedly was, after a while the human palate demanded new flavors.

The food animals might have largely vanished into the annals of culinary history, but humanity still remembered what they tasted like and desired faithful reproductions.

***

"Ah, here you are finally," Mickey had said, swiveling his wheelchair around towards them when they walked into his office.

Mickey Sanderson was in his sixties, but of course now looked about thirty years old. He was a slight man with platinum blonde hair and an elongated face.

That night, Mickey had had a visitor with him; someone neither Ethan nor Zoe had met before. This unfamiliar person was a tall woman with long black hair and pale gray eyes. Everything about her had screamed 'cop' or 'soldier.'

"Ethan and Zoe, meet Paula Neyman," Mickey had introduced them. "Paula . . . Ethan Hackman and Zoe Patterson."

Paula had smiled and had shaken their hands with a firm but feminine grip. "Uncle Mickey has told me a whole lot about you two. It's a pleasure to finally meet you both."

"Same here," Ethan said. Paula was very attractive; but nowadays that was routine enough; everyone was young now, and youth was in itself a form of beauty. On meeting Paula, Ethan had felt the routine male attraction to a pretty woman. He'd been just as certain that Zoe would view her as competition.

Zoe had frowned at Paula's statement. "What exactly did Mickey tell you about us?"

Paula had shrugged. "Mostly how *you're* the daughter of Senator Trevor Patterson, and that you hate humanity's modern life of stylized cannibalism, and would love to have a chance to set things right. To blow society up, if you could."

That had shocked Zoe. "You told her that much about me?" she'd asked their host.

Mickey had grinned back at her. "Nothing to worry about. Paula's my niece. She thinks the same as you and Ethan do about AFI."

"Oh, that's a huge relief," Zoe had said with a smile at Paula. "Welcome to the club—it's great to know that we're not the only ones who see something wrong in the fact that nowadays one can buy human meat at the mall along with tampons, cellphones, and sneakers."

"Sometimes I'm certain I'm simply dreaming this whole life we live now and that I'll wake up in the morning and it'll all be over," Paula said. "It makes no sense whatsoever to me to walk into a supermarket and find human body parts for sale—arms, legs, brains, hearts, breasts, penises and vaginas, kidneys and livers, tripe—whatever I wanna buy. Including those disgusting trays of zombie eyes that I always"—she giggled—"and I really mean this, I *always* at first mistake zomb eyes for grapes and wonder what fruit is doing in a butcher's display. When that happens, it takes me a few seconds to remind myself that this isn't the past anymore." She'd laughed, and then sighed in a very ladylike way. "I really do wish this was the past. Sure, we had lots of bad stuff back then—terrorism and pedophilia and all that—but definitely not supermarket chains offering skinned human corpses—male, female, and child—for sale, and allowing housewives to select which part of their bodies they want to purchase. . . . And don't even get me started on dining at restaurants."

"We're lucky we don't have pets anymore," Mickey said, "Or else we'd have 'canned zombie' pet food."

"It's getting more insane by the day," Zoe had said. "Last time Ethan and I attended a wedding, the chefs had barbequed a whole zombie for the guests at the reception. Can you just imagine that? They had a human being roasting on a spit like he was a pig."

Paula had laughed softly. "Well, technically zombies don't really qualify as humans anymore," she'd said. She'd gestured around the office; her fingernails a blue slash through the air. "The latest proposed amendments to the constitution designates zombies as 'things,' not 'people.' They're not even animals anymore. Once that law makes it through congress, rats and bugs will have more rights than the zombies do."

"They plan to include even the newly-infected who haven't turned yet," Mickey interjected in an enraged voice, his fingers tightening like vises on the wheels of his chair. Mickey occasionally got very worked up; it was his way of venting his frustration at having lost both of his feet in a motor accident. "This is clearly ChoZo's doing. What's next—outright cannibalism?"

"Not yet—but it's clearly not far off," Ethan had said, just to add something to the conversation. "Crazy as it seems, there's already rumors of a 'Man is meat' lobby in the Senate. And where the USA goes today, other nations follow tomorrow."

"No," Zoe had immediately objected. "Non-zombified human meat has no life-extending qualities. The so-called 'Man is meat' lobby is just VASL propaganda to embarrass the government."

"Hmm, I don't know 'bout that," Mickey had said reflectively, scratching the stubble of beard on his chin. "Unreliable and paranoid as they undoubtedly are, the Vegan and Seafood Lobby are great at gathering intelligence."

Ethan had laughed. "Not those guys, man. The Vegan and Seafood Lobby are great conspiracy theorists. They're the sort of guys and dolls who think Elvis isn't dead but now lives on Mars and works for NASA."

His comment had triggered some laughter.

"Hey, where's Michelle?" Ethan had then asked. "Best to have all of us conspirators together." Michelle was Mickey's daughter. She was a very reserved girl who assisted him with running the research institute. Normally she hung around her father like a spy satellite.

"Oh, she had a bad headache and had to retire early," Mickey had explained. "Since Paula was here I told her to go right ahead." His guests had still all been standing and so he then indicated the chairs set around the table beside them, on which stood a bottle of wine and four empty glasses. "Everyone, please sit down. We've a lot to discuss."

When the three had seated themselves, Mickey had then slid his wheelchair up close to the table. Paula had poured drinks for all of them. While she did this Ethan had tried to get the measure of the woman. In addition to being Mickey's niece she had to be both reliable and very discreet, or Mickey wouldn't have told her as much about them as he had.

One thing Ethan had quickly noted about Paula Neyman was that she moved with very little wasted motion. And something about her eyes also let him understand that she was a dangerous woman; possibly a deadly one to tangle with.

Zoe had seemed to be sizing her up too, but from a normal female perspective.

Ethan had looked away from Paula. The table in Mickey's office stood next to an open window that faced the compound's front gates, and Ethan had had a good view of the zombie pens that lined the compound's walls. Just as with the rest of the building, the cage lights had been switched off for the night. Similarly the captive undead were silent. The zombies would be vegetating now—rocking back and forth in either a sitting or standing position in that almost plant-like state of reduced alertness that served as sleep for them—but they would instantly regain full alertness the moment a human being came near them.

"So what's this summons all about?" Zoe had asked after a sip of red wine and with a petulant look on her face. "Tonight's Saturday. Ethan and I were supposed to go clubbing." To that intent, she'd visited the salon during the day and gotten both her hair and her nails done.

Mickey had frowned. "I think it's time for us to go into action against the government."

Zoe had first stared at him in surprise, and then she'd burst into a fit of giggles. "Against the government? Mickey, are you crazy?" She'd laughed so much that she spilled her red wine on her red pants.

A cold smile had stolen over Mickey's features as he watched her laugh. Zoe had finally realized that he was serious. She'd placed her wineglass down on the table and while tapping it with red fingernails, asked: "Are you serious?"

Ethan had just waited. He'd been as surprised as Zoe but had managed to control himself better.

Mickey had nodded. "Yes, I am serious." Still smiling, he'd then turned his focus to Ethan. "Tell her about ND."

Zoe had stared at Ethan. "What is 'ND?'

"It's actually pronounced 'End,' " he'd told her with a sigh. Under the influence of alcohol, he and Mickey had already told Zoe their sad and depressing tale at least six times. How, as part of a team of researchers tasked with finding a way of extending human life out at Assured Future Innovations' research facility in Athens, Ohio, a young biochemist and his elderly pharmacologist friend and mentor (meaning himself and Mickey; even in recollection he liked to keep them both anonymous) had created a dangerous viral variant, which turned people into the exact precursors of the zombies that thronged the world today—bright green eyes, purple-and-green streaked bodies, a total collapse of rationality, and a ravening lust for human flesh.

AFI had then decided to destroy this 'zombie serum,' but the samples had somehow gotten lost en-route to the disposal facility. Nothing had happened for a year afterwards, and he and Mickey had thought they could rest easy, but then one warm May morning, the news was suddenly full of reports of people going crazy around the world.

Ethan didn't like remembering this. "I really don't feel like talking about that tonight," he'd protested.

"Well, *I* want to know about ND," Zoe had insisted.

Ethan had looked to Mickey for help. But Mickey had merely shaken his head and mouthed, "No, you tell her," back at him. And meanwhile Zoe had had an expectant and slightly pissed-off look on her pretty face, a look that demanded a worthwhile exchange for her giving up her night of partying. Paula had sat relaxed in her chair, sipping wine and looking cool and sexy.

"Okay," Ethan had grudgingly agreed and looked at Zoe again. "Well, baby, of course we had volunteers for our commendable work of trying to make people live longer. AFI found us people from somewhere, no questions asked . . . bums, junkies, the homeless . . . We injected them with our test serums and paid them well . . ." He'd smiled sadly at his girlfriend. "But I'm digressing, aren't I?"

She'd nodded. "Baby, cut to the chase."

"Okay, I will. Along with our missing zombie-creating virus, we had also developed an antidote to it. That's what we called ND."

Zoe had stared at him in shock. "There's a cure to the zombie plague? But why didn't you mention it all this while?"

He'd sighed. " 'Cos it doesn't exist anymore. ND went missing at the same time the virus did." Before continuing, Ethan had paused and taken a sip of wine. "I'd best explain in more detail. ND was dangerous too. A quarter of those who took it died. We know because we tried it on those we'd unwittingly turned into zombies. And you need to remember that because of the delay before the virus's effect became apparent, we had *a whole lot* of infected test subjects."

Zoe had nodded impatiently. "And the rest of them? Ethan, what happened to the others you tested ND on—the ones who didn't die?"

Ethan had winced at the memory. "Oh, baby, you didn't wanna watch it. They'd lie on the ground for about a week, twitching, moaning and foaming at the mouth, and then they'd be okay. The viral shit would've vacated their systems and they'd be fine again—sane, normal people like everyone else." Once more he'd sighed. "But for those six or seven days? Their damn moaning was the worst part of it . . .

"So, yeah," he'd concluded. "Back before we had the zombie outbreak, ND would never have gotten FDA approval . . ."

"But now . . . with four billion people trying to eat the few remaining survivors . . . and being eaten by them . . . ND would be a godsend," Zoe finished for him.

"Yes, it would have been," Ethan had agreed. "Only, the problem is that it's gone too. We lost our ND samples at the same time as . . ." Then he'd stopped addressing Zoe and had looked at Mickey instead. "Are you . . . is there . . . do we . . . ?" The idea was so unexpected that Ethan hadn't even dared hope it was true. "Have you found a way to resynthesize ND? According to what I remember, AFI requested that we send them all of our research paperwork for both the virus and ND, so that no one would be able to . . . but then they told us the information had all gotten lost . . . the files burnt up during the initial zombie outbreak . . . and . . ." He'd stared questioningly at Mickey.

Mickey had nodded back at him. "Yeah, man, I know both where there's some samples of ND and the research papers too."

"What?" Ethan could only stare at Mickey. After a while he'd realized that his mouth was hanging open.

Mickey had nodded again. "Yeah, it's true. Back when AFI requested that we send them all the ND samples and paperwork that we had, I held back several vials of the stuff. My intention was to see if it was possible to tweak it further to get rid of the undesired side effects. But at the time we were busy perfecting that 'wondergel' that regenerated burnt skin, and so into a storage vault the samples of ND went, along with my Xeroxed copies of the manufacturing process. The samples have been there ever since. The zombie plague hit before I could resume work on them, and we had to do that emergency evacuation of the premises."

Ethan had thought on that. "Man, why are you just telling me this? We could've gotten it out ages ago. This worldwide mess need never have occurred."

Mickey had shaken his head. "Too dangerous. At first we weren't sure what was going on. You and I didn't even realize it was our 'missing' virus samples that had caused the zombie apocalypse. And afterwards, Ethan . . . I apologize for saying this, but even when the truth came out I really didn't know who I could trust." Before Ethan could protest this, Mickey had added: "There's only four people who can access that vault—Me, you, Fernanda Rodriguez and Diane Smith. And as you know, Fernanda died in the zombie outbreak while we were evacuating the lab and Diane's now a high-ranking ChoZo minister; last I heard about her, she's a bishop."

"But you and I . . . we've been together from the get-go," Ethan had protested. Then he'd nodded that he understood. "But yeah, I get your point—we only get one shot at this, right?"

"It gets worse than you think," Paula had said, speaking for the first time in the conversation. "Two months ago, Uncle Mickey uncovered documents that prove AFI were responsible for the zombie apocalypse."

"What?" both Ethan and Zoe had said. "What?"

Paula had nodded her head. "Yeah, it's true. Those zombie virus samples you and Uncle Mickey sent for destruction didn't get lost in transit. AFI 'stole them' as it were and used them to trigger the zombie outbreak."

"But that's impossible!" Zoe had said in a worried voice. However, she hadn't sounded convinced.

Ethan had stared hard at Mickey. "Is this correct? Our bosses engineered everything from the offset, all the deaths, all the misery, everything?"

"Yeah, I'm afraid so," Mickey had replied, reversing his wheelchair away from the table and piloting it over to the nearby window and staring out into the night. "One of the most telling pieces of documentation my spies dug up shows that the owners of AFI registered the company name Ambrosia Flesh Incorporated two months before the zombie outbreak. Worse still, 'ambrosia flesh' became a legally patented product around that time too. So 'ambrosia flesh' wasn't a new concept; the bastards knew exactly what they were doing all along."

Zoe had shaken her head in disbelief. "You're saying AFI tested your zombie virus on some people, realized what its effects were, and got a patent for zombified human meat before the zombie apocalypse hit?" She'd pointed her raised wine glass at Mickey and shaken her head. "C'mon, you guys, I'm not drunk, but even if I was drunk that defies my credulity."

"Mine too," Ethan had quickly agreed. "I refuse to believe that the USPTO would accept a patent for human meat . . . in the old days."

Paula had laughed. "Here's another riddle for you—haven't you ever wondered how it was that the zombie apocalypse began everywhere on exactly the same day—the fifth of May?"

Ethan had had no reply to that. He had wondered about it a lot. In the classic movie zombie outbreak scenario, the level of infections started small, in some isolated research station and then spread exponentially. "You're suggesting AFI seeded the virus around the world?"

"No other explanation makes sense," Mickey had replied. "You know, I think once the bastards realized what they had, they spent the interval between when the virus was supposedly lost and the day the zombie holocaust began tweaking the virus to ensure that after the initial incubation period was over, the next wave of infections would occur almost immediately—there had to be little or no delay in folks transforming into zombies once they'd been bitten or the world governments would have been able to control the outbreak by simple quarantine measures."

Ethan had just stared. Beside him, Zoe had begun trembling with rage.

"Here's another bothering question for you," Paula had said. "Didn't it amaze you at the time how quickly our government shut down all of our nuclear power stations? Despite the level of national emergency, we didn't have even one—not even one—nuclear meltdown nationwide . . . or worldwide for that matter. This is a worldwide fact: there was not a single case of WMD discharge. Not even from those nations that actively sponsor terrorism. The only problem we had was the zombies themselves."

Yes, Ethan had already been suspicious of how quickly the US government had managed to turn off all of the country's nuclear power reactors and lock down all military facilities, almost as if it had been expecting the disaster. But that couldn't be, could it? Nobody could be crazy enough or ruthless enough or evil enough to turn approximately sixty percent of the planet's population—the present estimate of zombie numbers was four billion undead—into mindless meat machines.

"AFI has always been much bigger than we could possibly imagine," Mickey had told them. "My research shows that they're like the fabled Illuminati—they've been working behind the scenes for centuries, using entire governments as pawns to achieve a single master plan. Their name may have changed through those years, but their evil mission hasn't."

"And now it's time to take the fight to the big boys," Paula had said with a smile on her full lips that hinted at barely constrained excitement.

"But how?" Ethan asked. "For certain I'm in. But how do we retrieve the sample?"

"That part is simple," Mickey had replied on that cold night when the world's future had seemed to hang in the balance. "You and Zoe have both been drafted to join a research team that will be traveling to Athens, Ohio in three weeks from now."

"Really?" Zoe had asked in surprise. "Ethan and I haven't heard anything about that."

Mickey had nodded. "You'll find out next week. You, Zoe will be in Admin and Ethan with the researchers; they want his on-site opinion on the location of those proposed Midwest zotein silos in Ohio. It's a short trip for both of you—once the outpost is properly set up you'll be recalled back here. But in the meantime . . ."

Ethan had smiled as he understood Mickey's plan. "All we need do is get the ND samples out of the lab and airlift them to you along with regular zombie research stuff we're shipping home."

"Exactly . . ." Mickey had said with a replying smile of his own. "Once you switch the sample tags, no one will suspect a thing." He'd reversed his wheelchair from the window and parked it back beside them at the table. "You three get me those ND samples and I'll do the rest."

That statement had made Ethan first look at Mickey and then point a finger at Paula in surprise. "Three? She's coming along with us?"

Paula had nodded. "Of course I am, dude. I'm a weapons expert. You two amateurs need someone to watch your backs."

Ethan had looked at Zoe. Zoe had shrugged back at him.

***

The immediate problem then had been how to get Paula included in the scientific expedition that would be traveling to Ohio in three weeks time. Paula didn't work for AFI and there was insufficient time to both employ her as a guard and have her assigned to the trip.

And Mickey had been adamant that she travel with them. "A mission of this magnitude and consequence requires at least one weapons specialist," he'd pointed out to Ethan. "And neither you nor your girlfriend fit the bill."

Mickey had of course been right. Even though he'd had his once-deficient eyesight laser-corrected, Ethan still wasn't a great shot. And for all her tomboyish bravado, Zoe was at best a very bad shot; she was clear proof that real life isn't a spy thriller. Even at close range it was ninety-to-one odds that she would miss hitting you except she actually had the gun point-blank in your face.

So they definitely needed Paula along on the trip.

But for a while, as their departure date neared, it had really seemed like there would be no way to swing it. Meanwhile, Paula—who'd secretly flown in from Miami—had hung around but remained out of sight.

It was Zoe who came up with the solution. "Hey," she'd told Mickey over the phone, "my office just got info that they're sending over a female priest from Boston to accompany us to Athens. What if we . . . you know?"

(Each AFI outpost was required to have at least one ChoZo minister, to 'pacify the souls of the zombie dead.')

And so, two days later, while motoring west along I-90 towards Springfield at night, ChoZo Reverend Alice Brown had come upon a stalled car at a turnoff just after the Wells State Park.

A bleeding woman had stood by the car, flagging her down.

Reverend Brown hadn't been worried about stopping out along this deserted highway. There were no zombies in this southern area of Massachusetts. To ease the job of trapping and 'processing' the undead, AFI had set up a massive number of blockades along the northern Massachusetts state border, with emphasis towards the western part of the state. Doing so had created a 'food corridor' that effectively 'funneled' all the northern zombies down through Maine and eastern New Hampshire to the northern Boston neighborhood of Charleston—where the USA's biggest zombie processing plant was located.

And so, on that pleasant and starry night, Reverend Brown had halted beside the bleeding woman. "What's the matter, miss?" she had asked concernedly.

"Help me, please," the woman had wept. "It's my brother . . . our car stalled and he got out to have a look at the engine and the hood slammed down on him and I can't get it up and he's not moving and . . ."

Reverend Brown and her passenger, a man she was giving a lift to, had immediately gotten out of her car and hurried over to the parked Toyota. The situation had been exactly as described by the distraught woman. The hood was partly down and a body lay beneath it, pressed onto the car engine.

"Quick, help me get the hood up!" the bleeding woman wept.

However, before Reverend Brown could bend to the task, the supposedly stuck car hood had lifted and she'd found a revolver pointed in her face, the gun held by a man whose face seemed oddly familiar to her. A moment later she collapsed dead on the highway, her brain destroyed by a high-caliber bullet fired at point-blank range.

"Stop him, Paula!"

The dead woman's passenger had turned to flee, but before he'd taken a step he was grabbed by the woman who'd flagged them down. While twisting to throw her off of him, he saw a brief flash of silver and then the blade of a knife was buried in his right eye. He'd felt a brief shocked agony before she finished him off by slamming the heel of her hand against the grip of the knife and driving it deep into his brain.

The woman had let go of the dead man. He'd fallen on top of the Reverend's corpse. Then she'd gestured to her male companion, who, his revolver now dangling by his thigh, had been staring in shock at the dead bodies. "Ethan, snap out of it. Help me get them into the trunk of my car."

And that was how Paula Neyman had joined the trip to Athens. That night the real Reverend Brown's corpse had been fed to the zombies at the Zombie Research Institute.

Using their connections, Mickey and Zoe had already made fake ID for Paula, and so when she turned up in Springfield the next day as Reverend Brown, no questions were asked. As planned, she had also arrived late, right when the convoy was in a hurry to depart.

***

Ethan still hadn't gotten over the experience of murdering someone. Sure, he consoled himself that it had had to be done, but he worried that they might need to kill more people before they retrieved the ND vials and got them back to Mickey.

"All who eat zombie meat are guilty of murder," Paula sometimes said. Ethan tried to get into that frame of mind too, but it wasn't easy.

The other thing that bothered Ethan as the convoy neared their destination was what Mickey had told them before they'd set out:

Mickey had said it was imperative that they acted now as he suspected that the dreaded Mr. Tricks, US head of AFI Intelligence, was onto him.

"I don't know how soon his dogs will come calling," Mickey had said. "But mark my words, Ethan, I'll be ready for them when they do."

CHAPTER 8

Attack on Sanderson's House

"Doc sure has a swell place out here," Gorehound said as the Hog Family's white RV drew up to the front gate of Dr. Sanderson's palatial residence.

The house wasn't secluded, but there were no neighbors to speak of. Agawam, MA, formerly a city with twenty-nine thousand residents, now only housed five hundred people, most of whom resided in the east of the city, which lay directly across the Connecticut river from Springfield, where AFI had their main New England offices, and which had the comparatively 'huge' population of three thousand inhabitants. Dr. Sanderson lived out here because his Zombie Research Institute was just up the road. As to why he didn't just live on the institute premises, the Hog Family had no idea.

As was usual with the Hogs, Gorehound was driving. He was good with cars and shit—Hogwash couldn't even change a tire right.

Motorbikes were more Hogwash's thing. Give him a souped-up Harley any day and watch him leave law enforcement in his smoke. Hogwash sometimes felt real sad that the good old days were gone now, the times when bikers would ride two or three side-by-side down the highways, owning the road. Anyhow, after he'd almost crashed their Class-C camper two or three times, Gorehound had banned him from even looking speculatively at the vehicle's steering wheel.

And their ladies Scary and Jenni? Jenni couldn't drive, but Scary was almost as good a driver as Gorehound. Scary Hog was given to road rage though, and since the family didn't want to be stopped by the police when they had a cargo of kidnapped and/or mutilated people in their RV, she too was banned from the steering wheel.

So Gorehound always drove.

Just like she was doing now, Jenni generally rode shotgun. Gorehound looked over at her. He caught her eye and winked. She turned and looked pointedly away, out of the window on her side, at the gate of Dr. Sanderson's house.

She was mad at him because he'd slit the throat of the guy who'd groped Scary last night at the bar.

"Hey don't, honey, I wanna saw his legs off too," Jenni had protested, but Gorehound shook his head. "You can have your fun at Doc Sanderson's with the rest of us," he'd told her.

"Hey, then at least let me slit his throat!" she'd protested, her eyes gleaming nastily, while their now totally handless victim trembled in shock on the table.

Gorehound had considered letting her do it, but then he'd thought better of it. He knew his wife very well; if he'd given her the knife, she'd be torturing and cutting the guy for the next hour or so (Jenni was sadistic like that) and they'd really needed to get a move on over to Doc's house.

So, with a warning look at her not to interfere, he'd slit the asshole's throat, and then, for emphasis, had stuck the knife in the guy's belly while he bled to death.

Jenni had instantly begun giving him the silent treatment.

Crazy damn women, he thought now, wishing he could just smack some sense into her. Once or twice when Jenni got like this, he'd come really close to beating the living crap out of her. But she was his best friend's sister, so he always kept his anger in check.

"Okay, guys, this is it," Hogwash said from the back. "Mask up, everyone."

Gorehound picked the rubber pig-head mask off the front seat and slipped it over his head. As the latex hid his face he felt like he was switching identities—becoming someone else—someone even more brutal than his normal personality. He looked across at Jenni, who'd done the same. Now she looked creepy as hell. The hog-head masks were eerily realistic and very scary. Anyone seeing them would likely poop their pants before figuring out they were just rubber.

When everyone was masked up, Gorehound hit the car horn to summon the AFI security guy manning Dr. Sanderson's gate. The guy must've have heard the RV approach, because the door in the guard post opened before Gorehound had even gotten his fingers off the horn.

The guard was tall and muscular. He strode quickly over to the RV, his hand dropping to his holster when he saw the pig masks worn by its driver and passenger.

His reflexes weren't fast enough, however. Before he'd drawn his service revolver, Jenni had the barrel of a gun pointed in his face.

"Drop it," she told the guard.

When the guard had dropped his revolver, Hogwash opened the RV's side door, got down, and pointed a shotgun at him. "Now, you and I are gonna go and open the gate," he told the man. "Don't try anything dumb."

"Who the hell are you people?" the guard asked as Hogwash shoved him towards the guard post.

"We're here to ask Doc some questions. That's all you need to know. This ain't got a thing to do with you, so don't try to be a hero."

Gorehound watched them go. "So far, so good," he said.

Jenni was still ignoring him and didn't reply, but Scary, who'd been riding in the back with Hogwash, now leaned between the front seats and said: "Yeah—"

"Shut up, both of you," Jenni said. "We got trouble. Oh, shit—that sonofabitch."

Over at the gate, the guard had made his move. He'd stepped quickly through the entrance to the guard hut and then attempted to slam its steel door against Hogwash's arm. But the pig-masked intruder had been too quick for him. Hogwash kicked the gate back open, pulled the guard out, and flung him to the floor as easily as if he was a child.

A moment after trying his heroics, the guard was staring up at the shotgun muzzle pointed right at his face.

"I warned you, you sonofabitch," Hogwash growled, the rubber mask making his voice sound almost like a hog's grunts.

"Please, please!" the guard pleaded.

But Hogwash pulled the trigger anyway and the guard's head vanished, pulverized into the concrete floor.

"Oh, damn that fool," Jenni said angrily as Hogwash bent to wipe a splatter of the dead man's brains off of his left boot.

"No harm done," Gorehound said, placing a hand on her thigh. "We were gonna kill him anyway. No witnesses, remember?"

He winced when she brushed his hand off like it was poisonous. "Yeah? But now he's fucking alerted the whole house that we're here."

"Calm down, bitch," Scary said. "No one's in the house except Dr. Sanderson and his daughter. And Tricks said he'd disable telecoms to the man's house. He can't call for help." She began laughing. "And with no feet he definitely can't go running off anywhere."

Jenni calmed down. Hogwash had meanwhile vanished into the guardhouse. Gorehound stared at the dead man. The sight—no head, just a messy red splatter of blood, mingled brains and hair and destroyed meat above his lower jaw—amused him no end. Gorehound liked the results of violence. It was like painting a canvas with human colors; leaving one's mark on the world as it were.

After a short delay, the front gate swung open and Gorehound drove through onto Doc's driveway.

***

Michelle Sanderson had been fellating her father when the gunshot sounded. The noise startled her so badly that she clamped her teeth together on his penis.

"Ouch!" Mickey gasped and shoved her away from him. He examined his erection, saw that it was unharmed except for a few red tooth marks and then scowled at Michelle. "What the hell did you do that for?"

"Did you hear that?" she asked him in turn.

"Hear what?" Mickey hadn't heard a thing. He was in no mood for distractions of any kind. He'd been totally adrift in the pleasure her lips and tongue had been giving him.

Mickey had been overworking himself through the week and he just wanted to relax today and make love to Michelle. He and she had been lovers since her mother's death in the car accident that had also cost him his feet. They truly loved one other, even if it was a flawed and outlawed love. Of course, not even their closest friends understood the real reason why Michelle obstinately refused to leave his side or date men of her own generation.

Their loss is my gain, Mickey always thought.

Now he growled at the distraction. Michelle had heavenly lips; when she wrapped them around his penis it always felt like he was floating through paradise.

"I think it was a gunshot," Michelle said. Sex forgotten for the moment, she scooted off the bed and hurried naked to a bedroom window, her large breasts bouncing as she went. She peeked down through the blinds.

"There's a white camper driving in through our front gate," Michelle informed her father and then she hurried away from the window. She reached the foot of their bed, grabbed up her denim shorts, and hurriedly pulled them on.

"What's the matter?" Mickey asked. "What's got you so worried?"

She turned to him in alarm. "There's a guy wearing a pig mask down there. He's the one who opened the gate for the camper. Meaning Andy is dead."

"Shit! Has to be Tricks' goons." Mickey's erection, which had already drooped to half-mast since the interruption of he and Michelle's sex play, now wilted completely. "Quick, quick—call the cops!" he barked at Michelle while she slipped a tee shirt over her breasts. "I'll activate the special house defenses."

Michelle picked up her cellphone and began dialing. Mickey slid to the side of the bed and maneuvered himself into his wheelchair. At times like this lacking feet was a total pain in the ass.

He got the wheelchair moving, and sped it out of his bedroom and down the hallway to his study, reaching the hidden digital console just as he heard the RV pull up outside the front porch.

Oh, dammit! he thought in a sudden panic. *I can't remember the access codes for the defense system!*

"Hello!" Michelle was saying into the phone down the hallway. "Hello! Somebody please pick up the damn phone!"

The front and rear doors were on a separate security circuit from the rest of the building, one accessed by a simplified code that Mickey did remember. He entered that code and then spun his wheelchair around and zoomed it out of the study again and headed back for the master bedroom.

He had to find his gun.

"Hey, will someone answer this damn phone!" Michelle was swearing at her cellphone as he reached the bedroom. "Pick up the phone, goddammit!" Then she paused and stared queerly at him for a moment.

Mickey didn't understand what the matter was. "I need my gun," he explained. "I wasn't able to secure the house. I set the defenses for the doors, but—"

"Dad, you're still naked," Michelle interrupted with a roll of her eyes. "Put some pants on. It'll be horribly embarrassing if the intruders break in and realize exactly what you and I were up to when they got here. Particularly since you've got my red lipstick on your dick."

***

Mickey Sanderson's seemingly unquenchable lust for his daughter was yet another reason why he wanted to put a stop to the worldwide consumption of zombie meat. With parents and children exactly the same physical age nowadays, strange romantic and sexual situations were constantly arising, particularly since the un-aging elders were all experiencing a restoration of their libido.

'Zombie-agra' some people called it.

However, Michelle, who was motivated entirely by heartfelt love for Mickey, clearly did not view their incestuous domestic situation the same way he did. Even with the 'feeding on zombies' atrocity removed from the equation, she would still want her father as her only lover.

Parent-child cohabitation in all its variations was nowadays much more common than the media realized.

***

Jenni pointed to the front door and then gestured to Gorehound. "Kick the door down, baby."

"Despite his relief that she was finally talking to him again, her husband restrained himself from doing so.

"Let's wait for the others to get here," he told her, gesturing back to where Hogwash and Scary were getting a few things out of the RV. "I dunno exactly what the matter is," he went on, "but I've a feeling something's wrong here."

"Yeah? Like what?" Jenni asked. "Don't tell me you're scared." The pig mask she wore her made her voice come out all 'oinky.'

The accusation of cowardice stung Gorehound. "Listen, baby," he explained patiently as Hogwash and Scary strode over to them, the former carrying two machetes and the latter a can of gasoline, "there's no way that Doc Sanderson and his daughter didn't hear the gunshot that killed the guard." He gestured towards the gate. "And you know Mr. Tricks has disabled their telecoms."

Jenni's pig mask cocked sideways as she considered his words. "Oh, you think they're maybe lying in ambush?"

Gorehound nodded. "Exactly that."

Hogwash and Scary had now joined them on the porch. "Yeah, we don't wanna walk right into a fusillade of gunfire," Scary agreed. She shook her gasoline can. "Let's just fire up the place; smoke them out that way."

The four seemingly pig-headed humans stood there for a few moments longer, and then Jenni stepped towards the front door. "I can't believe what I'm hearing. You're all scared of *two* people?" She looked at her husband again, her eyes bright and excited in her mask's eye holes. "Honey, let's frigging do this!"

But, although Gorehound was delighted that Jenni was no longer pissed off at him, he felt it was best to err on the side of caution.

And so he stepped forward, grabbed her gently by the shoulders, and then gazed as intently into her eyes as his porcine headgear would permit.

"Listen, hon," he said quietly, trying not to anger her again. "I know you're in a hurry to get started on this, but I think it's best we do like Hogwash and Scary are suggest—"

"Let go of me!" Jenni shrugged him off and grabbed the doorknob.

When she grabbed hold of the doorknob, Gorehound caught sight of motion out of the corner of his eye and leapt backwards, colliding with Hogwash and Scary, both of whom had not yet moved from where they stood.

Jenni never knew what hit her. Nor did the others, for that matter. All that they later recalled was something like a coil of wire wrapping around her and contracting, and then Jenni lay on the floor in twenty or more pieces, completely sliced up.

There was a moment of general disbelief while the surviving members of the Hog Family regarded the bloody mess on the floor which up to ten seconds ago had been Jennifer Mary Hogan ('Hog' having been shortened from 'Hogan').

But then that frozen moment passed. Hogwash and Scary both turned and stared at Gorehound, who then screamed, "NOOOOO!" in a distraught voice, turned around, and ran down off the front porch heading for their RV.

Not knowing what he had in mind to do, after a short pause Hogwash and Scary dashed after him. And then they both stopped and stared again, because Gorehound had leapt up into the front of their RV and had gunned it up. Moments later he had the vehicle speeding towards the front of the house.

Still dazed and confused by the completely unexpected turn of events, Hogwash did a quick calculation, realized that he and his girlfriend were both standing directly in the path of the onrushing vehicle and then yanked Scary out of its way.

The RV sped past them like a freight train. There was a massive crash of impact as metal hit masonry, and then the front of the house disintegrated and the RV was parked inside the building.

Hogwash retrieved Scary from the driveway where they had both fallen, and then grimaced at the damage.

"Wow," was all he could say in a subdued voice that reeked of awe.

"Well, I guess Doc Sanderson's front door is open now," Scary said as they got to their feet. "I just hope your brother-in-law survived the crash."

**

Inside the house, Mickey Sanderson had been hiding in the living room with a pistol in each hand. The security device on the front door only worked once, and after that he knew he would have to face the intruders face-to-face. He'd already noticed that there were four hog-headed people to deal with, clearly Mr. Tricks' goons, although two of them seemed to be women.

Mickey had felt satisfaction when one of the women triggered the door trap. In the morbid silence that had followed the woman's exit from her mortal coil, he had looked over at Michelle, who was positioned by the hallway entrance and nodded to her to get ready. She had nodded back, indicating her readiness. Their plan was for him to distract the intruders while she escaped from the house through one of the rear windows and fetched help. It angered Mickey that he had been unable to remember the code that secured the entire house.

But so far so good, he thought. *There's only three of them left now. If I can catch the others unawares too, then Michelle might not need to even fetch help at all. We can just call the cops to mop things up.*

But then, in a completely unanticipated reaction, he had watched one of the pig-masked people run back to their vehicle. His satisfaction that they were fleeing had been short-lived.

"Shit!" he yelped when he saw the RV speeding towards the house, coming directly at the window he was peeking through.

As fast as he could, he swung the wheelchair around and attempted to get out of the way of the oncoming vehicle. Mickey had limited success, however, because one of the living room couches was in his way. And so, as the RV crashed into the living room it clipped the side of his wheelchair, spinning it out of control and flinging both the wheelchair and Mickey up over the couch that had been blocking his flight.

As Mickey hit the ground and was knocked unconscious, he felt relief that he had taken Michelle's advice and put some pants on.

CHAPTER 9

Arrival

Though thronged by zombies, the AFI convoy made it through Athens without further incident. But that didn't mean it didn't encounter strangeness.

"What the hell is this?" Paula asked as they rolled through a dark tunnel that looped over the road.

"I think it's one of those zombie aggregations we keep hearing about on the news," Zoe replied.

Paula nodded. "Oh, like those 'zombie trees' that start when they become stuck to the ground? But it's so damn big."

"Yes, I've never seen one this big before," Ethan agreed.

The tunnel, a meat tent marbled with bluish veins, ran on for fifty yards, then ended as abruptly as it had begun and they were out into the light again. Ahead of them another similar projection hung over the road.

"Must be some compound in the soil here making them grow this huge," Ethan added as the truck ahead of them zoomed into the dimness and they followed.

This tunnel extended for longer, a dark greenish mass that seemed to blend with the trees on their right and the houses on their left, as if it were foliage for the former and paint for the latter. The tunnel had an almost human smell to it. Its arc over the road wasn't smooth, being lower at some points than others, and once, Paula was forced to swerve the pickup truck to avoid ramming into a stalactite-like projection that ended in a zombie arm.

"You should have just run through that thing," Ethan said as their back wheels bumped over a tree branch lying in the road.

"Sorry, but it looked way too creepy, a hand dangling down like that from above."

"It's particularly creepy because there aren't any zombies in here," Zoe said. "Like the tunnel's eaten them all up."

A hand projecting from a tunnel of liquefied and malleable flesh. That surreal image remained in Ethan's mind as they reentered the light.

A quick look around revealed a large expanse of similar zombified formations nearby, but then they made a right turn back onto the main highway and that strangeness was left behind them. A few seconds later they were ascending a bridge and crossing a wide river. 'Hocking River' the GPS said.

"Welcome to the southern part of town," Paula said as they descended the bridge. "Museum's coming right up on our right."

A short drive past a roundabout and they were at the OHIO Museum Complex and Kennedy Museum of Art.

Ethan sighed at the massive number of zombies that thronged the place like living statues scattered on the grass. The zombies were literally everywhere here.

The dual museum complex was a huge sprawl of connected brown brick buildings, some of which were three or four stories high; with several even taller than that. The complex extended for almost a quarter of a mile—impossible to completely secure with the few men available—and so the security advance team had just cordoned off the far-east wing of the premises with a metal-and-wood barricade and let the zombies have the rest of the place.

This secured area consisted of about five buildings, with the main offices being in the tallest building which had five floors, the upper floor windows of which afforded the occupants a great view of the northern part of the city across the Hocking River.

The zombies seemed to have been 'vegetating'; they came alive as the convoy approached, but of course weren't fast enough to apprehend it.

The convoy rolled through a hastily opened gate in the barricade and parked beside the other vehicles in the compound. The perimeter gate was secured behind them and everyone got out. The guards in the foremost vehicles had clearly radioed ahead for assistance because there were already men with gurneys waiting to attend to the injured.

"I thought we'd seen the last of this crap," Ethan said after watching one bleeding man being wheeled past them in a hurry.

"Me too," Zoe said. "Still, it'll soon be over for good." She shook her head in disgust. "You know, we could easily have avoided all the bloodshed. A scientific expedition of this size and importance should rate at least one of those big military troop transport helicopters."

"Not enough trained chopper pilots yet. The big shots—your daddy included—have hogged all of the available ones."

"My father's not to blame for this mess."

"Honey, no single person is to blame for this mess—we all are."

She flung him a meaningful look. "Oh yeah? Well, some people I know have a higher proportion of that blame than others."

Despite her anger she looked rather comical to Ethan; a breeze was whipping her light brown hair about her face and she was having a devil of a time taming it.

Then she left him and hurried off to assist the medical staff with moving the injured.

"I'd better go too," Paula said, after walking around the hood of their pickup truck. "They'll need a priest to administer last rites to those who don't survive surgery." She nodded at a gurney being wheeled past them, its female occupant already showing signs of turning into a zombie. "She'll need last rites too before she's guillotined."

"But . . . do you think it's wise? I suggest you keep a low profile. What happens if you can't remember one of the prayers?"

Paula laughed coldly. "Don't worry about that. Ever since Uncle Mickey discovered the plans for this expedition I've spent my nights boning up on ChoZo liturgy and doctrine. Makes a nice change from masturbation. I could pass an exam on it now." She pulled a copy of Zombook from her robe. "And for anything I'm not sure of, I got the user manual."

"Okay, if you say so." Ethan nodded and Paula left too. He'd not missed her 'masturbation' comment. Was it just his imagination or was she sexually interested in him?

Oh, I hope not. No way will Zoe put up with that.

He looked around for the scientists they had arrived with. The medics were assisting with the injured, the others were supervising the unloading of scientific equipment. Professor Ricardo Cortez, head of the expedition, was conversing with his assistant Dr. Mary Chang. Watching them talk to each other, Ethan felt relief that he wasn't in a position of authority here; he was just along on the trip to give his opinion on the construction and situation of AFI's proposed zotein silos.

Until they made their move to retrieve the ND vials, Zoe and Paula would both be busier than he was.

The convoy had been badly hit by the zombies. Seven guards were being wheeled away/carried off for treatment. Ethan did a mental calculation, he'd seen four guards die when they'd been surrounded by the zombies. No, five—he'd forgotten the man he'd noticed in the side mirror: two male zombies had been ripping out the man's neck, while a female one had been eating his penis.

How many guards started the trip with us? Twenty? Ethan could see only four unharmed ones now. *The pickup truck ahead of us carried eight men before the attack, and just three afterwards. And that depletion in number happened just in the thirty minutes it took us to drive through the northern part of the city.*

It was a sobering realization of how deadly this trip already was.

Mickey was right. We've no margin for error here at all. None whatsoever.

He walked towards the barricade. On their arrival here, he had noticed the original chain-link fence that bounded the Museum premises lying flat on the ground, its support posts knocked over and uprooted. This new barricade he was approaching was now standard issue for traveling AFI expeditions; prefabricated steel-grid squares linked by steel webbing, the whole mass supported by a combination of steel and wooden poles. The grid squares were three-foot-a-side and could be interlocked to a height of nine feet. Their outer surface was supposedly too smooth for zombie hands to gain purchase on.

The barricade gate was a sturdy construction of wood and plastic bars with two metal locks, once more standard AFI issue. Unlike the fence that shook on each zombie impact, the gate seemed impervious to them. A glance around revealed another gate in the south wall of the barricade.

Ethan reached the barricade and peered through a section of its connecting mesh. Attracted by the convoy's arrival, the zombies had gathered and were already pressing against the barrier. Ethan reeled back from their ravenous expressions and their excited growling like the rumble of giant stomachs, their wide green eyes like green apples or giant grapes pressed into dough, gnashing jaws that dripped their poisonous saliva, and those teeth, so long now that their lips could no longer cover them. Ethan tried to remember the results of those lab tests with ND so long ago. Had the cured zombies' teeth returned to normal or not? He didn't think so and anyhow he didn't see how that could even be possible.

If this gamble of ours succeeds, the world will need to either develop a new standard of beauty for a whole lot of people, or provide free dental care for most of its population.

A fat male zombie lunged hungrily at the barricade. Ethan reflexly leapt back and almost collided with a guard.

"Sorry, sir," the man said, and got out of his way.

"How secure is this structure?" Ethan asked the man, whose looks and vocal accent immediately marked him as Latino.

"It does the job, sir," the guard replied. "But we still shoot a few zombies who manage to get over it."

The man wore the regulation black AFI uniform with an additional ChoZo patch over his right breast. He was armed with a light machine gun and carried several refill magazines for it attached to his belt. He also had hand grenades clipped to his belt. The sight of all the weaponry did nothing to help Ethan's confidence in the wall of steel that separated them from the zombies, who were now pressed about five-thick behind the barricade, and whose revolting smell—of grimy flesh, moldy clothes, and possibly their last human meals—the fence didn't hold back. The zombies moved and the barricade shook, but it held.

The guard's blithe response had worried Ethan. "I thought zomb can't climb over these barricades."

The guard grinned, showing a missing lower left tooth. "They can't, sir. But when they get hungry enough . . . sometimes they climb up on top of each other and the ones who climb fall over the barricade." He gestured over to the north side of the complex, the area that faced the river. "We process all the ones that make it through. Those we don't cook are stacked up on pallets over there, ready for transport back to Massachusetts when the trucks make a return trip for further supplies."

Ethan couldn't see the stacked undead from where they stood; the pallets and bodies were concealed by a building.

"But there's nothing to worry about, sir," the guard said, tapping his machine gun for emphasis. "All the sleeping quarters are on the upper floors and we've reinforced all the doors and windows on the ground floor so the zomb can't make into the houses. Also, there's a sentry post on the second floor to take out those zombies that do make it over the barricade at night." He laughed. "Silenced rifle of course, so the rest of us can get some sleep."

Ethan took another look at the zombies pressing against the barricade. Was it his imagination, or had their numbers actually increased in the short interval that he'd been speaking to this guard?

Feeling slightly nauseated, he thanked the man and walked away from the barricade. He proceeded slowly back towards their truck. He was very unsettled by the living death that encircled the museum,

Time to unpack our gear, he thought, feeling that the action would take his mind off of the zombies.

He had just gotten the suitcases out of the pickup truck when Zoe joined him.

"Come on, quick," she instructed him with that telltale glint once more in her eyes, that look which spoke of her having sex uppermost in her thoughts. With the stench and noise of the undead all around them, and blood stains from the wounded dotting the museum parking lot, Ethan wasn't in the mood for sex. He did however feel an intense rush of love for Zoe, an emotion provoked by a heightened awareness of their shared mortality. Looking into her eyes, he realized that he loved her enough to die protecting her.

What happened to Holly and Jenny won't ever happen to her, so long as I have any say in the matter, he decided with grim determination, and not for the first time.

He handed Zoe a backpack and a laptop case, picked up two suitcases, and together they headed for the main building in this secured section.

The interior of the five-story building was lit by electricity, courtesy of the generator Ethan could hear humming somewhere out back, probably mounted on a truck.

"Our rooms are up on the fourth floor," Zoe informed him as they entered the elevator.

Ethan was silent as the elevator ascended. His previous lack of interest in making love to Zoe was however fast vanishing, because, seeing as they were the only riders in the elevator, she had grabbed his crotch and was squeezing it.

By the time they reached the fourth floor and got out, Ethan was erect in his pants. When the cage door opened he felt very embarrassed, when the red-haired woman waiting to enter the elevator took a good look at the tightness of the crotch of his pants and winked before stepping past them.

"Have fun," the redhead whispered in his ear as she passed him. Then, giggling, she shut the elevator door.

Zoe, several yards ahead of Ethan down the corridor, was unaware of the exchange between them. But then, she turned around, walked back to Ethan and grabbed him by the elbow.

"Come on, come on, darling! I can't wait," she chided impatiently, and thereafter pulled him along behind her.

Once through the door of their quarters, Zoe offloaded her burdens onto a table, shucked off her pants and panties, and then, even before Ethan had had a chance to form a proper impression of the room, she lay back on a cot with her legs spread wide. She was already dripping, the uppermost parts of her inner thighs creamed white.

Ethan dropped his suitcases on the floor.

"Eat me!" she gasped, pulling him down between her legs and then rubbing his face into her sex.

As he fed her lower mouth his tongue, her grip on his hair and ears was so intense that it felt as if she was trying to stuff him into her womb.

"This isn't working!" she gasped after a minute or so of cunnilingus. "Come inside me quick!"

Ethan was more than happy to oblige her. While licking her vagina, he had been undoing his belt, and now he slipped down his pants and mounted her.

"Yes, yes, yes!" Zoe gasped as he slid into her. "Yes, yes, yes, yes yes!"

Neither of them lasted long after that. Once it was over they lay together on the bed laughing.

"I know everyone in the building heard us just now," Ethan said.

Zoe giggled. "Oh yes, whatever will Professor Cortez and Doctor Chang think of us now? We may have just put the fate of their mission in jeopardy."

Ethan relaxed. Sex with Zoe always relaxed him. But really, it was more than just that. Their relationship had become a major stabilizing factor in his life. Her love was something he was uncertain he could do without anymore. If Zoe Patterson left him now, would anything else be left to his life?

I can endure that sort of loss once, but definitely not twice, he thought. *At the moment, though not exactly a shadow of the man I used to be, I'm definitely not the man I once was. I'm not yet functioning at my full emotional capacity.*

Only now did he look around their room.

"In case you're wondering, the bathroom is down the hallway," Zoe said languidly. "We're all sharing it."

"There are only two beds in this room," Ethan said. "Where is Paula supposed to sleep? Or, are they expecting you and I to share a bed anyway?"

Zoe got up, wiped herself clean, and began to pull her panties back on. "She's not rooming with us. Remember, she's a priest and will be expected to spend time in prayer and meditation, which we lovebirds can only be expected to distract her from." Her facial expression turned serious. "Honey, please try to remember that she's not 'Paula' here; her name is now Alice Brown."

Ethan facepalmed himself. "Oh my God, I keep forgetting that. I had better watch my mouth and not give the game away."

"Yeah, just one slip of tongue from you could put our entire mission in jeopardy."

"Correction noted, honey. But with that settled, where is Paula's room?"

Zoe pointed at the door. "She's right opposite us. I think they assumed that since we arrived together in the same truck we might want to room near each other."

CHAPTER 10

The Interrogation

"Hey, Doc, wake up."

Doc Sanderson, now securely duct taped to his wheelchair, stirred just a little, so Hogwash slapped him hard across the face twice.

"Hey, I said wake up!"

"Stop hitting him!" Michelle protested.

Gorehound, who had also passed out temporarily after crashing the RV through the front of the house but had now revived again, scowled at Michelle "Shut up, you, or you'll be the one getting hit."

The fact that all of them were wearing pig masks and looked scary as hell reflected on the girl's face. She immediately subsided into silence again and watched with teary eyes.

After giving her that warning, Gorehound ignored her and tried to focus on what was happening to her father. Michelle was duct-taped too, so there was no chance of her escaping from the house. Scary had told Gorehound that when she and Hogwash entered the building, they had found Michelle bent over her father, weeping.

The bitch clearly loved Doc then.

Just like I loved Jenni, and now she's dead and it's their fault. And they're both gonna pay for that.

He looked around the living room. Its front wall was mostly destroyed, with the RV still parked in the middle of it. Wood, concrete, and plasterboard were scattered all around the RV, along with the broken remnants of a coffee table and a television that had been in the vehicle's way. Some of the ceiling and light fixtures had come down too.

I must've been crazy, he thought. Oh, yes, Gorehound really had felt madness overtake him in those immediate seconds that had followed his wife's death. *And how the hell did I survive the crash without breaking at least one bone or developing a concussion?*

"Yeah, dickhead, wake up; stop wasting our time!" Scary was telling their captive in the wheelchair. She was laughing, kicking Doc's leg stumps for entertainment.

Either the pain from Scary's kicks, or the blows to his cheeks finally roused Doc Sanderson. He awoke in stages, looked around in disbelief, and then sighed on seeing that his daughter was a captive also.

Gorehound, meanwhile, was adrift in turbulent emotions. Of course, most overwhelming of all was the sense of sadness and loss already settling into his black heart because of Jenni's death.

But there was something else now added to it, something that Gorehound did not understand. While unconscious he had either dreamt or had a vision, he was unsure which it had been. But in his dream/vision he had been in another place—Earth, but in the far, far, far-flung future, so far in the future that that time would make no sense to people living now.

And in that eternal future, he had been a man being bred as a cow.

In that future, humankind was no longer the dominant species on Earth. No, the zombies had evolved. The future zombies did not eat man, they ate a vegetable called a 'blood potato.' But horrifyingly and disgustingly, this vegetable called the blood potato was grown in the flesh of human beings, humans who were called humancows and were herded like cattle, and who were also food for each other. The blood potatoes were planted in their bodies as if their bodies were soil, and indeed all the captive humans were named 'Soil' and 'Earth.' When the blood potatoes were harvested from a humancow's body, the man/woman died and their body was cooked and served as food to the other humancows.

In the dream/vision, Gorehound had been a humancow ripe for harvesting. Doped up on drugs, he had lain on a conveyor belt in the slaughterhouse, waiting for the bolt gun shot to his head that would end his life. He had awoken from his dream just after he had died in it, when his head was being cut off so that his brains could be scooped out of his skull and discarded as toxic waste, because brains were poisonous to the zombies.

Remembering the dream now, Gorehound shook his head and winced

It had been a very dumb dream for sure, total nonsense, and yet it had been so vivid, so real, as if he had seen a vision of mankind's actual horrible future.

He refocused his attention on their captives.

"Now, Doc, we're simply here for some information," Hogwash was just saying. "And why did you have to go and kill my younger sister?"

"You lot are trespassing in my house," Doc Sanderson coldly replied him. "You had better leave peacefully or I will call the police."

That made Scary laugh. "Police? Doc, we work for the police. They sent us here."

On this admission, Doc looked up at Hogwash, who nodded down at him. "Yeah, Doc, that's right, we do. And . . . killing my sister aside," he pointed back at Gorehound, "that's her husband, by the way, and I'm certain that he's shortly gonna have some extremely harsh words with ya 'bout you making him a widower—but like I was saying, yeah, we work for the cops."

Gorehound nodded at the mention of his name. He jerked the snout of his mask. He liked the anonymity that the masks gave them, and also the suggestion that he was no longer a man, but a brute. So yes, this bastard Doc Sanderson had just killed Jenni, and he would have his revenge on the man, a bloody and violent revenge. But first they had to be professional and get the business at hand out of the way.

And then the beast in me will come out to play.

"What do you want from us?" Doc Sanderson asked.

Hogwash shrugged at the question. "A good friend of yours and ours named Mr. Tricks doesn't trust you."

Scary nodded. "Tricks says you've infiltrated the convoy AFI dispatched to Athens yesterday, and he wants to know why you're so interested in it and what your plans are."

Gorehound nodded his approval. No, Mr. Tricks hadn't mentioned that the convoy had been infiltrated, but Hogwash, who had a good mind for this sort of thing, had suggested they use this tack in their investigation. The question was simply a leading question, of the sort that is often used in police interrogations and courts of law. Doc Sanderson's reaction to the suggestion that the AFI convoy had been infiltrated would determine what questions they would ask next and what they would do otherwise. If Doc's reaction indicated that he and his daughter knew nothing, then all was well and good. The Hog Family could kill them at once and report back to Mr. Tricks that there was no cause for alarm.

But such was not the case, because once the leading question was posed, Michelle Sanderson immediately gasped in horror. And although she quickly realized her mistake, and attempted to cover it up with an outburst of coughing, her captors had already realized that they were on the right track.

"Okay, so now we've established that you have indeed infiltrated the convoy to Athens," Hogwash went on, giving Doc Sanderson no chance to either accept or deny the accusation. "Our next question is—why'd you do so? What are you looking for out there? What is so important in Athens, Ohio that you went skulking behind your superiors' and fellow researchers' backs?"

"I'm honestly disappointed in you, Doc," Scary said. "National hero like you—"

Hogwash laughed. "An international hero actually."

"—Yeah, and behaving like a common traitor. You should be ashamed of yourself."

"Can I talk now?" Doc Sanderson asked.

Hogwash stepped back from him. "Sure, Doc, be our guest."

Speaking from his seat beside Michelle, Gorehound wagged a finger across at the captive scientist. " However, I would advise ya to tell the truth, else there'll be dire consequences." To give Doc an idea of the kind of consequences he meant, he dropped his hand to Michelle's toned thighs and squeezed, which produced a loud yelp of protest from her, and an aggrieved grimace on her father's face. "Remember you just killed my wife, and I'm very pissed off at you two."

"Okay," Doc said. "There's nothing serious afoot. I'm just . . . Listen, I need some old research books from Ohio University and—"

"Stop lying, asshole!" Hogwash punched Doc Sanderson hard in the face. The blow broke Doc's nose, and blood began gushing from his nostrils as his head lolled back, and his eyes glazed over.

"Don't—" Michelle protested, leaning forward.

"Shut up, bitch!" Gorehound growled and backhanded her, knocking her back onto the couch.

Then he got to his feet. Standing up, he realized that he still felt rather disoriented from the car crash, like after imbibing several whiskeys on an empty stomach. Stepping carefully over the destroyed coffee table and scattered glass shards, he walked over to join the others beside the stunned doctor. While in transit, he paused in front of the RV. Nah, it didn't look like they'd be driving it away from here: the windshield was cracked into a glass spider's web that hung halfway out of its frame; and the front of the RV was so dented he considered it a miracle that he still had legs to stand on.

"So, Doc wants to do this the hard way," Hogwash said when Gorehound had reached them. "I suggest we live up to his expectations."

"Yeah, so what now?" Gorehound asked.

Hogwash laughed. "I say we give Doc Sanderson here a taste of his own medicine. Good Book—I mean the one before Zombook—used to say an 'eye for an eye and a tooth for a tooth,' right?"

The others nodded. "Yeah, but I never went to church back then either," Scary said. "What has that got to do with this?"

Hogwash pointed at Gorehound. "Our version is called 'a wife for a daughter.' Seeing as Doc just murdered your sweet, lovin' wife Jenni, I say it's only fair and square that that you rape his pretty daughter, preferably to death too."

"No!" Michelle squeaked from the couch.

"No, please don't rape her," her father pleaded through his daze.

Gorehound too was shocked by the suggestion. He hadn't been expecting this. He'd thought Hogwash would suggest that they begin torturing the captives. That was something he was looking forward to doing.

Scary apparently read his body language, because she laughed out loud. "Hey, Gorr, what are you so reluctant about? Grab the bitch and fuck her to death! Tear her ass up!"

"I'm not in the mood," Gorehound protested.

Hogwash laughed like that was the funniest thing he had ever heard. "Dickhead, you'll be in the mood once she gets her pants off. Jenni almost sanded my ears off with her complaints about how randy you always are." He sighed. "She almost gave me an inferiority complex."

"Jenni won't like it," Gorehound protested.

"In case you've forgotten so quickly, Jenni's dead," Scary instantly countered. "It doesn't matter if she likes it or not." She chuckled. "Bitch def'nitely won't be getting it anymore where she's gone to."

"Hey, Gorr, what the hell are you waiting for?" Hogwash asked in a no-nonsense voice. "We ain't filming porn here; this is a serious AFI interrogation."

"Okay," Gorehound reluctantly agreed. "I'll rape her to death." Then he glanced nervously at the front door, behind which he visualized Jenni's splattered remains, and added. "But I'll do it inside, in one of the bedrooms. I don't want Jenny watching."

Hogwash looked first at Scary and then Gorehound. Then he shrugged. "Okay, yeah, cool. I agree with you that my dead sis does deserve some respect. Wouldn't be nice to hump another woman right beside her grave."

That said, he handed a new gleaming machete to Gorehound, who then crossed back over to where Michelle lay and, after cutting apart the duct tape securing her ankles together, brutally jerked her up off the couch.

"Please, please no!" Michelle protested with tears streaming down her face, as Gorehound shoved her ahead of him. "My father is telling you guys the truth! All he's after in Ohio are some old research journals that are now out of print!"

"Move your ass, bitch," Gorehound laughed, smacking her buttocks with the flat of the machete blade, and steering her out into the hallway.

"Please let Michelle go!" Doc Sanderson pleaded. His mouth and chin were covered with blood from his broken nose, as was his bare chest and the crotch of his pants.

He shook himself in his wheelchair, but the effort was pointless and pathetic, the Hog Family had so tightly taped him down, he could have been an Egyptian mummy.

"You tell us the truth," Scary Hog said, "and our giant-dicked friend won't rape and kill your sweet li'l princess."

"But I don't know anything," Doc Sanderson pleaded with tears in his eyes now. "I really do not know anything. Mr. Tricks is totally mistaken about me. I'm no damn traitor. I'm one hundred percent dedicated to both AFI and ChoZo and committed to improving life in our modern world."

"Well, in that case . . . one brutal rape coming up!" Hogwash gleefully announced.

***

In the nearer of the bedrooms, Michelle Sanderson was flung face-down on the bed. She rolled over quickly, preparing to put up a huge fight to avoid being raped, although considering that the man called 'Gorehound' was almost twice her size and was carrying a machete, she didn't see how she could escape what was about to happen to her. Worse still, her hands were bound behind her, so she had no use of them to resist him.

The man looked hideous. In addition to his wealth of scary tattoos, his pig-head mask was horribly realistic, ridged pink latex with fake tufts of hair and white boar tusks and a smear of painted blood on the underside of the leering snout. The fact of his wearing a Church of Zombie tee shirt—a severed human foot on a plate, with the green inscription "Digestion is Salvation" circling it—only increased Michelle's horror.

This douchebag represents everything wrong with the world today, she thought.

'Gorehound' stood regarding her for a few seconds, no doubt sizing up her juicy nubile body. She was perspiring fiercely, with sweat drenching her top, which she realized really emphasized her large breasts.

Michelle knew that no matter what this evil man did to her, her father wouldn't tell the intruders the secret they so desperately desired to know. He and she had agreed on this: compared to the fate of humanity's so-called zombies, their own lives were inconsequential.

I agree with dad! If we're able to restore life on Earth to what it once was, our deaths will have been worth it. All that matters is Ethan, Zoe, and Paula finding the vials of ND. Even if dad and I both die here today, Ethan's a scientist too— he'll be able to duplicate ND and use it!

The one thing Michelle would miss when she died would be her love relationship with her father. She had no excuses for their incest and didn't think she needed any. She'd been in love with her father since she was a little girl (oh, back then he'd been just so handsome and sweet!), and now that zombie meat had made him young again and fate had removed her mother from the picture, it had seemed only natural to both she and Mickey that they date one another.

So I guess there is something good to be said for eating the zombies after all.

Her captor stepped forward and knelt on the bed.

"Touch me and I will bite your dick off!" she threatened as he began peeling her shorts off. "I mean it! I will eat your penis and swallow and digest it!"

"Shut up and stop kicking!" he growled back at her.

Michelle didn't stop. She kept on kicking until he punched her in the belly. Winded and with her eyes gaping from the pain, she went both limp and silent.

Lying there with her shorts off, her legs spread wide and her vagina exposed, she was surprised to see that the man wasn't undoing his belt. Instead, he moved up her body and whispered in her ear.

"Now, listen up, I'll make a deal with ya," he said.

Michelle was perplexed. "What kind of a deal?" she asked cautiously. Maybe if she didn't make any more fuss he'd settle for a blowjob. That was definitely preferable to being 'raped to death' like his companions had suggested.

"Lower your damn voice, bitch—I don't want the others hearin' us." After Michelle had nodded to this, he went on: "My wife just died and I really don't feel up to having sex with you at the moment, talk less of raping you. So what we'll do is this—you're going to make a lot of racket as if I am raping you in here."

Unable to believe her ears, Michelle quickly nodded. "Okay, that's fine."

"We got a deal? Pretend and I won't rape you for real."

"Yeah, sure."

"Hey, Gorehound, what the hell is taking you so long in there!?" came the other male intruder's voice from the living room. "Get on with it, wilya?"

"Yeah!" came the woman's voice. "Doc here is getting impatient! Ha ha ha!"

"Alright, get on with it," Gorehound said. "And make it real convincing except you want my dick shoved up your ass until you bleed to death."

Michelle cringed at the threat. She utterly hated anal; even with her father; it just seemed such an unsanitary practice.

She began screaming as if she was dying: "Oh my dear God, no! Stop, stop, stop it, you pig! No, no no, it's too big—Don't!"

"Yeah, like that," Gorehound nodded down at her. "And here's a little encouragement for ya," he added, then slashed her shallowly across both thighs with the machete, so blood welled up from the cuts and streamed down onto the bed.

Michelle's eyes widened from the pain. "No—stop raping me— you're much, much, much too big! Oh, my God, it hurts so much!" she screamed, much more convincingly now.

Outside in the living room, she heard her father pleading with the other intruders to let her go. It was almost amusing.

***

Punctuated by laugher and pleading from the living room, the phony rape in the bedroom went on for five minutes. During all that time Gorehound prayed none of the other two would come into the bedroom to see how he was getting on with raping Michelle.

He was particularly worried about Scary, who was a bit of a voyeur.

It isn't my damn fault, he thought. *At the moment, I don't even have the ghost of an erection. Shit, Hogwash is one stone-cold sonofabitch to expect me to get it up under these circumstances. I'd've expected him to at least show a li'l concern that his younger sister is dead. But no, he and Scary are acting like we're at a goddamn Christmas party.*

Gorehound had to hand it to Michelle though; the woman had really put her heart into her performance. No doubt the fifteen or sixteen shallow machete cuts now adorning her body (particularly the four on her breasts) had helped her enthusiasm, but she'd screamed herself hoarse in the process and now lay limp and exhausted on the bed.

She looks like I really have been raping her, he thought in satisfaction. *I'll explain the lack of come by saying I made her slurp it all up. The bloody cuts on her make things seem convincing too.*

"Now, remain here and behave, or else . . ." he threatened needlessly—she was so exhausted from yelling that there was no way she could have gotten up to go anywhere.

After smearing some of Michelle's blood on his tee shirt, Gorehound left her sprawled on the bed and hurried outside to the living room, pretending to zip up his pants as he stepped out of the hallway.

Gorehound was amused. Things in the parlor weren't exactly as he'd left them. Part of the reason that Doc had been pleading for mercy had been Hogwash and Scary working him over with knives. The man was covered with gashes; he looked really pale now.

"The bitch dead yet?" Hogwash asked.

Gorehound shook his head and scowled in fake disgust. "Nah, she's got a huge pussy—doubt she even noticed my dick inside it." He took satisfaction in the miserable look that came over Doc Sanderson's face at his statement and waved his machete at the man. "Doc said anything useful yet?"

Scary shook her head. "Nah, he still insists he's a real American hero and that Tricks is messed up in the head for thinking he'd betray Zombianity."

Gorehound sighed and pulled Hogwash aside. Leaving Scary guarding Doc, he led Hogwash over to the far side of the crashed RV and whispered to him: "So what do we do now? We know the guy's hiding something, but he don't wanna talk. Are we gonna knock them both out and hand 'em over to Tricks, or what?"

Before replying, Hogwash scratched the snout of his mask as if it was an actual part of his body. "Doc's too well known for us to do that—there'd be a public outcry," he reminded Gorehound in a harsh whisper. "Which is why Tricks sent us here in the first place."

"So, what we gonna do? Tricks won't pay us if we kill 'em without getting him the info."

"I got an idea," Hogwash said. "Go fetch the daughter from the bedroom."

Hoping Hogwash knew what he was doing, Gorehound trudged off to the bedroom.

"Hey, you, get up!" he said as he pushed the bedroom door open.

Gorehound picked Michelle up, slung her over his shoulder and carried her back out into the living room.

***

"Okay, here's how we're gonna do this now," the other pig-masked man explained to Michelle. "Seeing as we already tried it one way and that didn't work, this time we'll do it the opposite way."

Michelle had no idea what the brute was talking about. The pain of her wounds was horrible. Yes, Gorehound hadn't raped her, but maybe it might have been better if he had, because the cuts on her breasts hurt just as badly as she imagined an unwelcome penis in her vagina would have. If Gorehound hadn't been holding her upright now, she'd have slumped to the floor from pain and exhaustion.

She looked at her equally bloodied father, and tears filled her eyes. Her father's face was defiant, but the blood all over him nullified his defiance. One of the intruders (she was sure it was the woman) appeared to have been whittling away at the skin of his stumps; his leg stumps were both peeled and bloody and there were red scraps of skin on the floor around his wheelchair.

Is the human race worth us both suffering pain of this magnitude?

"See, bitch," the other man (was his name actually 'Hogwash?') was telling her, "now, you're either gonna tell us what your daddy wants in Athens, Ohio, or we're gonna cut his dick off."

The brutal threat immediately made Michelle cringe. *No, not dad's penis!* Michelle loved her father's penis. The idea of her father and lover without his exceptional manhood, the horrifying thought of that stellar male organ that had given her so much pleasure and ecstasy being detached from his body, hit the wall of Michelle's defiance like a barrage of tank fire.

Gorehound laughed. "Yeah, Doc, seeing as you refused to tell us what we wanted to know when I raped your daughter, I guess we'll just have to cut off your dick then."

Her father could only gape. Scary was already slicing open his pants.

"No, not his penis!" Michelle yelped in fright. "Anything but that!"

Scary laughed and ripped the torn fabric aside to reveal Mickey's manhood. "Ooh, is daddy's little girl in love with daddy's big dick? Hey, is this a lipstick smear? Has daddy been fucking his little princess?" She grabbed Mickey's penis by the glans and stretched it out to its full length. "Well, either way, kiss goodbye to it!"

"No, don't!" Mickey protested when Scary pressed her knife against the base of his manhood. "Please don't!"

Scary looked at Michelle expectantly. "Or have you got something useful to say to us, bitch?"

"Yes, yes, yes!" Michelle said and broke down completely in tears. She couldn't help herself; saving the zombies or not, she couldn't let her father be castrated. She just couldn't. "Okay, okay, I'll tell you everything you want to know, just don't cut his penis off."

Hogwash nodded. "Alright, start talking, bitch, and your dad's dick lives to see another day."

"No, don't tell them anything!" Mickey protested. "Don't, Michelle! I'm not worth—!"

"Shut up!" Hogwash said, slamming a punch to the side of Mickey's head that knocked him out cold. Then, his eyes like flint in their mask holes, he nodded to Michelle.

"Go on, woman, or else . . ."

Relieved to see that Scary had lowered her knife, Michelle began talking. While Scary recorded her confession on her cellphone, Michelle told the Hog Family everything they wanted to know about Ethan and Paula and Zoe's quest to retrieve the vials of ND from the vault at Athens.

Afterwards, Hogwash nodded. "And you're certain that what you're telling us is the truth—the honest-to-zombie truth? You lot are trying to cure the zomb of their infection?"

Michelle nodded. "Yes, yes, we are." Hating herself for trading the fate of the zombies for future sexual pleasure for herself, she nonetheless stared defiantly at the three intruders. "There, now you know what you want to know. Now, please leave my father and I alone. We're going to be in enough trouble with AFI as it—Hey stop that! What are you doing to dad?"

"It should be obvious," Scary gleefully replied. "I'm pouring gas all over him!"

"No, stop!" Michelle gasped as the pig-headed woman doused her father and his wheelchair in gasoline. "No, don't do that!"

But Gorehound was already flicking a lit match at the unconscious man.

Mickey Sanderson caught fire like a torch and was burning fiercely in seconds. Then he suddenly woke up and began howling in pain. As his skin peeled off, a stink of roast meat mingled with the gasoline smell already in the living room.

Michelle first gaped in disbelief at their captors. Then she began screaming, making more noise than her burning father: "Why!? What are you crazy people doing!? Why kill him!? I already told you what you want to know!"

"This is payback for you killing my wife," Gorehound explained in a sad voice.

"But . . . but . . . Urrgh!" Feeling a sharp and sudden pain in her belly, Michelle glanced down and saw that Gorehound had stabbed her with his machete. She looked at him in horror as he pulled the machete out and stabbed her again, deeper this time, sending its wide blade all the way through her body so it stuck out of her back.

Behind him, her father was burning with his mouth open, unable to even scream out his agony anymore; smoke welled from his mouth and nostrils as if they were chimneys. His eyes had popped and were dribbling down his skinless face.

Gorehound was already swinging his machete at Michelle's neck.

"I'll see you all in hell!" she yelled and spat in his face as her head began to separate from her shoulders.

***

Why would they want to cure the zombies? Gorehound asked himself. Some people were truly crazy and deserved to be locked away, he'd realized while listening to Michelle rant.

Or else . . . why would anyone in their right mind want to cure the zombies?

Gorehound liked the state of the modern world. In addition to the fact that the current relative lawlessness in the world meant less hassling from the police and lots of leeway to be as violent and as evil as he liked to other people, he loved being young and strong again. Before the benefits of zombie meat were discovered, Gorehound had been fifty-two years of age and just been diagnosed with type 2 diabetes. Eating zombie meat had rolled back the years and also rolled away his disease. The news nowadays was full of verified medical accounts of folks' cancers having regressed and vanished.

Zombie meat was truly the modern miracle.

Why anyone would desire to take that miracle away from mankind was a mystery to Gorehound.

***

As Gorehound had suspected, their RV was too bashed up to start up.

After they had all retrieved their essentials from the vehicle, they made their way over to the front porch, where Scary poured gasoline over Jenni's sliced-up remains and set them ablaze.

They kept their pig masks on for this ceremony.

"A befitting funeral pyre for the girl," Hogwash said after they observed a minute's silence beside Jenni's burning body parts.

Then, racking his memory, he spouted some ChoZo doctrine that those who died in the service of Zombianity would ascend to a Paradise where they would have zombie flesh to eat forever and a day.

Gorehound didn't believe that shit for a minute. But at least Jenni had gotten a funeral of sorts.

The Hog Family now removed their masks and stood outside the Sanderson house, watching it burn. Smoke was spilling out from the living room windows and the bedrooms seemed to be burning too.

Hogwash called Mr. Tricks on his phone.

"Tricks says to just let the place burn down," he informed the others once he'd gotten off the phone. "He says he's in conference with Senator Patterson at the moment, but that he'll dispatch an AFI chopper to fly us to Ohio to arrest those three traitors before they can do any damage."

The flames consuming the house grew fiercer and the Hog Family retreated a distance because of the increasing heat, and also in case their RV exploded. Finally they stood outside of the front gate, beside the headless corpse of the security guard they'd killed on their arrival, and waited for their helicopter to arrive.

"Hey," Gorehound asked, after they'd been staring down the empty street for a while. "When you got off the phone you said Tricks was in conference with Senator Patterson."

"Yeah, that's right," Hogwash agreed. "What about it?"

Gorehound jerked a thumb back at the burning house. "The dead chick said one of those three who went to Ohio was Zoe Patterson. I'm just wondering if she's any relation to the senator."

Hogwash scratched his jaw. "You know, I didn't consider that. She mightn't be tho'. Patterson's a common enough surname."

Scary pressed up against Hogwash. "It don't matter. We can always ask her when we catch her. If she is the senator's daughter, we'll just make certain not to have any witnesses present when we gut her."

They all laughed at that.

Behind them, their Class-C camper finally blew up, and Doc Sanderson's house came crashing down in a pile of masonry and debris.

CHAPTER 11

Rearrangement

With a surviving US population of barely 30 million people, it was considered wiser and more logical to aggregate the survivors in fixed localities and let the rest of the country run wild (or go to shit) as it were. Boston, New York, Washington D.C., Miami, Los Angeles, Dallas, Salt lake City and Chicago now each had populations of 2 million people, with the remaining 14 million current residents of the United States of America being concentrated in smaller cities with populations of between two hundred thousand and half a million people each. As much as possible, the chosen human settlements were coastal, or at worst situated near large or flowing bodies of water, so that it would be easy to evacuate the population in the case of an emergency.

Zombies couldn't swim.

At present, except for government workers and farm staff, ninety-five percent of the US's human population had been evacuated to these cities, leaving the majority of the country to the zombies.

When the next elections rolled around, the plan was to simply let everyone vote based on what state they'd been shipped/trucked/flown in from.

CHAPTER 12

The View From the 4ᵗʰ Floor

There was a knock on the door of Ethan and Zoe's room.

Startled out of his half-dressed afterglow in Zoe's arms, Ethan hurriedly got out of bed, pulled up his pants and then called out, "Come in."

Paula entered. She looked both depressed and tired, and her blue priest's robe had spots of blood on it.

"You look completely ragged," Zoe said.

Paula nodded. "It's a morgue down there. Three of the wounded guards died and one became a zombie, so I've been performing funeral rites." Then her eyes narrowed slightly. "You're looking good though," she told Zoe. "Almost as good as if you didn't just make the same grueling trip over here that I did. In fact, you look as if you just got through having sex."

"Oh, she did," Ethan said.

Zoe shrugged and giggled. "I was just so pent up that I had to come; or else . . ."

"Wish I was that lucky," Paula said. She then crossed to the larger of the room's two windows and looked out of it.

"A guard I spoke to mentioned a zombie pile out front," Ethan told Paula. "Can you see it from there?"

Paula looked down and then nodded. "Yes, I can. Wow, they've a whole lot of zomb meat stored down there."

Ethan and Zoe walked over to join her. Paula was right. There was a literal pyramid of headless zombies stacked below them, its height reaching up to the second floor. And as they stood there watching, a fresh headless body was being added to the pile, the pale nude female form indelibly marked with the trademark green and purple lines.

"That's the girl who just turned," Paula said.

Out beyond the grim spectacle stood the barricade, and outside of that was the press of zombies. The panoramic view afforded Ethan from this fourth floor vantage point showed the true extent of the zombie horde; there were thousands of them out there, clothed, dressed in rags, naked; undead adults, kids, and crawling babies, all summoned by the communal desire to eat the living.

It was truly a chilling sight to behold, and Ethan didn't stare at it for long. Though just as gruesome a sight, the pile of headless undead below he and the girls was at least harmless.

Characteristic of normal zombie storage facilities worldwide there was no smell of decay. Zombie meat never spoiled. According to the scientists, unconsumed zombie flesh would keep literally forever. This was merely another fact of the new world, where man now ate man; or at least what had once been man.

It was surreal, seeing possibly two hundred headless human bodies arranged below them like this, with the bodies' unnatural coloration creating the impression that one was staring at a painting. Of course, if one had a look into the room where all the zombie heads had been kept, the impression would be even more bizarre.

"The cooks say they're shipping the bodies back to Springfield within the next two days for processing," Paula enlightened them.

"Surely there's no need for that," Zoe objected. "We've an excess of meat in Massachusetts as it is. Better they keep this lot here for when Ethan's storage silos are ready and then they can grind them up into zotein."

"The problem here is storage space," Paula replied. "Because zombies keep making it over the barricade, their number keeps piling up down there, and if they don't start shipping them away, they'll soon run out of space to keep any more in the compound, or space for anything else for that matter. Apparently, the original plan was to expand the barricade to enclose four more buildings once the guards who traveled with us arrived. But seeing as we lost most of their number, that plan is no longer feasible, so . . ."

"Someone clearly wasn't thinking clearly," Ethan said, pointing down at the barricade outside of which the undead throng gathered and waited. "There's no need to ship the bodies back to where they already have an excess of them. I'll have a talk with Dr. Chang about this. A much better solution, and a practical one too, is to simply dump the zombie bodies over the barricade and let them pile up out there. The meat won't spoil, and in addition the bodies will serve to reinforce the barricade and prevent the zomb from getting in."

"But if you do that, then the living zombies may be able to climb over the dead ones," Zoe pointed out.

Ethan mused on that for a short while. "You have a point there, honey. Maybe a better approach is to stash the bodies in several of the nearby museum buildings. Anyway, I still see no reason to truck them cross-country to Massachusetts. And also . . ."

But now his attention had been caught by something else, something a whole lot stranger that the zombie pyramid below them.

***

Dusk hung over the region. Having lived in Athens for five years before the zombie holocaust, Ethan was very familiar with the layout of the city. He didn't recall ever seeing it from this perspective though, from the south and staring from a height across the river. The hills surrounded everything, covered with greenery the color of the zombies' eyes; guardians of the graves that never were. The hills fenced off Athens, Ohio from exterior view, but also shut out the exterior world. The hills and the sky, the city and the zombies; that was all there was here and now.

From this height and position the northern landscape was much like a Google Maps image: three-dimensional and with the layout of a video game. At points the hillside seemed terraced and the occasional bare outcropping of rock that broke through the greenery had the appearance of a frightened face seeking to escape captivity.

The thing that shouldn't have been in the landscape was the green mass that stretched across the city like melted, moldy candy. There was no mistaking what it was; even at this distance and elevation, Ethan could tell it was the same zombie aggregation they had twice driven beneath during the convoy's frenetic race to safety through the city.

But so big? Viewed from above, the extent of the green thing was daunting, covering as it did a full third of the entire city north of the river. Now he understood why the advance team had warned them off motoring east along Route 50 to get here—all of Route 50 that he could see before the horizon darkened his gaze lay underneath the green mass. What else lay under that mass, he couldn't even hazard a guess. He remembered the single arm that they'd seen dangling from the ceiling of the second tunnel they'd driven through and shuddered.

"Utterly unbelievable," he said aloud without meaning to. His gaze was dragging back across the landscape towards the west, where the tops of buildings erupted out through the green mass like the hands of drowning men. Most of the woods in that area were submerged in the green too, but occasional green mushroom caps marked the tops of the highest trees.

"What was that, baby?" Zoe asked, snuggling close to him.

Ethan wrapped an arm around her shoulders and with his free hand, pointed north. "The real problem here is that my old research lab is somewhere in that green mess."

"Oh shit, I was worried you were gonna say that," Paula said. "Which building is it—can you tell from here?"

Ethan shook his head. "Nah, our lab had just two floors, with a basement level, and from what I can see, it's only the three-or-four-story buildings that are breaking through the aggregation. So we're going to have to drive under it to find the lab." He forced a laugh. "I can't even see my old home anymore. It was over on the east, near the university, now it too is buried beneath that green stuff, or maybe the green expanse is blocking off my view of Mill Street."

Paula nodded. "So, I'm sure I've heard it all before somewhere, but I wasn't actually paying attention then, 'cos I've forgotten everything I heard; but please, run it by me again: how actually do these things— these zombie aggregations—come about?"

Zoe looked up at Ethan and nodded. "Yeah, how? Does zombie skin contain a glue or something?"

"Close . . . real, close," he replied. "Like sharks, zombies must keep moving because if they remain in one place for too long, being partly plants, they tend to become rooted to the ground there and start growing as if they were seeds."

"Did you just say they're partly plants?" Paula asked with a frown. "I recall Uncle Mickey saying something similar, but like, I wasn't paying attention then either."

"Please don't ask me to explain how or why we did it," Ethan said. "But, yeah, there's a little plant RNA and DNA mixed up in the zombie virus. But here's a little bit of the 'why' of it anyway: Seeing as the goal of our research was to extend human life, our reasoning was logical enough. Some tree species—giant redwoods and yews, for instance—live many times longer than humans—thousands of years in fact. So . . ."

He let his words hang in the air. The sun, already invisible in the east because of the hills around Athens, was setting fast, and the loss of daylight filled him with a deep melancholy, as though his soul were graying along with the sky.

Athens . . . Why Athens, of all places? With the crystal clarity of hindsight, Ethan mused over the ironic significance of the name of the city where AFI had located their research laboratory: *Greek mythology . . . gods who in their passions and unrestrained behavior were exactly like men . . .*

Maybe Zoe and Paula felt the same as he did, because neither of them commented until he resumed his explanation:

"The thing is, the plant DNA we inserted during our synthesis now seems to have a strange side-effect; one that makes the zombies take root. It doesn't happen to all of them, and we've no idea why it happens to those it does happen to, but every now and then, a zombie becomes rooted to the ground somewhere—roots grow out of its feet and legs and burrow themselves into the soil and after that the zombie remains immobile at that spot."

"So, it doesn't attempt to walk away?" Paula asked.

Ethan shook his head. "Once a zombie grows roots it seems to lose all locomotory ability. It also loses its hunger—you can stick your hand in its mouth and it won't try to bite you." He coughed. "Now that's weird enough, right? But once one zombie has become thus rooted, it seems to attract other zombies to itself and they in turn became rooted around it and fused to it, with their bodies liquefying and becoming a single unit. That mass of zombies is now a 'zombie tree' that continues to grow and grow and attract additional zombies to join its mass . . . until . . . ." He gestured out over the north of Athens again. "Until there exists a strange living mass like that one down there. Well, that's the theory," he added quickly. "I for one have never believed that the undead could concentrate themselves that much, that a 'tree' could grow this large. The few examples of the process I've previously seen were 'trees' of just a few zombies—fifteen or twenty at most, not that thing . . . That thing down there can't be called a zombie *tree*—it's a zombie *forest*."

"Must be something in the soil around here," Paula said, and Ethan remembered earlier thinking the same himself. He didn't know whether or not the assumption was right.

"Given enough time and enough zombies to combine with it might cover the entire city," Zoe said. "Maybe the whole county even." She shivered against Ethan, "Now there's a scary thought."

Ethan nodded. "Yeah, like a crazy banyan tree."

"A *what* tree?" Paula asked, turning to him with a perplexed look.

"It's an Asian tree that keeps spreading and spreading," Zoe replied her. "It keeps growing and growing, but it's limited to swampy areas."

Ethan was neither surprised nor put off by the fact that Paula Neyman didn't seem to understand much about science. He'd already realized that she was a woman of action, not one of thought. She fit the stereotypical mode for the perfect soldier. She was clearly very intelligent, but her mental focus was concentrated on missions and goals, not on processes and the mechanics of things.

Paula nodded and looked back out of the window. Her profile was sharp, chiseled by the dusk, and Ethan once more realized that, despite the coldness in her gaze, she was really quite a beautiful woman. Her jaw was shapely and her cheekbones high, her nose regal and beautifully formed, her lips full. Even her eyes had a pleasant aspect to them, if one didn't gaze too deeply into them; for then one became aware of a world-weariness, a jadedness that radiated out from her soul to mar her facial features.

Paula, who now looked twenty-three, had been fifty-two before the zombie outbreak, and had participated in many 'wet' CIA covert operations around the globe. Her body may have reset itself to youth, but her eyes revealed her soul's true age.

Unconsciously, Ethan compared her to Zoe. Zoe's beauty was of a different kind, simple, unadulterated, and uncorrupted. She was the rich-girl prom queen, a woman born with a platinum spoon in her mouth, and it showed in the happy glow of her eyes, in the haughty sweetness of her smile. Zoe was indisputably pretty. Her features were regular and well-balanced, and her skin had the sort of glow to it which, in addition to celebrating her restored youth, also attested to the fact that she took good care of it.

Add to this the glorious mess of brownish hair that topped Zoe's body and ringed her shoulders . . . it was a devastating combination for a man to deal with.

And she's mine . . . all mine, Ethan thought with a surge of gratitude to the Divine Engineer. Then he felt slightly foolish for having experienced that emotion.

Who was he grateful to? God? Before the zombie holocaust had happened, Ethan's feelings about God had been ambivalent—the Almighty may or might not exist. But since the death of his family, and what he considered the death of the world? Well, it seemed to Ethan that if God did exist, he must be a sadist; he saw no other explanation of a Divine Engineer watching the human race go through what it had and doing nothing. If there was ever a time humanity had required divine intervention, it was the present.

And . . . now? Ethan felt uncertain. He and his two companions were so close to fixing things, to restoring the world to the way it once had been, that he found it hard not to believe there was a divine hand at work somewhere, aiding them. As far as his faith was concerned, it depended on the turn of a favorable card, on their getting the upper hand in the world's current poker game.

God would win redemption with Ethan when the human race did.

***

A sudden knock on the door made them turn away from the window.

"Come in," Ethan said.

A guard entered and bowed slightly. "Sorry to disturb you, sir, but I was ordered to fetch the priest."

"Yes, what's the matter?" Paula asked, stepping away from the window and walking toward him. "Has someone else died?"

"Oh, nothing so serious, Reverend," the man replied with a polite smile. "It's just that a zombie fell over the barricade a short while ago and we've decided to have her for dinner. We need you to perform the rites of transition. The blessing and atonement."

Surprised by this, Ethan jerked a thumb backward at the window. "But you have lots of stored zomb meat downstairs. The nutritional value is exactly the same."

The man nodded. "Yes, sir, we do, but just like with fish, zombies always taste better fresh. And besides, this zombie is a very young one. The doctors say her flesh will accelerate the healing process in those injured today." His blue eyes revealed his clear anticipation of the delicacy.

Ethan sighed. Zombies didn't either age or regress in age. Kid flesh was both sweeter and more tender and was thus more desirable than that of adults, and as such fetched a better price in the market. And its healing powers were indisputable. As to what was to be done when all the zombie children had been eaten, some social media influencers (possibly all employed by AFI) were already suggesting that the lowest-income tiers of society be hired as 'breeders' in 'baby factories' to replenish the supply of young ambrosia flesh, seeing that all that would be needed would be to inject their children with the zombie virus once they had reached a desirable age. This suggestion was being met with much approval from the rich, who would naturally be exempt from such a plan.

The Vegan and Seafood Lobby were understandably scandalized.

Another, much less popular suggestion, was that every couple in the Church of Zombie be required to donate their firstborn child as kid flesh. Just last week, Zoe had told Ethan a rumor she'd heard, that ChoZo had already added this 'scripture' to the forthcoming edition of Zombook. However, Ethan didn't believe this; there were still lots of young zombies for the world to feed on, enough for fifty years at least.

Paula retrieved her copy of Zombook from the bed where she'd dropped it and then joined the waiting guard at the door. "Let's go," she told him.

The man bowed slightly again and departed. Paula left the room after him, her blue robe swishing around her.

The pair had left the door open. "Wanna go watch?" Zoe asked. "It's boring up here. Nothing to do except look out of the window, at the zomb who want to eat us."

"I'd prefer not to go," Ethan said. But then, seeing that she disliked his reply, he reconsidered. "Oh, alright, let's go. But don't blame me if I throw up."

"You're just a pus—"

The door opened before she could finish and Paula walked back in. Before Ethan could inquire as to what had brought her back upstairs, she strode over to Zoe's side and pulled her away from him. Then she whispered something in Zoe's ears that made Zoe's eyes gape wide open in shock, while she simultaneously seemed to be trying not to blush.

Then, smiling to herself, Paula was gone again.

"What's the matter?" Ethan asked. "Has something gone wrong downstairs?" But that couldn't be the case. Paula had been smiling when she'd left.

Zoe was still blushing and now she burst into loud giggles. "I can't believe what she just told me! You won't believe it either."

"What did she say?" Ethan asked.

"She told me that if you and I are up for a threesome later, to let her know," Zoe said. Now she really looked embarrassed.

"A threesome?" Ethan laughed to hide his own surprise. *I was just thinking how beautiful she was, and now this.*

He saw that Zoe was looking curiously at him. "Well, are you?"

"Am I what?"

"You know . . . up for a threesome with Paula?"

Ethan realized that he was treading on eggshells here. "I don't know, are you?"

"What do you mean—am I?"

"Do you like Paula enough to . . . ?"

"Baby, I've never done it with another girl."

"Do you want to?" Ethan had never had a threesome before either and found the idea both attractive and repulsive. True, he'd be having sex with the lovely Paula, but he'd also be sharing his beautiful Zoe with her. Such a tryst could be viewed either as a win-win, or a win-lose situation.

Zoe looked in turn embarrassed and then confused and then a little angry. "Hey, why are you making me decide this?" she finally asked him. "You're supposed to be the man here."

Which he figured was simply her way of saying: "Yes, I do very much want to have sex with Paula, just to have a girl-on-girl experience, but I need for *you* to *make* me do it, so that if I dislike eating her pussy I can blame you afterwards for the disaster."

Ethan blamed neither Zoe nor Paula for their current heightened states of sexual arousal. The only reason he was himself not horny all the time was because their mission weighed so heavily on his mind. If his two female companions were able to compartmentalize their thoughts effectively enough to achieve sexual desire, he found himself unable to do so; and yet once Zoe prodded him, his body instantly responded to her desire. The entire world now existed in a state of high libido. Nobody was to blame, or maybe zombie meat was the real culprit, because ambrosia flesh was what had made everyone young and therefore randy again. People didn't call it 'zombie-agra' for nothing.

"Okay, so you're saying you'll go along with whatever I say we do?" he asked.

She didn't reply. She looked like a female bomb primed to explode.

"You know," he said, "we'd better hurry if you want to watch Paula give that young zombie her last rites."

Zoe seemed to immediately forget about Paula's sexual proposition to her. Or maybe Ethan had simply given her an escape from her embarrassment. "Yes, yes, baby," she enthusiastically replied. "Let's go."

As they walked down the corridor to the elevator, Ethan just knew that he, Zoe, and Paula would end up in bed tonight.

CHAPTER 13

A Trip Through the Sky

The sky was as black as a witch's cat. The AFI chopper buzzed through the night like a monstrous bee.

Inside the aircraft cabin, Hogwash, Gorehound, and Scary sat in silence.

Scary was leaning contentedly on her boyfriend. Gorehound sat by himself opposite them, deeply wrapped in his thoughts.

Helicopters and airplanes made Gorehound nervous. His wasn't the usual worry that the aircraft would crash, but rather, he worried about getting his head caught in the rotor blades and having it cut off. A violent man himself, a helicopter's rotors reminded him of a group of whirling machetes, and having more than once used such machetes on a person's neck, separating their head from their body, or hacking their arms and legs off, he had an extremely vivid picture of what could happen to him.

Despite all of his bravado Gorehound had a very well developed guilty conscience. It hounded him ceaselessly, that one day, be it sooner or be it later, he would have to pay the price for his many sins. Despite this assurance of his impending damnation however, Gorehound found it impossible to quit the evil lifestyle he led.

And where his rational (or irrational) fear of nemesis was concerned, airplanes were even worse than helicopters: Gorehound had seen one too many action movies in which during the climactic scenes, the film's villain had been fed through a jet's engine, entering it solid and shortly afterwards exiting it as a paste of minced meat and blood.

Worst of all were those movie scenes in which the villain appeared to have been completely pureed by the engine propellers and exited it in a bright red liquid spray or in a shapeless blob like spilled milkshake or smoothie which then splattered messily against the side of the aircraft.

But still, that dreaded someday appointment with the Grim Reaper notwithstanding, the business of death must go on. Gorehound, Hogwash, and Scary made money from violence, from dealing in murder and brutality. It definitely paid the bills.

Once, way back in high school, Gorehound had had dreams of becoming a medical doctor and helping heal the world, but that simply hadn't worked out. By his senior high school years he'd fallen in with the wrong crowd and gotten big-time into truancy and drugs, until his dreams of attending medical school were simply part of his drug haze.

Time passed quickly when you were always stoned; one day he'd awoken and he was thirty years old, with no skills to speak off, and so he'd gotten into drug running; working up and down the east coast and in westward to Illinois. And then after a while the law had caught up with him and he'd done time.

He'd met Hogwash in prison. Someone had been trying to rape him in the carpentry shop and Hogwash had literally saved his ass, though he'd gotten stabbed in the arm for his efforts. But that was nothing compared to what they'd done to the guy who'd been trying to sexually molest him.

Gorehound and Hogwash had first bound and gagged the sonofabitch, then they'd taken their time with torturing him.

First of all they had forced the scumbag to drink about three liters of water, and then, when as was expected, he began complaining about his need to pee, they had slit the head of his penis in the shape of a cross with a knife, and then laughed as he was forced to piss out both blood and water. Then, after tightly securing a rubber band around the base of his penis to prevent him from bleeding to death, they'd cut off his fingers and toes joint by joint, and then stuffed all those severed digits up his anus. The mutilation process had taken ages but had been deeply satisfying.

When finally, their victim had had no fingers or toes left, they'd drowned him by sticking his head in a bucket of water and left him for the screws to find.

Since that day, Gorehound and Hogwash had been like brothers. Once out of the slammer they'd formed the Hog Family, dealing drugs and handling strong-arm stuff for local loan sharks and the Boston mob. Gorehound had fallen for Hogwash's sister Jenni and married her. Scary had lived down the street, but was always dropping in to buy drugs from them.

And then the zombie apocalypse had hit.

Jenni, oh Jenni. Hogwash didn't like thinking about her. Her memory hung behind him like a ghost. Was that what a ghost was—a vivid memory that refused to leave one alone? Gorehound was hurting inside. But his pain wasn't the sort that a 'normal' person would feel. Had Gorehound undergone a recent psychiatric evaluation, he'd have been confirmed a sociopath. He'd murdered and mutilated too many people for Jenni's death to upset him too badly. But when he thought about her his guts twisted up and he suddenly felt like crying; a feeling totally alien to his personality.

So he thought about Jenni as little as he could. Instead he was focusing on their mission to Athens, on arresting those three idiots who wanted to cure the zombies.

He still couldn't believe anyone could be so dumb as to want to do that.

Outside the chopper it was almost dark now. When they had set out from Springfield, Gorehound had also found it distracting enough to stare down at the world, at the empty towns and wandering zomb herds. But now the world below had faded into a gray twilight blur and he had just his thoughts to haunt or comfort him.

"How much longer to Newport?" Hogwash asked the negro helicopter pilot. Even though Mr. Tricks had gotten them this helicopter at short notice, they didn't have any priority. Despite its importance in the modern scheme, even AFI Intelligence was being hit by the shortage of aircraft pilots with good security clearance. This chopper, for instance, was already scheduled to fly to Newport, Delaware to drop off crates of scientific supplies and pick up stuff to fly back home.

"Two hours," the black man replied after checking his instruments. "We'll be in Newport for about an hour-and-a-half—we can all have dinner and stretch our legs while they refuel us and load us up with stuff to take to Springfield. And then it's onward to Ohio, to maybe arrive there at about eleven or near midnight. We spend the night there, refuel and fly back to Massachusetts in the morning."

"That's fine. Wake us up when we arrive there."

"Sure, buddy."

Hogwash shrugged at Gorehound and then laid his head on Scary's and proceeded to fall asleep.

Gorehound smiled at them. He wished he could relax too. But that simply wasn't going to happen. By his calculations, they had about five hours of flying left to do tonight and he'd be awake every single minute they were in the air, worrying about having his head chopped off by their helicopter's rotary wings.

But soon they would be in Athens, Ohio. He smiled at the thought. Ethan Hackman and his companions weren't expecting them. It would be no problem at all to arrest the traitorous trio and bring them back to Springfield, though Gorehound wasn't looking forward to the flight back home either.

However, he was looking forward to the opportunity to hurt those three a great deal. Breaking Ethan Hackman's legs would be good compensation for this discomfort the asshole was currently making him endure.

CHAPTER 14

Death in the Kitchen

The zombie for dinner was in the kitchen. She was young, twelve or thirteen years of age at most—the stage gourmands referred to as 'ripe'—right at the beginning of puberty when the spurt of sexual hormones both gave the kid flesh an exceptional flavor and also produced its desired healing properties.

The girl was dressed in the filthy and tattered remnants of a blue dress that barely covered her. Considering that she'd been wearing this same dress for two full years now, in the heat, the snow and in the rain, it was a wonder any of it remained. Her hair might have once been blonde but it was so muddy now it looked dyed brown.

The zombie girl was plump, which was also desirable, because her body fat could be harvested and amongst other things, used to make the sacred oil Paula was about anointing her head with.

Aside from Ethan, Zoe, and Paula there were six others in the kitchen; four cooks and two guards, the job of the latter being to keep the zombie restrained until she was dead. At the moment very much alive, and totally oblivious as to why she was in here, the kid was doing her best to reach Paula and bite her. She was prevented both by handcuffs and by a restrainer in the shape of a set of tongs (but which ended in a hoop) around her neck, by which the guards controlled her movements.

"Digestion is Salvation," Paula intoned.

"Digestion is Salvation," all those in the kitchen, Ethan and Zoe included, responded while bowing.

"Digestion is Salvation." This time while speaking, and while also avoiding the upward snaps of the zombie's jaws, she sprinkled a few drops of sacred oil on the girl's head. The oil's sickly-sour smell filled the kitchen.

"Digestion is Salvation," came the response again.

Then, while tracing a 'Z' on the girl's forehead with her fingers, Paula pronounced the blessing: Though she was holding her copy of Zombook open to the relevant pages, she didn't look at it while speaking. The ChoZo litany was not hard to recite. It was simple enough that even the zombies seemed to understand it:

"There is no God above us,
Heaven and Hell are both here on Earth.
There is no Truth.
There is only Flesh,
Eternal life through Flesh,
Delicious and nourishing and purifying zombie flesh,
Through the consumption of which mankind will live forever."

"Amen," everyone recited.

Paula smiled at the zombie girl, which seemed to incite her, because in her desire to take a bite out of Paula she now jerked furiously against the metal hoop around her neck and succeeded in tugging the two guards restraining her forward. The girl snapped her teeth at Paula's neck, but Paula quickly staggered back out of range, with drops of zombie spittle barely missing her face.

The guards got the girl under control again.

"Hey, guys, remember to muzzle up the next one," Ethan said.

"Yes, sir!"

Frowning now, Paula told the girl: "Fear not that thou shalt have no grave; from flesh you came and into flesh you shall return."

"Amen," Ethan and the others intoned.

That was all. The girl was immediately maneuvered around to a large sink which had been fitted with a guillotine. The guards fitted her head into the guillotine, a chef thumbed the switch and the blade 'thunked' down, separating head from body.

The cooks now 'processed' the girl's corpse for dinner.

Once her head had been removed, one chef emptied a blue liquid over it.

"What's that they're doing?" Paula asked Ethan. Her expression was calm, but Ethan could clearly see the worms of displeasure writhing beneath her pale skin; she looked like she was about to cry. Alarmed by this, he glanced quickly around at the two guards, but neither man had noticed that their priest seemed saddened by what she'd just set in motion.

"It's an enzyme that neutralizes the poison in her spit," Zoe informed Paula. "The zombie virus can't survive in corpses and would normally die in two hours, but since we want to eat her now, we have to speed the process up and denature the toxin." She laughed. "We don't want to eat her brains or tongue and turn ourselves."

Meanwhile, two cooks pulled on latex gloves and then carried the headless corpse across to a specially-constructed island, where her blood could drain out while they butchered her.

While the man and woman who had moved the corpse onto the island undressed it and powerwashed it with a jet of hot water, the blue tint of which hinted at it containing the same enzyme that had been poured over the severed head, the chef who had activated the guillotine rolled over a cart of knives and bone saws.

"We've elevated murder to a high art," Paula whispered to Ethan in disgust, as the cooks expertly flayed the girl's corpse, getting most of her skin off in a single sheet. "The speed at which they've just skinned her has to be some kind of national record."

"Don't worry, we'll soon put a stop to this madness," Ethan whispered back.

"Yes, we will, honey," Zoe agreed hotly, but then she discretely squeezed his ass.

One of the cooks held the girl's skin up to the light as if assessing its value.

"I'm wondering how long it'll be before we all start using zombie-leather bags and boots," Paula said.

"No one has yet found a way to bleach out the green and purple stripes from zombie skin without weakening its texture," Zoe explained with a low laugh. "It's driving the fashionistas in Paris and Rome bonkers, but for now they and the rest of us are stuck with artificial leather, or whatever cow leather still remains from the old days."

As at other times, Zoe's rather blithe acceptance of the zombie's death bothered Ethan a little. Where Paula sounded disgusted; Zoe sounded bored. But he understood that it was just her privileged upbringing rearing up its head. In his experience, those who had led a sheltered life, buffered by money from the everyday concerns of the rest of the world, found it hard to show empathy with individual suffering. It was easier for them to relate to the indigestion of their pets than to the pneumonia of the homeless. Zoe was demonstrating that trait now.

And what about myself? he pondered while watching a female chef cut the zombie's liver out of her. *As hard as I try, I find it difficult to regard zombies as human. I see a 'thing' there on the butcher block, not a person. I'm fading too; soon I'll be as unaffected by their plight as everyone else.*

He sighed, which made Zoe look at him, so he smiled to reassure her.

"Hey, I'm ready to leave now," she said.

"Yeah, let's go," Paula said curtly. "My work here is finished." Across from them the cooks had begun slicing the flesh from the girl's bones. Beyond them stood a tub filled with other stripped zombie bones.

No part of a zombie was ever wasted; everything was nutritious. Whatever part of a zombie wasn't eaten (including its bones, teeth, nails and hair) was processed into the food supplement powder called 'zotein.'

"Thanks, Reverend. We'll see you all at dinner then," the cooks waved as they left the kitchen.

Ethan's gloomy train of thoughts continued while they exited.

Yes, I eat ambrosia flesh like everyone else does. Yes, I'm young and healthy and handsome now. Yes, I'm worried that once I cure the undead, I'll grow sick and age again. But . . . but . . . but . . .

CHAPTER 15

New Arrivals

As Ethan, Zoe, and Paula exited the elevator on the fourth floor, they heard the noise of aircraft rotors overhead.

When they reached Ethan and Zoe's room they saw the source of the noise—a helicopter was landing on the roof of the two-story building next to theirs. That building had an extended helipad, with seemingly enough space for two aircraft to fit in. A short bridge extended from beside the heliport's refueling rig to the floor beneath theirs.

It was dark now, but the compound's external lights were on, and the helipad also had its landing lights turned on.

They watched as the helicopter's rotor blades stopped spinning and its four passengers alighted from the cabin. The two men were scientists Ethan thought he recognized; the two women he didn't know, but both were dressed like senior AFI executives.

"Those four seem to be high-ranking," Paula said. "Ethan, just how important is this research outpost of yours supposed to be? Athens seems to me to be just another middle-of-nowhere town."

Her voice still sounded strained from seeing the zombie girl butchered downstairs, and after asking her question, she walked away from the window and lay on one of the cots, staring at the ceiling with her hands folded behind her head.

"Best I let Zoe answer that," Ethan said. "She's Admin, while I'm just a lowly scientist."

He and Zoe remained standing by the window while she replied Paula: "This place shouldn't be important, but I think it holds sentimental value for the AFI execs. After all, this is where it all began, so to speak. But, on paper at least, Athens occupies a strategic position for the situation of zotein silos . . ."

While she explained, Ethan watched the expedition heads Professor Cortez and Dr. Chang welcome the newcomers with a deference that confirmed the four of them as VIPs; possibly even the ones who'd green-lighted this expansion project.

And then his gaze moved beyond them, dropping to the barricade behind which the zombies had once more become agitated by the noise of the helicopter.

The zombie press was so thick against the barricade now that Ethan again became scared that the barrier would collapse and flood the hungry horde into the museum premises. Their throaty growls made them sound like hungry lions. Open mouths, green-veined tongues, and eyes like 'go-signals' for the famished.

Darkness had shrouded the north of the city and Ethan could neither make out the extensive green aggregation nor the buildings that projected through it, but looking in that direction drew his mind back into Zoe's conversation with Paula and the supposed reason he was here in Athens—the construction of zotein silos.

"AFI zombie hunters have no difficulty finding prey," Zoe was explaining. "Zombies find them instead. The problem is that the hunters need to separate 'good' zombies from 'bad' ones." She laughed. "Of course, this isn't a literal distinction, as all zombies can be eaten, no matter their state of disintegration. But when hunting at a distance from the cities, there's limited storage space in each meat wagon, and to maximize this space, it's best to transport only those zombie bodies in prime physical condition—that is, undamaged— back to AFI's meat processing plants."

Ethan considered taking over the explanation, but then decided to let Zoe continue.

But the sight of the zombies packed around the barricade bothered him and he stopped watching them, instead turning and looking into the room, staring at Paula.

He first studied her face, which was still twisted up in displeasure, and then her slim body down to her bare feet. She had a small tattoo of a deer on her left calf muscle. Her feet were large, but finely shaped, her toenails painted bright blue, though their paint was chipped by her shoes. His interest in her body wasn't sexual, it was meditative, something to replace the presence of the zombies in his mind. He tried to let his appreciation of Paula's contours and beauty flush away his fears, but it was hard going. But then, out of the blue, he did find something to divert and amuse him: how at the moment neither Paula nor Zoe looked sexually aroused enough to want a threesome later.

Paula in particular looked as asexual as a nun; which was even more amusing since she was masquerading as a priest.

"If zombie meat doesn't ever decay, what the hell do you need silos for?" she was asking. "Why even go to the added expense of grinding the undead up?"

"It's supposedly an investment in mankind's future," Zoe explained. "Since zombie flesh doesn't spoil, all the tattered zombie remains that now litter the country everywhere are good for eating and will continue to be so for decades, possibly centuries, to come. But despite their undeniable nutritious value, they don't look appetizing at all, and in their current state—what with the amount of 'fresh and intact' zombies roaming the countryside and abandoned cities—the consumer won't be persuaded to eat them. And so AFI collects those zombie remains and processes them for future consumption, grinding them up—bones, hair and all—and stores the resultant powder and pellet mixture as 'zotein.' " She laughed. "We at AFI may be assholes, but we're conscientious assholes. Even though at the current rate of consumption there's clearly no chance of us having a shortage of zombie flesh, AFI are taking no chances concerning the future of the new, permanently-youthful human race. And though the Church says otherwise, it's a business decision, not an ethical one."

"Yeah, but the silos still need to be constructed." Paula said.

Ethan decided to join the conversation. "Not as many as you think—at least not yet," he explained. "We're still filling up all the silos previously used to store corn and other grains, for example the old Heritage Cooperative ones in Marysville. Here—Athens—will be one of the first locations where a full-fledged AFI silo facility will be built. We've projected that in four or five years we'll have covered miles of the surrounding countryside with storage containers." He paused and laughed coldly. "And then, those zombies now clamoring outside to be let in, will all be 'in'—ground up and stored in silos."

"It's nasty logic, but impeccable," Zoe pointed out. "Why keep millions of zombies alive when they're a lot less trouble dead? And the recovered heartland territories can be used for farming again."

"It takes a horrible mind to conceive of a plan like that," Paula said. "To kill million of people and store them as powder."

"Oh, they don't plan to kill and grind up all of them," Zoe said with a laugh. "Just about fifty million or so, enough to clear out most of the breadbasket. The rest will be allowed to wander where they will, so long as they don't come near the cities."

"They'll be safe till we feel like eating them too," Ethan said. "And speaking of eating," he added, "how about if the three of us head downstairs to the dining room? I don't think dinner's ready yet, but hopefully they'll have some beers we can drink."

He looked at Zoe, who nodded. "Yeah, let's."

"Okay," Paula agreed. "But you guys have to keep an eye on me in case they do have beer, or I might get raging drunk."

"Paula, you were in the CIA," Ethan said patiently. "By your own admission, you did all kinds of crazy shit while with them. Completely illegal violent shit. And now you can't handle the sight of a young girl being killed?"

Paula swung her feet off the bed. "It's different," she protested angrily, while slipping on her shoes. "I don't know how it's different, but it is." Then she looked sad. "No, I know exactly how it's different—that kid we're having for dinner tonight could have been me. She could have been any one of us three, if the zomb had bitten us today—just like that other headless girl we earlier watched get dropped on the corpse pile outside."

Now tears really did come to Paula's eyes, and Zoe left Ethan's side and went to hug her.

"And now we're going to eat her," Paula added, with tears running down her cheeks. "Is this all the human race has come to, to be food for one another?"

Ethan nodded. "Now you're making me depressed too. Come on, ladies, let's go get drunk."

CHAPTER 16

Dinner

Dinner was zombie stew.

After a couple of beers apiece, Ethan, Zoe, and Paula ate with the others in the dining room.

In one corner of the hall stood a life-sized wooden cutout of a smiling zombie, with a speech balloon that read: "Eat me—I'm the healthiest meal you'll ever have."

The dining room was full of people. Some of the diners seemed glum, but most, including the contingent of newly-arrived scientists and the four guests who'd just landed in the helicopter, laughed with friends as they ate.

A lot of the diners' laughter was forced; it was the thanksgiving of the reprieved, of those relieved to have survived today's deadly ride through the city. And those who hadn't been on that deadly trip were very aware of the terrible 'undeath' that waited just a few yards away; as they ate they heard the growling of the nearby zombies like it was the amplified unsatisfied desire of their own bellies.

Ethan, Zoe, and Paula had more beer with their dinner. Ethan sipped from his can and figured that at least for the moment, things didn't seem too bad.

Watching the other diners in the hall, however, quickly reminded him that there was something very wrong about this scenario—this modern world in which no one looked over thirty years of age and most people seemed closer to a mere score of years. This dining room seemed like a college setting; filled with the young and the boisterous. Only a person's eyes—revealing their many experiences or lack of them—sometimes let the cat out of the bag as to one's actual age.

"Well, you must agree she tastes utterly delicious," Zoe quipped, after forking some meat into her mouth. "That zombie chick's death gives me great pleasure. She didn't die in vain."

"Please stop," Paula said. "You'll make me sick."

"How exactly have you survived this long since the zombie apocalypse?" Zoe asked her, in a seeming continuation of Ethan's earlier and similar query. "You're as young and beautiful as the rest of the world, so you've clearly been eating ambrosia flesh like everyone else has. So what's with all your revulsion all of a sudden?"

The three of them had a table to themselves a short distance from the others, but were speaking in whispers anyway.

"I'm sorry, but something about this place really gets to me," Paula replied. "I think it was the sight of all those bodies outside your window. Yes, you're right. I've almost been killed by zombies several times—I've fought against them and killed them too—and I've eaten lots of them. But I've never seen a body pile like that before . . . all headless . . ."

Zoe laid a hand on Paula's. "It's okay, girl. You just need to chill out. We'll discuss it later, okay?"

Paula smiled. "Yeah, I'll like that." She seemed world-weary all of a sudden, and Ethan felt it too. Still, he broke off a chunk of brown bread, dipped it in his bowl of zombie stew and continued eating.

Yes, Zoe was right; the dead girl tasted utterly delicious. Absently, he wondered what Paula's vagina would taste like later, because she and Zoe were now eyeing each other seductively.

CHAPTER 17

The Arrest

Trouble came shortly after dinner. Ethan was lying on a bed in their room watching the ceiling fan make its lazy rotations. Zoe sat perched on the window sill near him and was staring out at the barricade and the zombies. Paula was in her room, changing from her religious robes into something more comfortable after using the bathroom down the corridor.

And then the racket began.

"What the hell?" Ethan said, on hearing the first banging noises. His initial worry, that the zombies were breaking through the barricade, was soon laid to rest. The noise was coming from inside the building.

"The noise is coming from Paula's room," Zoe told him. "Sounds like there's a fight going on in there."

They both hurried out of their room to see what the trouble was. They opened their door just in time to see a guard with a bloody nose tase Paula, who, dressed in just her panties, immediately slumped down to the floor. Before she could rouse herself, two more guards quickly handcuffed her and hauled to her feet. There was a fourth man out there in the corridor, whom Ethan quickly recognized as the helicopter pilot who'd brought the VIPs.

"What's going on?" Ethan asked the guard with the bloody nose. "Why are you arresting the priest?"

"She's an imposter, sir," the man angrily explained. His nose was clearly broken, twisted awkwardly to the right of his face.

"Impostor?" Ethan looked at the man in confusion. His immediate concern was he and Zoe's possible guilt-by-association from their being with Paula all day long. He needed to say something to defuse any suspicions the guards might have, and quickly at that. But for the life of him, he couldn't think of anything to say.

Thankfully, Zoe quickly came to their rescue.

"Hold on a minute," she said as the guards began hauling Paula away. Other doors along the corridor had opened now, with people peering out to see what the commotion was about; one man had even stepped out of the bathroom with soapy hair and a towel wrapped around his waist.

"I don't understand how she can be an impostor," Zoe went on. "She arrived at AFI HQ in Springfield yesterday morning, identifying herself as Reverend Alice Brown. I saw her ID myself. How can—?"

It was the helicopter pilot who replied her. "She *is* an impostor, ma'am," he said.

"But how can you be so sure?" Zoe went on. "We rode with her for two days and she seemed legit in her ChoZo convictions."

The man frowned impatiently. "Because, ma'am, the real Alice Brown is my mother."

Paula's mouth fell open. "Your mother? . . . So . . . ?"

The guard with the broken nose nodded. "Yeah, ma'am. This woman here"—he nodded at Paula, who dangled limply between the guards restraining her—"clearly did something to the real Reverend Brown and then took her place. We don't know what or why."

Ethan nodded too. "I suspect she's with the Vegan and Seafood Lobby. You know what sort of assholes they are."

"Yeah," the guard readily agreed. "No problem, we'll find out soon enough."

The pilot had already turned away from them and was angrily asking Paula: "Hey, bitch, what did you do with my mom?" When she didn't reply or even look at him, he gripped her chin and forced her head up so that she was looking at him. "I'm talking to you, lady— where the hell is my mom?"

Paula began laughing. The pilot balled his hands into fists, but managed to restrain himself from hitting her. Instead he stood there with his hands by his sides, looking both incensed and frustrated, while the guards dragged Paula away. Then he stamped off after them.

Once the corridor was completely empty, Ethan ducked inside Paula's room. "Keep watch in the corridor," he told Zoe.

He quickly went through Paula's suitcase, which lay opened up on her bed. He located the suitcase's two secret compartments and removed their contents, leaving only her two pistols and their boxes of spare ammo. He stuffed the other objects into his pockets, shut both secret compartments again, and then rearranged Paula's clothes, lingerie, and cosmetics exactly like he'd met them. Then, at a signal from Zoe that the corridor was still empty, he stepped out of Paula's room and crossed back into theirs.

"Thank heavens you thought of doing that," Zoe said. "I'd completely forgotten about that stuff she was carrying." Then she frowned. "You didn't bring her guns, baby?"

He shook his head. "No need. When the guards search her stuff they'll expect to find something suspicious. If they don't find anything unusual, they'll get suspicious that she has collaborators on the trip. The guns should satisfy their curiosity." He began pulling the objects from his pockets and placing them on the bed. "Once the guards find Paula's guns, they'll likely assume she's here to assassinate someone."

Most of the objects Ethan had removed from Paula's suitcase were explosives—egg-sized-and-shaped bombs with a small digital timer window, but which Paula had assured them were each powerful enough to warp a truck into twisted shreds of steel. She also had a bunch of skeleton keys and something that looked like a cellphone, but with a display screen on both sides of it.

"Okay, what do we do now?" Zoe asked. "We both know Paula is as tough as nails, but if they fly her back to Springfield for interrogation, she'll sing like she's Mariah Carey."

Ethan nodded. "We'd better call Mickey and warn him."

Zoe got out her satellite phone and dialed first Mickey Sanderson's home number and then his private one. While they waited for Mickey to pick up, Ethan felt time stretch like a rubber band; each second seemed to last forever.

After ten minutes Zoe lowered the cellphone in disgust. "Half of the time I can't connect . . . and when I do the line goes straight to voicemail."

"Had to happen sometime."

"What do you mean?"

Ethan shrugged. "Honey, things have been going so well of recent that a fuckup was long overdue."

Zoe draped a towel over the explosives on the cot. "What do we do now? I assume we have one day tops, before AFI have Paula back home; and then we're cooked geese."

Ethan picked up his gun from the table where he had left it since their arrival here. "There's just one thing we can do," he said calmly. "We'll have to free Paula and make a break for it."

"Tonight?"
"Tonight."

CHAPTER 18

Interrogation No. 2

"Now, lady, are you gonna tell us how and why you're impersonating the real Reverend Brown, or are we gonna have to fly you back to Springfield so our bosses can interrogate you?"

"I've no idea what you're talking about. My name *is* Alice Brown."

"Yeah, right, and your own son doesn't recognize you?"

"I'm telling you guys, she's not my mother!"

"That man is schizophrenic, keep him away from me! Hey, can't two people share the same name?"

"Lady, you're not the lady reverend."

"Oh yes, I am."

"No, you are not my mom. What have you done to my mom, you bitch?"

"Calm down, Ronald. We'll get to the bottom of this. If she refuses to talk now, the boys in Massachusetts will identify her by her fingerprints; then we'll start a search for your mom."

"Hey, if I'm not that psycho's mom, who the hell am I then?"

"We don't know, lady; you tell us. You know, you really should cooperate with us. Do that and we'll go easy on you. No matter how you slice it, this is the end of the road as far as you're concerned. Just tell us who you're working for."

"And if I refuse?"

"Well, we might just throw you to the zomb. We'll claim it was an unfortunate accident."

"Hey, don't you dare do that before she tells you where my mom is!"

"Fucking calm down, Ronald. Let me handle this. Hey, Tony, get the kid out of here, find him something to drink. And then go see the medics and have your nose looked at. You look like you just fought Mike Tyson after he maybe just found out he was broke. Now, lady, where were we? Listen, just tell us why you're doing this. Who the hell put you up to impersonating the good reverend, and why?"

"You guys are crazy! I don't know why you're doing this to me. I'm not working with anyone. I really am a ChoZo minister."

"Listen, lady, I'd love to believe you, but Ronald says you're not his mother, and you'd expect him to know, wouldn't you?"

"Well, if you don't think I'm myself, who the hell am I then?"

"We think you're a VASL spy. Maybe you came here to kill those execs who arrived by chopper."

"I'm not a goddamn Vegan Fish-head spy, you jackass—I'm a real ChoZo priest."

"Okay, have it your way then. You leave for Springfield tomorrow morning. You're certain to have your fingerprints in AFI's criminal database."

"Whatever, but you've simply got things mixed up; and that kid Ronald is certifiable. Hey, and can I have some clothes? This guy here keeps staring at my tits. Hey, baby, you wanna lap dance? I used to be a stripper."

"Joey, stop ogling the woman. You and Donny fetch her things from her room."

CHAPTER 19

Break in . . . Breakout

Ethan and Zoe made their move three hours later, when the camp's generator had been turned off for the night and its buildings and the world were in darkness.

In the interim, the AFI guards had returned and searched Paula's room, and had taken away her suitcase and clothes.

"I'm frightened and jumpy," Zoe admitted after the noise of the guards ransacking Paula's room had subsided and their footsteps had faded away down the corridor. "I was expecting them to kick down our door and arrest us too."

"It means Paula is keeping her mouth shut," Ethan had replied. "Good for her, but better for us."

"Yeah, she's one tough lady. So now they'll find her guns like you intended."

After that they'd played a nervous waiting game as the hours slowly ticked by, both of them still worried that suspicion might yet fall on them before they could put their rescue plan into action.

But nothing bad had happened, and now their time to act had come.

"Let's go," Ethan said finally. "The sooner we do this the better."

"Yeah," Zoe quickly agreed. "If we wait any longer I'll be too nervous to go through with it."

Each of them had dressed in the darkest clothes they had and sneakers. They both also had a backpack of gear with them. Ethan's most prized possession was the ultra-heavy-duty battery he needed to power the digital lock on the research institute vault. The fist-sized battery would power the vault's lock twice for a duration of three minutes each time. More than enough time to retrieve the vials of ND, but they had to get to them first.

After peeking out into the corridor and confirming its emptiness, they set off for the stairs at its end. No electricity meant the elevators weren't working. They both carried flashlights, but in this case the building's darkness was an ally, not an enemy. They also both wore their guns holstered at their waists.

"I really hope you're right about Paula being on the second floor," Zoe whispered as they descended the stairs.

"Me too. But I'm sure that's where she is." Ethan's assumption was based on the guard he'd spoken to earlier in the day, near the barricade, saying the night guard had a room on the second floor. Ethan figured that was where they would be keeping their prisoner.

He paused and peeked out onto the third floor landing. Seeing a woman walking away from them, he ducked back into the stairwell. "At any rate, if Paula isn't there," he whispered to Zoe as they resumed their descent, "we'll try the ground floor of the building next door with the helipad."

"Why?"

"I saw a few guards walk in there earlier. Looks like they use the place for storage or something. Anyway, once we sound the alarm, we'll have freedom to search the entire building."

"Second floor coming up," Zoe said.

The second floor corridor was empty.

"I need to knock out or kill the night watchman," Ethan said. "We can't take the chance on him noticing us mining the barricade."

Zoe, her eyes large as a cat's in the dimness, nodded. "Okay, baby, but be careful."

Ethan kissed her and stepped out into the corridor.

The guard room had the only open door along the corridor. From his post, the man had a clear view of the eastern main gate and also had two night-vision-enabled monitors that revealed the compound's north and south walls. Ethan understood that the man wouldn't be on sentry duty all night; but he was in here alone till his relief came.

Ethan stepped inside the room as quietly at he could. But he wasn't quiet enough.

"Hey, who's there?" the guard asked while turning around, with his right hand instinctively reaching for the gun on his desk.

Ethan whacked him hard in the head with his flashlight. The man went limp and slumped out of his chair onto the floor. He had a deep bleeding cut over his right ear, but Ethan hadn't killed him; feeling his neck revealed a strong pulse.

Ethan shoved a rag into the man's mouth as a gag, bound his wrists behind him with electrical cord, did the same to his ankles, and then hurried back to Zoe.

"Have you done it, baby?" she asked.

Ethan nodded. "He's out cold. The coast is clear."

Downstairs, they paused for a moment in the foyer of the building to prime the little egg-sized bombs. Zoe shone her flashlight on them while Ethan attended to the task. Priming them was a simple procedure. Pressing the green stud on the tiny display set the amount of delay time before the bomb went off, and also placed it on standby until the red button was pressed. Then one got the hell out of there.

Ethan set each bomb for three minutes.

"I doubt these things are anywhere near as powerful as Paula claims," he said.

"Stop worrying about that," Zoe said. "So long as they let a few zombies into the parking lot, we're good. All we want is a distraction, not to kill everyone."

"When we began this, we were clearly the good guys," Ethan said. "But now we've already murdered two innocent people, and we're getting ready to possibly kill a few more now. How can we justify ourselves?"

"Anyone who eats zombie meat is guilty of murder. We're merely the judge, jury, and executioner." Zoe gestured impatiently. "Hurry up, before someone rapes Paula."

"If that's what bothering you, don't be in such a hurry," Ethan said absently. "Paula might just encourage them to rape her. And if we interrupt her at a critical moment, she might hurt us both."

"You're kidding, right?"

"Yeah, I am," Ethan agreed. "I'm as nervous as you are." He frowned at his girlfriend and then nodded. "Okay, let's do this. I'll mine the fence while you locate a truck we can escape in. Remember what we agreed on—first try the pickup truck we arrived in. I don't recall Paula taking the keys out of the ignition after she parked it."

Zoe nodded quickly. Ethan knew she was scared of being too close to the zombies, and as such was relieved that he'd be the one mining the barricade.

He kissed her and then they both slipped out of the front door. There was a cheese-colored slice of moon in the sky and the night

121

breeze was cold as winter. Zoe headed right, across the yard to the car park. He headed left toward the barricade.

His first port of call was the area of the barricade near the helipad building. Hoping that the helicopter pilot who'd fingered Paula as a fake wasn't standing up there beside his machine, he stared cautiously up and then decided to move further away from the building to place the first bomb.

I wonder what that guy would think if he knew it was I and not Paula who killed his mother to get her here?

It was an unpleasant thought. Ethan activated the egg bomb (the red stud had an identifying grove in its top for such dark situations as this) and placed it beside one of the fence posts. Peering between the posts he saw the zombies rousing from their hibernated state as they sensed him nearby. Their reek of filth choked him. With the noise of the undead rumbling in his ears, and while hoping it didn't become loud enough to warrant investigation from the slumbering guards in the building, he hurried forward to place the next bomb. Before doing so he looked back at the building. The only light visible was that in the unconscious guard's window.

Poor guy's still asleep on the floor.

Ethan looked towards the parked vehicles for Zoe, didn't see her there, looked around the yard, and then finally located her nodding and waving at him from the front door of the main building.

That was fast, he though with relief, giving her a thumbs-up.

Returning his attention to his own task, he activated and placed the second bomb, then hurried on to place two more beside the barricade's main gate, one on either side of it. The plan was to escape when the zombies entered the enclosure, but once that happened he and the girls clearly wouldn't be able to get down from their vehicle and open the gate. So the gate had to go. The gate seemed very sturdy though. Ethan hoped Paula's little bombs were powerful enough to knock it over, or else they would have to ram their way through it.

He still had three more bombs, but the consistent dread of being so close to the zombies in the open at night was draining him of courage. (He really didn't blame Zoe for not wanting to help with this part of their task.) So he hurried away from the east gate to place a final bomb over by the south barricade gate, the one beside the generator truck.

But after doing so he still had two explosives left. After considering what to do with these two remaining bombs, he activated them both and dropped them there by the south gate also, but one of them rolled away from him and vanished in the grass near the wall of the building. Ethan was about to go looking it, but then decided against doing so and instead ran back around the side of the house.

Zoe was waiting by the front door. "You finished, sweetheart?" she asked.

"Yeah, it's done," he nodded while wheezing for breath. "We just have to wait for the first explosion. I'm taking it you've found us a ride out of here."

Zoe nodded enthusiastically. "Same pickup truck Paula drove us here in. Key is still in the—"

'Kaboom!' The explosion silenced her. It was so loud, it felt to Ethan like someone had dropped him right into the middle of a discharging thunderbolt. He stood there in the foyer gaping at Zoe, and then, their ears still ringing, they both hurried to the window and pulled the drapes aside.

"What the . . . ?" Zoe gasped. About five yards of barricade were missing. The front wall of the helipad building was also dented. And there was a large hole where the zombies had been, formed because their bodies had been shredded in the explosion.

"Wow, Paula wasn't lying about the strength of those things," Zoe whispered in awe. "I don't think we still need to sound any alarm."

Already, those zombies that hadn't been shredded were spilling though the wide gap in the barricade, flooding into the yard like an overflowing river of death.

Ethan grabbed Zoe's arm and urged her out of the foyer. "I grossly miscalculated the strength of those bombs! Come on, come on! We need to get back to the staircase! This place will soon fill up with—"

'Kaboom!' Ethan and Zoe didn't hang around to watch the next section of barricade collapse. They were already hurriedly climbing the stairs back to the second floor and faking looking as confused as everyone else who was spilling out of their rooms in bewilderment.

"Shit!" Ethan said suddenly.

"What?" Zoe whispered as they joined the milling people.

"We were so startled by the first explosion that we forgot to shut the front door behind us! The zombies will be able to enter the building."

Zoe stared at him in horror. "Oh, no. And, darling, it's too late to run downstairs and do it now."

CHAPTER 20

Zombies in the House

After that everything was utter bedlam and confusion. And when the last three bombs exploded, the corresponding vibrations that shook the building and accompanying crashing noises made Ethan think that he might have unwittingly caved in the south wall also, letting the zombies in by that way too.

The lights were back on now but were flickering erratically, as if one of those final bomb blasts out back had also damaged the generator.

Blending in with the general insane atmosphere and looking as innocent as they could (not even drawing their guns) Ethan and Zoe searched for Paula in the rooms along the second floor corridor. No one questioned their presence in the corridor as they opened up doors and peeked through them, and the reason for this lack of interest was obvious. Looking from a window in one empty room revealed the yard downstairs to be packed with zombies. Everyone was perplexed as to who had let the zombies into the camp.

Guards hurried past them with machine guns.

One man sputtered, "VASL sabotage," but no one replied.

"We need to hurry. They'll soon figure out it was us who did it," Zoe said urgently.

Ethan pushed the next door open, and was greeted by Paula's loud carnal moans. She wasn't being raped; she was having consensual sex with one of the guards. The man sat on a chair and Paula was riding him face-to-face. Her right hand was free, her left wrist was handcuffed to the metal cabinet beside her.

"Oh wow, Joey, yeah, baby!" Paula gasped. Then, looking over her sexual partner's shoulders, she saw Ethan and Zoe and stared at them in surprise, with sweat dripping off of both her forehead and her breasts. "Oh gosh! I wasn't expecting you guys tonight. What's all the commotion out there?"

This room had no windows. Clearly why it was being used as a cell. Conscious of those outside in the corridor peeking in and seeing them, Ethan shut the door quickly.

"Postpone your orgasm—it's time to go," Zoe told Paula curtly.

"What's that, honey?" Paula's lover turned to look at them and they saw that the man was drunk. "Hey, who are you—"

Paula was sitting astride the guard's thighs, and now, in a combat move that Ethan had never seen before, she leaned back so her body was lying flat on his thighs, lifted both of her feet off the ground, and as the drunken man's penis popped out of her vagina, she wrapped her legs tightly around his neck. His eyes bulged as she tightened her legs, throttling him.

The guard tried to free himself from her stranglehold, but then, wriggling like a snake in her horizontal position, Paula jerked her knees first left and then sharply right. There was an audible 'crack' as the guard's neck broke, and then he slumped back dead, with blood dribbling from both corners of his mouth.

Paula unlocked her ankles from behind his head, sat up again while lowering her feet to the ground, and then stood up off the dead man.

Ethan averted his gaze from both the dead man's softening erection and the trails of female excitement that glistened on Paula's thighs. "Where are the keys to the handcuffs?" he asked her.

She pointed to her right, at a key that lay beside a light machine gun and a white baseball cap on a desk. "That one."

Zoe fetched the key and freed Paula's arm. Paula rubbed her wrist for a few seconds, then she located her suitcase in a corner of the room and began pulling some jeans on. Over her shoulder she asked: "Whatever did you guys do? It sounds as if the entire planet is going crazy out there."

"We let the zombies in so we could bust you out," Ethan replied. He was bothered by the way Paula was dressing beside the guard's corpse without the slightest display of emotion. Also, her found her matter-of-factness disturbing. Even if she hadn't known what was causing the explosions outside and couldn't see them because this room had no windows, she hadn't seemed bothered by the noise at all. When they'd opened the door, she'd been fully engrossed in having sexual intercourse.

When we got here she was gasping in ecstasy—she wasn't faking—and now . . . Now, it's as if she just used the man as a sex toy to kill a few boring hours. And the way she killed him, like she was merely switching off a vibrator . . .

"We misjudged how powerful those bombs are," Zoe admitted while Paula zipped up her pants and then slipped on a tee shirt. Then she slipped on a pair of hush puppies.

"Oh, they definitely pack a punch. How many did you use?"

"Seven."

Paula's eyes widened. "Seven? With that number, you could demolish this entire building. Maybe even collapse half of this entire museum complex if you place them right."

"We may just have done that," Ethan said. "When the last bomb went off it felt like it destroyed the entire south wall."

Paula extracted her guns and boxes of ammo from concealment. "I'm lucky they hadn't found the secret compartment yet." She looked at Ethan and Zoe. "Okay, let's go. No, hold on a sec." She walked over to where the dead man's machine gun lay on the desk near the white baseball cap, and, after slipping her own guns into her waistband, picked it up. She cocked the machine gun, slipped on the baseball cap, and then nodded to Ethan to open the door.

Ethan did so and peeked out into the corridor. "Empty. At the moment all the action is happening elsewhere."

They stepped out into the corridor. "With the way the lights are flickering now, it'll be unwise to take the elevator," Zoe pointed out.

Ethan nodded. "Back to the stairs then."

"Tell me," Paula asked as they headed towards the stairwell, "how were you planning on us getting out of here?"

"Same way we got in," Ethan replied. "Our truck still has the keys in it. Once we reach it, we're out of here."

"Sounds good, but let's check it out first," Paula said. She was showing no sign of fear whatsoever and Ethan now realized why Mickey had insisted she travel with them. *Zoe and I aren't professionals. Sure we may have rescued Paula, but we're winging it and are already in over our heads. But Paula is trained to operate in crisis situations like this.*

Following her lead, they ducked into the room next to the stairwell and shut the door. Then they hurried over to the window and peered down into the front yard.

"Oh, no!" Ethan was horrified at what he'd done.

Downstairs was utter, complete carnage. The zombies were running riot down there, eating people like they were at a human buffet.

About half of the barricade was missing and the zombies now filled the unprotected enclosure like fans swarming a soccer pitch after their team's victory. The noise was raucous, both the ravenous zombie growling and the screams of their victims.

Standing at this second-floor window, they were right over the action; they had a ringside view to the slaughter, like being there in person at the Coliseum while the lions ate the Christians.

The entire yard was swamped with the undead. They were everywhere in sight. Arms outstretched, they trudged relentlessly forward with their classic slow-mo gait, their lack of speed neutralized by the fact that they were endless in number and their prey had nowhere to flee to. The zombies seemed to be in the building too. Noises of gunfire—both the single bark of pistols and the rapid-fire tattoo beating of machine guns—filled the air, like punctuation marks in the fatal paragraph of zombie hunger.

"Scratch Plan A," Paula said calmly. "No way in hell are we reaching the parking lot without being torn to shreds."

Neither Ethan nor Zoe disputed that. Even if one discounted the mob of undead around the building itself, the zombies were also packed thicker than sardines around all the vehicles.

Ethan felt like kicking himself. *If only I realized the bombs were that powerful. But . . . but they were so small!*

Right next to their intended transport, half of a guard's body lay on the front of a pickup truck, with about ten zombies hunched over it and munching on it.

Not far from there, a blood-splattered zombie was eating a woman's head. It had already eaten the flesh off of her skull and the head was only identifiable as female because it still had long black hair. Ethan even thought he recognized the dead lady.

Then a bullet blew the zombie's head apart. Similar cases abounded near the front of the building; zombies eating what remained of people, then their heads exploding from a stream of bullets. The dead zombies would collapse to the floor but more would instantly take their place, lurching forward with their huge green eyes ablaze with hunger.

They watched as a guard was pulled away from his defense post.

"Screw you undead bastards," he screamed as the zombies began eating him. "I'm not food. I'm not gonna become one of you!" That said, he stuck his revolver into his mouth and pulled the trigger.

"Shit, NO!" he screamed a moment later, on realizing he'd run out of bullets and couldn't kill himself. Then the zombies covered him and his screams became even louder.

The undead had clearly gotten into the building on its damaged south side. Looking that way, Ethan and his companions saw a screaming woman in a shredded nightgown flee towards the destroyed south gate. There was an unaccountable bare patch of yard in her path—totally clear of zombies for as far as they could see—and she ran for it, trying to get out into the woods. At first it seemed that she would make it, but then, an almost liquid-looking gust of black smoke blew around the side of the building and got in her eyes and she tripped and fell and stunned herself on the concrete. Before she could recover her senses, the zombies were all over her.

Wincing, and not wanting to witness the woman's death, Ethan looked away, but only to see something equally bad.

Right below them now, Professor Cortez was being torn apart; one of his feet was in the mouth of a zombie girl who, her face covered in his blood, was biting off his toes. Ethan grimaced as the scientist's head separated from his shoulders in a shower of blood.

"Oh, my God, no! This is what we've caused?" Zoe cried. "Paula, we just wanted to get you out of there!"

"It was for a good cause," Paula replied. Her voice was still calm, but her expression was grim. "Well, turnabout really is fair play. We had zombie for dinner and now they're having us for dinner."

"We need to get out of here before we actually do become zombie dinner," Zoe said worriedly.

"It really looks like we're screwed—or stewed," Ethan couldn't resist saying.

Paula shook her head. "Well, taking a truck is definitely out, but we're not yet trapped here."

Ethan looked quizzically at her. "You're thinking of barricading ourselves on an upper floor?"

She shook her head. "No. We'll take the chopper that brought those VIPs. But to reach it, we'll need to climb to the third floor."

"The helicopter?" Ethan hadn't considered that mode of exit. "Yeah, it's still up here—I haven't heard any noise of it leaving yet.

Okay, let's do it. But we'll need to capture the pilot and make him fly us away from here."

"Only if he's not already become zombie food," Zoe added worriedly.

Paula smiled. "No need, I can fly a helicopter—it's one of my many talents."

While Ethan and Zoe stared at her in surprise, she walked calmly to the door and gestured to them. "Come on. I don't think we're the only ones thinking about using the chopper!"

Ethan and Zoe un-holstered their guns. Then, along with Paula, they stepped out into the corridor and broke into a run for the stairwell on the north side of the building.

"We're lucky they built that bridge from the helipad to the third floor of this building," Ethan said as they ran up the stairs. "There's no way in hell we could have reached it from outside!"

"They were possibly thinking ahead to a crisis like this, when they might need to make an emergency evacuation," Paula said.

"Zombies ahead!" Zoe shouted as they burst out on the third floor landing and entered the corridor that led to the helipad walkway.

Ethan had already seen them. A group of four zombies were walking towards them. It was bad enough that the zombies were directly in their path and were blocking them off from their destination, but even worse was the fact that another zombie was coming up the stairwell behind those.

"Time to fight," Ethan said and began firing. He aimed high, for the zombies' heads—that was the only way to put them down. Beside him, Paula and Zoe did the same and the zombies' heads exploded.

The living trio rushed past the fallen undead quartet and Ethan put a further bullet in the head of the zombie who had just emerged from the stairwell.

They paused for a moment and Zoe peered down into the stairwell. "I don't think it's a good idea leaving this place open," she said.

"You're right," Paula agreed. They had returned her explosives to her and now she pulled out one of the egg-bombs, made a slight adjustment to it and rolled it down the stairwell.

"Run!" she told them once it had vanished around the stairwell turn. "I set it for thirty seconds!"

They ran. The helipad bridge was only twenty feet off and they spun onto it and dashed over the heads of the zombie throng below.

"Hey, stop right there!" a voice ordered immediately they arrived on the helipad roof. "Where do you think you're going?"

A guard was pointing a machine gun at them. Behind him the helicopter pilot who'd exposed Paula as a fake was refueling the aircraft from a nozzle connected by black serpentine hose to the miniature fuel dispenser unit at the roof's edge. A worried-looking man and woman were waiting to board the chopper. Ethan recognized them as part of the VIP contingent. He understood their fear; up on this roof they were literally surrounded by zombies, as if the undead were sea water and the building an island.

"We just want to leave too," Ethan explained to the guard. "The zombies have—"

Boom! Paula's bomb went off then. The noise was so distracting that Ethan was forced to turn around and watch the resulting destruction. It was shocking to see three stories of house wall collapse like Lego bricks. The masonry rained down like . . . like rain. It covered the zombies on the ground and also ripped the far end of the bridge off the wall.

The guard who was covering them with a machine gun had also been distracted, which was his mistake. By the time Ethan remembered him and turned back to him, Paula had gotten behind the man and had forced the muzzle of his machine gun up under his chin. She pulled the gun's trigger and the result was fatal. The guard's face and head disintegrated into a bloody mess; his brains exploded out of the top of his head like a mushroom cloud.

Beyond the guard, the male VIP now had his gun out and his female companion had ducked behind him.

"You can't take our helicopter," he barked in an authoritative voice, though his voice betrayed his fear.

"Yes, I can," Ethan replied and shot the man.

The VIP dropped his gun, clutched his wounded belly and staggered back. Unfortunately, he and his female companion were both standing at the edge of the roof, and as he lost his balance and fell over its low railing, he clutched her to stop himself falling. Refusing to let go of her even when she beat at him desperately with her fists, he wound up pulling her along after him. The woman screamed loudly as they both fell down to the zombies.

Ethan spun around. There still remained the helicopter pilot to deal with. Ethan felt panicky. They had to get the pilot before he flew the chopper away without them and stranded them here with the zombies.

Oh, my God, Zoe! In the excitement, he'd forgotten all about her. He looked around and saw that she was okay. She was pointing her gun at the pilot, but seemed unwilling to shoot him.

He was very relieved that Zoe wasn't shooting. Crap shot that she was, she would probably miss hitting her intended target, strike the helicopter's fuel tank instead, and blow them all sky-high.

The chopper pilot was watching them in rage. He had just returned the fuel nozzle to the dispenser unit; and now that he'd recognized Paula, he advanced angrily on her with his hands once more balled into fists. It didn't matter that she was holding a machine gun; he was too furious to care.

"You goddam bitch!" he screamed at her. "What the hell did you do to my mother?"

Paula dropped her machine gun and met him head on. "Your mother is dead!"

"I'm gonna feed you to the zombies!" Fists swinging, the man leapt at Paula. She ducked his punches. Each fist missed her, though he did succeed in knocking the white baseball cap off her head.

Still winging wildly, the pilot leapt at her again, but this time he collided with the two fingers that she speared into his eyes. He howled as both of his eyes popped and blood and pale goo squirted from their sockets. When Paula yanked her hand back, his eyeballs came out of his face, impaled on her fingers. She wiped them off on her breasts.

But even blinded, the pilot still grasped for her.

"I'm still going to feed you to the zombies, you bitch," he spat, with blood streaming down his face while he lurched in her general direction.

"Okay, maybe later, but you go first," she told him and then karate-kicked him over the edge of the roof.

The blinded pilot's screams when he landed amongst the undead were unreal, sheer unvarnished terror, filling the night.

All who consume zombie flesh are guilty, Ethan told himself. *Of course that includes us too.*

A fire had clearly started in the damaged building next to them, because now a thick cloud of smoke and dust was blowing out over the helipad.

After sending the pilot over the edge of the roof, Paula had clambered up into the helicopter cockpit and was busy starting it up. Ethan heaved a loud sigh of relief when its rotors began spinning, their initial shuffle of motion quickly becoming a noisy howl that cut through the surrounding zombie noise like the blades of a blender shredding tomatoes.

Looks like we've made it.

He looked around for Zoe, who had been staring over the edge of the roof at the zombies. He didn't see her; instead, he discovered that a previously unnoticed man, the other male VIP, was charging at him with a knife. The attacker was almost on him; he had no time to bring up his gun and fire, and it looked like he would be stabbed. But then Zoe streaked out of the smoke like a bullet and rammed into the man's side. They both fell to the ground, with the impact rolling Zoey off of him and away from him.

Shit, that was close, Ethan thought. He quickly shot the man and then ran over to help Zoe back to her feet.

"Ouch!" Zoe said as, ducking beneath the furiously whirling rotor blades, they both ran towards the helicopter where Paula was gesturing fiercely at them.

"Where the hell did that guy come from!?" He had to yell to be heard above the noise of the rotors.

"He was hiding behind the fuel tank at the corner of the roof!" Zoe yelled back as she climbed into the cabin of the helicopter. "He must have gone to take a leak there!"

Ethan climbed in too, and then looked outside. The VIP he'd just shot was not dead. He was lying on his back with an agonized and desperate stare on his face, and was stretching a hand towards the helicopter.

But the helicopter was already lifting into the sky. Ethan dispassionately watched both the bleeding man and the roof fall away below them.

"Where to now?" Paula asked from up front, her voice almost completely swallowed up in the rotor noise. "We need a place to stay for the night."

"How much fuel do we have?" Ethan asked. They were hovering maybe fifty feet above the zombies now and he could see the entire undead horde staring up at them, curious about the source of the noise in the sky. Their huge green eyes flashed like beacons, like landing strip lights inviting the chopper to crash amongst them.

It was a terrifying sight seeing that multitude of hungry faces, many with bloody mouths, gazing expectantly up at them.

"They look like they're expecting manna to rain from Heaven," Zoe said with a shudder.

Ethan hugged her tight. "I haven't yet thanked you for saving my ass down there," he said.

She snuggled closer to him. Looking at her face he could see she was already getting sexually aroused again. "Oh, anything for the man I love," she giggled.

"We've enough fuel for a trip of about three hundred miles," Paula called out over the cabin noise. "But we clearly can't leave the area until we've gotten the vials of ND from your old research lab. So my question remains the same: where are we going to spend the night? It needs to be somewhere around here, somewhere close by so we don't waste our fuel."

Ethan nodded. "Well, okay then. I think I know where we can hide tonight." He leaned forward and pointed past her shoulder, out of the windscreen. "Head out over the river towards the north of Athens. I recall that they had a helipad on the roof of the O'Bleness Hospital. The hospital is nearby, although it's most likely submerged in that green zombie mass. But I don't think it would have completely covered it."

CHAPTER 21

Death on the Roof

The incoming AFI helicopter reached the museum helipad amidst utter chaos. The far section of the tall building next to the helipad was on fire, a towering inferno whose night-searing flames illuminated the ghastly scene below.

The peaceful eastern museum enclosure that the Hog Family had expected to find was instead full of the undead. Even from this height they could see some of the zombies eating parts of people.

"Should we still land?" the black pilot asked worriedly.

"Yeah, land," Hogwash gruffly informed him. "Helipad looks safely isolated." He pointed past the man. "That bridge or walkway has broken away from the wall at an angle, so they can't get onto it."

Sweating profusely, the pilot swung the chopper down onto the rooftop. The man was clearly already uncomfortable because of the garish pig masks his passengers had donned just before their arrival in Athens. And now this; what was down there made it seem like they were flying into Hell itself.

"What the hell happened here?" Scary asked as they descended. "It looks like a total massacre."

"The shit's hit the fan," Gorehound said simply. He didn't like the looks of this. In addition to the zombies everywhere and the corpses they were eating, there were there three corpses on the helipad also. Gorehound didn't like it one bit.

Hogwash laughed. "Nah, bro. The world went to shit yesterday; we're cleaning the fan."

"We weren't informed about any distress calls or . . ."

"Sure they'd have sent an SOS," Scary said. "But you know how unreliable telecoms connections are everywhere. Even in the residential cities they're shite." She laughed. "They're probably only now realizing in Massachusetts that there's a crisis here in Ohio."

The chopper landed. The Hog Family opened up its cabin doors and alighted.

"Hey, you, you stay put, get it?" Hogwash warned the pilot. "Turn the engine off and wait. If you dare try to put this whirlybird back up in the air without us aboard it, I'll personally throw you alive to the zombies."

"Yessir!" the man agreed and gulped. Gorehound studied the negro's face as he reluctantly killed the engine. *Yeah, we'll need to keep an eye on him. He looks scared shitless; like he's really thinking of leaving without us.*

He glanced sideways at the nearby building. Burning fiercely on its other side, this side of it was open to the air, with half of its wall crumbled away around a giant hole that extended into its depths. Like Hogwash had pointed out, the concrete bridge to this helipad—which seemed to have originally connected to the third floor—was completely sheared off the wall and now hung out in space at an angle to the hole in the wall, with four or five yards of space between it and the nearest zombie.

The interior of the building looked like a doll house. With no walls and the house's lights dimly flickering, he could peer into the rooms and see the beds and everything. Most of those opened rooms now contained zombies, who were staring across at the chopper; they stared and clawed the air in hunger. Forced by pressure from those behind them, a few of them fell out of the opened rooms while the rest continued staring.

Gorehound flung a worried glance back at the helicopter, to ensure the pilot wasn't about ditching them and flying off, then he walked to the edge of the roof and stared down at the zombies. The noise of the aircraft's arrival had agitated them and they were pressed in a thick crush against the walls of the building.

They clearly can't climb the walls here, but how 'bout them getting in from downstairs? Gorehound worriedly looked across to the roof hut in the far corner. He relaxed when he saw that its steel door had been barricaded shut.

Damn, it looks like everyone at this outpost has been killed by the zombies tonight!

Even if they were safe from the zombies up here, the sight of them made him uneasy and he retreated from watching them.

"So, the zombies killed everyone downstairs," Hogwash was saying. "But then, who killed these guys up here?"

"Hey, this guy is still alive!" Scary called out. Gorehound looked around for her. She was over on the other side of the roof, kneeling beside someone propped up against the metal balustrade.

They hurried over to her side. The survivor was an executive of some kind; this was immediately obvious from the expensive suit he wore. He was sitting against the railing of the roof, and had clearly dragged himself there, as was evidenced by the long trail of blood that connected his body to a spot near the middle of the helipad.

The front of his shirt was wet with blood, but he seemed strong enough to interrogate.

Scary stepped aside and let Hogwash kneel beside the man.

"Who are you people?" the man gasped weakly, clearly scared of the masks they wore.

"We're with AFI," Hogwash informed him. "We work for the US Government."

"The government? Oh, thank God! Help me, I need a doctor!"

"What happened here?" Gorehound asked.

The man shook his head and seemed to have difficulty collecting his thoughts; maybe due to blood loss. "Someone sabotaged the barricade and let the zombies in," he gasped. The effort of giving them this information seemed to have worn him out for the time being. He slumped back against the metal balustrade, and gazed at his three rescuers, their bizarre porcine heads reflected in his eyes.

"Someone did this *intentionally?*" Scary asked, looking down at the zombies, who, undeterred by the fact that they could not reach the humans on the roof, still stretched out their hands towards them as if expecting them to sacrifice themselves to their implacable hunger by diving into their midst. Their throats and bellies rumbled like car engines during a NASCAR race. Several of the smaller zombies had clambered up onto the shoulders of the others, but thankfully, their hands still didn't reach the roof.

"Do you know who did it?" Hogwash asked. "Have you any idea who the culprit was?"

The wounded man first looked at them dully and began shaking his head, but then his eyes brightened as if a sudden understanding had come to him. "I think it was Hackman that did it," he said. "Do you guys know Ethan Hackman, the famous celebrity? He's the one who shot me and left me for dead here. He also stole our official helicopter. He may have been the one who let the zombies in too, though I have no idea why anyone would do a dumb thing like that."

"Dammit, the sonofabitch escaped us!" Scary angrily spat over the balustrade onto the zombies.

"Did Hackman leave alone?" Hogwash asked.

The wounded man shook his head. "No, he didn't. There were two women with him. One of them flew the helicopter. The other one . . ." The man wheezed in pain, then added, "The other girl looked very familiar. Some high-society bitch. I've met her before but I don't recall where . . . may have been at a cocktail party."

"Which way did they go?"

"That way." The man pointed past the helicopter, out across a shining body of water. Then he coughed up a splatter of blood. "Listen, guys, enough questions already. Please get me to a hospital before I bleed to death."

"In a little bit," Hogwash assured him. Then he, Gorehound, and Scary retreated for a short conference.

"So what now?" Gorehound asked. "Those two women with Hackman are clearly Senator Patterson's daughter and that other Paula bitch."

"We'd better call the boss and ask him what he wants us to do now," Hogwash said, pulling out his cellphone.

"Our next course of action is obvious," Scary said. "Hackman and those two bitches must have headed for Sanderson's old lab. We need to hurry after them."

Hogwash grimaced. "True, but unfortunately, cuz both we and Tricks assumed this was gonna be a simple 'fly in and arrest' operation, the boss didn't tell us the location of the lab, so now we don't know where it is."

"Shit, you're right," Scary agreed. "Okay, call Tricks, baby. Once we get directions . . ."

Hogwash dialed Springfield on his satellite phone and Gorehound looked over at the chopper. The pilot gave him a thumbs-up. Apparently the man had gotten over his heebie-jeebies. Good, that was one less thing to worry about. Dust and smoke were blowing out over the rooftop and they were surrounded by zombies as far as the eye could see. Dead ones too, he realized when his gaze took in the nearby pyramid of headless zombies, which was almost as high as the helipad roof. But the zombie pile was twenty feet away, too far for the undead to leap across from, though they weren't even trying to scale it.

"Hey, you guys, hurry it up!" the wounded man called out weakly. "I need to get to a doctor. My body's begun feeling unnaturally cold."

"Don't sweat it, we ain't forgotten ya," Gorehound replied him. "We're just callin' HQ."

Hogwash finally got off the phone. "Can't raise Springfield; reception's fucked up again." He spat in disgust. "Typical technical failure when you can't afford to waste any time."

"So what we gonna do now, baby?" Scary asked, leaning her pig snout tenderly on his shoulder.

"We clear the roof of the corpses and pass the night up here, then try to get Tricks again in the morning."

"But Hackman's already got a head start on us," Scary objected. "If we don't pursue him immediately he might get to that damn zombie cure before us . . . and then . . . ."

Hogwash gestured out beyond the roof and the nearby shimmering waterway. "I don't think Hackman planned to escape tonight, but something must've happened that made him fly off like that. And with him not expecting us to be after him, it's unlikely he'll try to hit the research lab tonight. So, with any luck we'll still arrive there before him and then we can ambush him."

"Yeah, I'm with you there," Gorehound agreed. He always appreciated how Hogwash could think things through clearly and calmly; the true mark of a leader. "Okay, so let's throw these bodies to the zombies."

"Hey, but what about me?" the wounded man asked. "I'm not gonna survive tonight up here on the roof."

Gorehound looked down at the man, whose face looked pasty in the moonlight. "Yeah, he's right," he told Hogwash. "Don't look like he'll make it through tonight without medical attention."

"We'll throw him to the zombies too," Hogwash said with a dismissive wave of his hand. "He's just baggage we don't need."

"What!?" the man shouted. "Fuck you! You pig-headed jerk!"

Hogwash headed for the man. "We don't have time to get you to a hospital tonight and then fly back here. I don't even know that we've got the fuel in the chopper to make the trip. So you're zombie food."

No one saw it coming, but the next moment there was a gun in the wounded man's hand. "Stay away from me, you pig sonofabitch! Stay back!"

Hogwash didn't take him seriously. "I'm gonna shove that firecracker up your ass and—"

Bang, bang, bang, bang! The man shot Hogwash. The first bullets hit Hogwash in the chest at almost point-blank range and staggered him backwards, and then the last bullet hit him in the left eye and blew off the entire left side of his head.

Then it was over and Hogwash lay dead on the rooftop with blood streaming from his shattered skull.

Scary screamed and rushed to Hogwash.

Gorehound first gaped at the dead man and then at the wounded one. The man swung the gun around and fired at Gorehound, but the firing pin clicked on an empty chamber.

And then, the next thing, Scary ran past Gorehound with a knife and began stabbing the wounded man—in the neck, in the face, in the belly, everywhere she could reach. Already weakened by blood loss, the man was completely unable to defend himself. Scary's blade entered his left check and exited his right cheek, the same thing happened with his neck. Even when he was clearly dead, she kept stabbing and slicing at him. She stabbed him so many times, his innards oozed out of him, themselves mostly sliced into bits.

Gorehound let her work the man over. He felt cold. *First Jenni and now Hogwash? Both dead in one day?*

Scary continued stabbing and slicing away at the dead man. Gorehound walked past Hogwash's corpse and banged on the helicopter cockpit.

"Hey, you, get the hell down from there!"

The pilot had been watching from the cockpit window. Shaking his head, he joined Gorehound on the rooftop.

"What the hell just happened?" he asked.

"Bad patient. Didn't like the doctor's prescription for his treatment." Gorehound gestured around at the corpses. Scary seemed to have exhausted herself with stabbing the man who'd killed Hogwash. Completely drenched in the man's blood, she was sitting beside him and breathing heavily, with a crazy look in her eyes. She wasn't weeping. She was much too tough for that.

"Gimme a hand with throwing the bodies over the rooftop," Gorehound instructed the negro pilot.

"Why do that? We're leaving now, aren't we?"

"No, we ain't. We're rooming here tonight. We leave tomorrow morning."

The pilot looked like he'd protest, but then he shut up and followed Gorehound across the roof and they began throwing the bodies over the railing. When they reached Hogwash, the pilot gave Gorehound an inquiringly look.

"Yeah, him too. Dude's sung his last song."

They picked Hogwash up and carried him over to the railing and dumped him over it. Gorehound turned around to find Scary standing behind them. She wasn't dangerous though; she'd left her knife stabbed into the heart of the man who'd killed her boyfriend.

Gorehound hugged her for a while, then he, she, and the pilot walked over and threw the dead VIP off the roof also.

CHAPTER 22

The OhioHealth O'Bleness Hospital's helipad was completely covered by the green zombie aggregation, but Paula landed the helicopter in the middle of its parking lot, which was clear of the green mass.

"You sure about this?" Zoe asked nervously as Paula cut the engines. "At least leave the engine running for a while, so we can leave in a hurry if we need to."

The rotors hummed down to a halt. The total silence created a strange feeling of peace in Ethan, as if all was suddenly well with the world again. He found it possible to forget that barely ten minutes ago, they had fled a scene of total carnage and zombie destruction; and that he was to blame for all those deaths back there.

If the end truly justifies the means; do the means justify the end? he wondered.

"Sorry, but we need to conserve fuel," Paula replied Zoe. "If this place isn't safe to spend the night in, we'll be out of here in five minutes. Long before the zomb can catch us and feast on us. It's also quieter to leave the engines off. No noise means we'll be harder to locate in case of human aerial pursuit."

Zoe frowned. "Yes. But I'd still feel safer if we could be in the air in seconds, you know?"

"It's alright, baby," Ethan told her soothingly. "I've a feeling we'll be fine here tonight." He nodded, indicating the compound outside the helicopter. "There's something weird about this place, but I'm not sure what it is."

"Well, for one thing, that damn zombie greenery surrounds us now," Zoe said.

"That much is true," Ethan agreed.

"And . . . there seem to be no zombies at all in this area," Paula added, turning around in the pilot's seat to face them both. "I noticed that as we descended. There aren't any of the undead near or around this green stuff."

"Well that's a relief," Zoe said.

"Yes it is," Ethan said. "But why aren't there any zombies nearby?"

He opened up the cabin door and stepped down, then reached up to help his girlfriend down too. Once Zoe was standing beside him, he drew his gun, and indicated that she do the same. He'd reloaded during their short flight here. Zoe hadn't, but then her Glock had a larger capacity than his revolver; in addition to which, she'd only fired it twice during their escape.

When Paula had joined them on the ground, they all looked around, shining their flashlights to clarify what little details the moonlight revealed.

Most of the O'Bleness Hospital's buildings were shrouded in zombie material. The liquefied green flesh was draped over the complex's roofs like a gigantic plastic drop cloth designed to keep the premises clean. It covered the upper floors and some of the lower windows too, but most of the ground floor was free of the stuff.

The yard's perimeter wall, however, had gotten a similar treatment. Except for a twenty-foot-wide space where gates might once have stood (or where a portion of the wall had fallen over, though there was no rubble in evidence) it was totally smothered in green, covered as if by a thick coat of living paint.

Ethan wanted to walk over and investigate the walls, but Zoe pulled him back. "No, baby, don't—we'll have enough time for that tomorrow."

"I just want to have a look," he began, but then saw Paula shaking her head at him.

"Zoe's right," she said. "We've all been through enough today. What's important right now is that there's no zombies here and I don't think we'll be noticed from the air; at least not before morning."

"Alright," Ethan agreed. "So where do we sleep? Out here in the helicopter, or"—he pointed to the hospital—"in there?"

"Hospitals have beds," Zoe said. "I feel like sleeping in a bed tonight. Not to mention that Paula might be wrong about the zombies not showing up here."

Paula scowled. "I don't think they will. But okay, you may be right. No point taking any chances after all we've been through."

"And besides, the weather's turning cold like it might rain," Zoe added.

"Okay," Ethan agreed, "now that that's decided, let's get some essential stuff out of the whirlybird and find somewhere to roost."

"Why'd you choose this place to land anyway?" Zoe asked him while she and Paula rooted through the boxes at the rear of the chopper cabin for food, water, candles and blankets. "Did you suspect that it would be free of zombies?"

Ethan, who was once more putting on the backpack he'd taken off to access his box of revolver ammo, shrugged his shoulders through its straps and shook his head. "No, darling. I had no idea the zombies don't come in here." He then pointed east. "But the lab we're headed for is right down that way. Say, ten minutes walk from here. Unfortunately, as far as I could tell before we landed, it's mostly buried beneath this green stuff too. We may or may not have difficulty reaching it."

"Hey, guys, we'll worry about that in the morning," Paula said impatiently, leaping down from the chopper with a hastily packed carton, and gesturing up to them. "C'mon, you two. Let's go get some sleep."

***

The hospital interior smelt like a long abandoned attic. Where the moonlight cut window-shaped squares on floor and furniture, its musty air shimmered with dust motes and bugs drawn to the light. Its floor was covered in ancient dust. The darker places rustled with rats.

Ethan shone his light around the reception area they'd entered. Dust-coated seats, a reception desk with a full set of equipment including notebooks, telephones and two laptops, a shattered TV that was also falling off the wall, tattered magazines scattered everywhere. An artist's gallery of medical charts and posters on the walls.

He shone his light on the floor and found, amidst the wide splotches of long-dried blood that decorated the white and gray tiles, two skeletons, both totally stripped of flesh, both with several bones missing. The second skeleton lacked a head. Ethan shone his flashlight around the room and even down two adjoining corridors; the missing skull was nowhere in sight.

Paula nodded at the corpses. "I don't think the undead have been in here in a long while. Ours are the only set of footprints."

"I pray it stays that way," Ethan said.

Paula pointed to a large cockroach crawling up the wall on their right. "We may have to share our beds with the roaches though."

"Ugh, don't say that," Zoe said. She grimaced when a large rat poked its head out of the darkness and, whiskers twitching, stared inquisitively at them. "You're making me wish I'd voted to sleep out in the chopper."

The rat vanished into the shadows beneath an impression of a bloody set of hands dotted with bullet holes.

"Let's go upstairs," Ethan said. "That way, if the zomb do break in, we'll have a fair chance of defending ourselves."

Upstairs was the same as downstairs, more dusty rooms and floors (though there were fewer rats up here), lots of dried blood smears on the walls, dusty hospital equipment, and several more completely fleshless skeletons. However, one difference up here was that the green mass overhead had blocked out several of the windows. Though empty, such rooms were as dark as night.

Finally, the trio settled on two second floor rooms on the north side of the building. Each room had a bed and an attached bathroom with a dusty toilet that could still be used even if it didn't flush. But more importantly, their windows weren't blocked off and afforded a clear view of the parking lot and the helicopter.

"In a real pinch, we can let ourselves down from the windows and run to the chopper," Paula said.

Zoe grinned at Paula. "Girl, you think of everything." Then she dumped her backpack on the bed next to Ethan's. "Okay, this is *our* room. You can have the other one. . . . Except if you think we should all share one room. We can bring that other mattress in here too."

Paula shrugged it off. "I'll be fine by myself."

"Okay, now please help me clear this corpse out of here," Ethan said.

The 'corpse' in question was the remnants of possibly the last resident of this hospital room. His bones, which had been heavily gnawed by rats, were at the bottom of the closet, over which hung a pair of pants and a shirt crisscrossed by spider webs.

"Don't look at me," Zoe said. "I'm not touching those bones; not even with your ten-foot-pole." She nodded at their companion. "Ask your one-woman-army to help you."

Ethan shrugged at Paula, who shrugged back.

While Zoe dusted the bed off, Paula and Ethan carried the bones out of the room and dumped them in the room opposite, which already had two skeletons of its own, one of which was still lying in bed as if it had died there; either during sleep or by zombie attack, or from a heart attack brought on by sheer fright.

After the bones had thus been dumped, Zoe and Paula walked off somewhere together and Ethan was left in the room with his thoughts. He sat at the head of the bed with an elbow on the windowsill and stared out into the night.

He was immediately filled with guilt at all the deaths he'd engineered tonight. Even the 'All who eat zombie meat are guilty' mantra didn't work to assuage his guilty feelings.

From this window, he could also see the gate space in the strange green wall that surrounded the hospital.

Hey, there still aren't any zombies coming in here to investigate our presence. And there's no way that they didn't hear us land. What's the deal here? Is something repelling them from entering the hospital premises?

This puzzle distracted him from his guilt, and when after quite a while, neither Zoe nor Paula had reappeared in the room, Ethan snatched up his flashlight. He figured an even more productive distraction would be to have a look at the green zombie aggregate that covered the hospital's upper floors.

Seeing as we'll be going under it tomorrow, getting a sneak preview is the smart thing to do.

But when he turned away from the window, Zoe was standing completely naked in the doorway of the room. And she had that tell-tale lustful expression in her eyes.

"Paula was wondering if you'd like to join the two of us in a spot of relaxation," she said while stepping towards him. Her words were playful but were also, just like her eyelids, heavy with sexual desire.

Ethan considered turning her down and sending her back to play with Paula.

But then he reconsidered. *The dead are already dead. Nothing I can think, say, or do will bring them back to life. Hey, I may be dead tomorrow too, might as well live tonight.*

He got up, walked over to Zoe, and kissed her. "Lead me on, sweetheart," he said.

Paula was sitting in bed, waiting for them. She was a gorgeous white statue spotlit by a rectangle of moonlight from the window in which the dust swirled in hypnotic patterns. She was just as naked as Zoe. Her body was wonderfully toned and her breasts were glorious alabaster cones tipped with drops of honey.

"What I want now is for both of you to make love to me," Paula said. Her voice was soft and deliciously vulnerable. At the moment she wasn't a killing machine, she was just the girl next door.

Zoe walked over to the bed and began kissing Paula and fondling her breasts. Ethan quickly undressed and joined them.

Paula grabbed him by the penis, hooked two fingers in Zoe's vagina and pulled them both down on top of her.

"Fuck me, both of you!" she gasped throatily, pressing Ethan's lips to her breasts with one hand while stroking him fiercely with the other and at the same time sucking on Zoe's tongue. "I want to make it with both of you before the end of the world."

There was very little said after that, just a whole lot of sucking, kissing, and penetrating.

CHAPTER 23

Life & Sex

There were cases of booze in the helicopter—part of a scheduled delivery elsewhere. The black pilot got out a few six-packs, and he, Gorehound, and Scary began drinking.

It got cold, so they built a fire with wood from an old packing crate they found near the helipad's refueling tank and sat around it. Scary and Gorehound had taken off their pig masks and left them in the chopper. Scary sat pressed up beside Gorehound, like she was freezing and he was the only who could warm her.

"You know I was in Iraq," the pilot said. "And I'se seen some utterly crazy shit in battle over there, but nothing—and, man, I mean absolutely nothing—compares to this out here." He gestured at the edge of the roof and the zombie horde beyond. "I know there's benefits to all this—but the one thing I dread more than anything else is waking up one morning and finding I've been bit by the zomb and that I'm transforming into one of them." He took a long drag from his beer can. " 'Cuz after that happens to you, you ain't even cattle— know what I mean, bro?"

Gorehound nodded. "Yeah, one bite from those things and you go from living forever yourself to becoming food for everyone else, who then lives forever at your expense."

"Damn right," the man agreed. "By the way, my name's Marlon .. . Marlon Rivers."

Gorehound nodded his acknowledgement and the man went on speaking: "And so, that's the reason why I'se scared to hang around here earlier. It ain't the fear of death; nah, I seen death in all its hideous forms in Iraq—sometimes things got so crazed over there that I gave up all hope of returning home to my mama. Total SNAFU, if you know what I mean. But that was just death . . . after a point I wasn't scared of the Grim Reaper anymore. In fact, while I was flying those retrieval missions to get our boys out of tight spots in which the projected success rate was like a million-to-one, Death and the Devil both seemed like close friends of mine; like they were both waiting for me to eat a bullet so we could drink a few cold ones in Hell together. And that was fine by me. But this . . . ?" Marlon gestured across the roof at the green-eyed multitude that watched them from the peeled-open rooms in the tall building next door. "This is just plain ungodly, no matter how long eating 'em is gonna make me live for . . . and no matter what the Church of Zombie says about it."

With a scared look in his eyes, Marlon stopped talking and drank his beer.

Gorehound nodded his understanding and drank too. He'd always imagined the Hog Family as being together forever and ever, for as long as Zombook and the Church said they'd all live. But, given the nature of their job, he now realized that had been naïve thinking.

"Yeah, dude," he agreed with the pilot. "Everything is so messed up now that I dislike talking or even thinkin' 'bout it."

He put some menace in his voice when he said this, and the pilot took the hint and didn't say anything else after that. Scary hadn't said a word since Hogwash's death anyway, and once the pilot also fell silent they all formed a conspiracy of silent drunks.

They drank and got drunker and the hours passed and the zombies growled and rumbled and reeked and finally vegetated around them, and once both Gorehound and the helicopter pilot wobbled over to the roof's edge and drunkenly pissed down on the zombies to show the undead their condescending opinion of them, while Scary laughed and laughed and laughed and laughed, and all three of them just managed to not fall over the steel railing into the hungry death below.

And then, much, much later, Gorehound found Scary sleeping beside him on the floor of the helicopter cabin. Why they'd both climbed up in here, he didn't know, but when he looked out of the cabin, their negro pilot was passed out cold beside the embers of their fire.

Gorehound now began feeling a familiar urge. He'd woken up with an erection and there was a woman lying next to him. He decided she'd do for tonight and began peeling her pants down her legs. He got them off and her top too, before she woke up.

"No, don't," she protested weakly. "Please don't!"

"Shut up and spread your damn legs," he countered, ripping away her panties to expose her sex.

She moaned when he entered her and at first that made perfect sense to him. He was a big man, and she was a small woman; she might have trouble accommodating his girth. But then he decided she was just being silly; as far as he could tell, Hogwash (God rest his evil soul) had been even bigger down there than he was, and he'd never once heard Scary complaining about the size of Hogwash's penis or even hinting she was sore down there. So maybe what she was upset about was that he wasn't doing it hard enough.

So he really put his back into his thrusts now and then she began responding, grabbing his buttocks tight and pulling him even deeper into her body, and weeping as he plowed her. She wept a river, as if she was trying to drown her sorrows. He grabbed her breasts and kneaded them roughly and her eyes widened as if she was seeing God, so he guessed that he was getting through to her now.

Scary wept so much while they were doing it that Gorehound had no idea if she came or not. But afterwards she went limp under him and seemed satisfied in some weird way that he found impossible to understand, possibly because he was as drunk as she was.

"All men are pigs," he heard her say before he fell asleep again.

CHAPTER 24

The Cat

Ethan awoke once in the night to relieve himself. Zoe was asleep in Paula's bed, but Paula wasn't in her room. A quick peek down into the yard revealed it to be as empty of the undead as when they'd arrived here.

He used the bathroom, and then walked next door to see if Paula was asleep in there.

Gun in hand, Paula was sitting cross-legged on the bed, staring out of the window. Apparently, old CIA field habits died hard. Not wishing to disturb her silent vigil, and still feeling sleepy himself, Ethan thanked Heaven for this beautiful guardian angel, and then padded quietly back to sleep by Zoe's side.

***

In the morning, Paula seemed inexplicably distant. She kissed Ethan readily enough, even sliding her tongue between his lips to taste his, but her mind seemed elsewhere, far away.

Meanwhile, Zoe was clearly embarrassed after their threesome. Back in their room again this morning, she was fidgety and seemed strangely vulnerable.

"Hey, honey, just chalk it down to experience," Ethan told her as he held her close. "We don't have to do it again—with her or anyone else—if you don't want to." He grinned. "But you can't deny it was very enjoyable."

Zoe threw him a cautious look. "I'm just worried that you'll wind up liking her more than you do me," she said.

He kissed her. "Darling, that won't *ever* happen."

His statement did seem to satisfy her and her behavior normalized after that. They picked up their things and went back to Paula's room.

The girls had thoughtfully brought up a loaf of bread and some cans of zombie spam (or zam) from the helicopter last night, and now prepared sandwiches for breakfast.

Paula sighed while opening the cans. "Zam, Big Zack burgers, Kentucky Fried Zombie—"

"Hey, I like KFZ!" Zoe protested. Then she giggled and kissed Paula warmly on the lips. "Oh, darling, I'm just kidding. I understand the problem. It really does seem hypocritical to eat the very monster you're trying to save. Like a poacher trying to rescue an endangered species."

Yes, Ethan agreed as he chewed his sandwich, it really did seem like a double standard to feast on the very creatures you were trying to help. But he knew that to save the zombies he needed to live long enough to do so, and he also needed to remain young and strong until the job was completed.

"Zombies truly are delicious," he said. "It really does seem sad to give this up."

Paula threw him a cold look. "Hey, don't you start. I've had enough of this chicken-flavored zombie crap to last me an eternity." She traced a line of text on a zam can with a blue fingernail: " 'Church of Zombie approved to help you live forever.' Personally, I'm looking forward to the day when I'll be able to gorge myself on fried chicken again."

"Well, no one can accuse the Church of slacking in their job of brainwashing the public," Ethan said. "Not with kids now being taught the essential principles of Zombianity from kindergarten."

Paula sighed. "Yeah. 'I eat therefore I am.' " She groaned. "And people once complained that mandatory school prayers were bad."

"You know, that should really be, 'I eat therefore I shi—' " Zoe's giggled reply was cut short when a cat ran into their room.

The sight of the creature almost made Ethan drop his sandwich. The cat dashed between Zoe's legs and vanished under the bed.

It was being pursued. Seconds after it had taken sanctuary behind the humans, a trio of large black rats appeared in the doorway. They paused there with their black bodies trembling, their horrid beady eyes staring up at the humans in fear, but not wanting to back off from killing the natural rat predator that they now hunted and which they could see cringing in fright under the bed, though it was hissing defiantly at them.

"Go on, scram!" Zoe said, flinging one of the emptied zam cans at them.

The rats scattered and ran off and the three humans were left with the mystery of the cat to deal with. And it was a mystery. Even in the cities, former household pets were almost impossible to come by. Out here in the zombie-ruled wilderness, cats and dogs were now considered as extinct as skunks, deer, moose, rabbits, raccoons, rattlesnakes, groundhogs, chipmunks and just about everything else untamed and on four legs that one could think of. In theory, you could still find the occasional squirrel and tortoise.

"Where the hell did it come from?" Ethan asked, bending forward and looking under the bed. The cat, its body still trembling from the chase with the rats, stood in the shadows with its back arched.

Ethan got down on his hands and knees and reached under the bed and stroked it. "Hey, kitty, kitty, come out, come out." Its fur was still standing on end, but finally it relaxed and came to him.

The cat was dirty gray in color, and quite thin and hungry-looking. It was male and half of its right ear was missing, apparently (judging from the shape of the wound) as the result of an encounter with zombie teeth. But that was an old wound, one long healed.

"Poor guy looks like he ain't eaten in days," Paula said, when Ethan lifted the cat up onto the bed.

"I guess with the rats around here so big, they're quite difficult to kill," Zoe said, pointing out a few more recent, if minor wounds on the cat's back which were clearly the result of rodent teeth.

"The smell of our breakfast must have attracted him." Ethan opened up a fresh can of zombie spam for the cat, which quickly devoured it.

They all sat eating their breakfasts, with Paula and Zoe each stroking their new feline companion from time to time.

The cat had clearly come to stay. Once it had finished eating its zam, it made itself comfortable by Ethan's side. He stroked it, but then got up. His mind was once more on their task. The cat's presence had cheered them all up, but they still had a job to do, and the sooner they got started on it, the better.

"We'd better get a move on," he said. "The sun's up and anyone who survived that mess at the museum has had more than enough time to alert AFI Intelligence. Three or four hours at least and this place will be crawling with troops."

Paula shook her head. "Not true. They've no way of knowing it was us who started things. They may come running . . . or maybe they won't. I suspect it's the latter. They'll merely send a recovery team to pick up the survivors."

"They'll be sure to investigate if they see our helicopter out there," Zoe said, pointing down at the aircraft. "I agree with Ethan that we need to be gone soon."

Paula mused on Zoe's statement for a moment and then nodded. "Yeah, you're right. Okay, let's go then." She looked at Ethan. "How far to the lab and back? How long will it take to get out the vials of ND?"

"We should be done in less than an hour. Maybe even forty minutes. We just need to reach the lab." He tapped his backpack. "Seeing as I'm carrying a backup battery, opening the vault is a question of seconds. Then we'll be back here and on our way home again."

"What are we gonna tell them about last night?" Zoe asked. "AFI are going to want some kind of explanation as to how the three of us escaped."

Paula laughed. "Don't you worry about that. I'll tell them that I prayed to Zombie God for his help and he parted the zombie horde before us."

Zoe laughed. At first Ethan grinned, but then he frowned on remembering that officially, Paula wasn't supposed to be traveling with them at all, and once back in Springfield, MA, they would be wise to keep her concealed from everyone.

And then he remembered the cat, which was now contentedly purring and rubbing itself against his legs.

"Hey, what are we gonna do with this little guy?" he asked the women.

"We'll take him with us," Zoe said without hesitation. "He came to us for protection. Leave him here and the rats are sure to kill him."

"We *can't* take with us," Ethan immediately objected. "Where we're going may be dangerous too."

"Oh yes, baby, he is most definitely coming along with us," Zoe said, her eyes narrowing like she was preparing for a fight.

"But he simply can't." Ethan didn't see the logic of them carrying the cat along with them. "If we run into zombie trouble, he'll be eaten for sure."

Zoe bent down and picked up the cat and stroked it. "No he won't. He's survived this long, hasn't he?"

"Please, baby, be reasonable."

Zoe, her jaw firm, shook her head. "This cat is coming along with us and that is that. If necessary, I'll carry him in my backpack!"

"Stop arguing, both of you," Paula said in amusement. "We'll just lock our cat up in the helicopter. That way we'll know he's safe and we won't have to watch out for him tagging along after us."

CHAPTER 25

Breakfast for the Zombies

He was back in the too-distant-to-mentally-comprehend future, riding across the desert on a wheelless motorbike. This desert was called the 'Worlderness,' and he was escaping from a tribe of zombie-worshippers who wanted to kill him.

Zombie worship was the theme here, even his clothes were made from zombie leather.

Then there was a tree—the universe's largest-ever lemon tree. He was climbing it . . . his companion was a girl who had plants growing in her body . . . suddenly there were zombies in helicopters after them both. Then they had reached Haeven (not 'Heaven') . . . and then suddenly zombies were falling to earth like rain . . . . and then he was in bed, having sex with the ugliest woman who ever lived, and she was telling him how much she loved him, while having an extremely loud orgasm and . . .

***

Gorehound jerked awake and realized that what had woken him was the helicopter pilot shaking his leg. The man was standing outside the chopper, leaning in, and he had a horrified look on his dusky face.

Gorehound rubbed the sleep from his eyes and looked around for Scary. She wasn't in the chopper. He looked back over at the pilot.

"What the matter? More zombies?"

The man gulped and shook his head. "Nah, bro, this is a lot worse than that. Get down and come have a look for yourself."

Worse than the zombies? Not bothering to pull on his shirt, Gorehound quickly buckled up his belt and got out of the chopper. Barefoot, he followed the pilot over to the east side of the roof. The zombies were still down there, but their numbers were much less than

156

last night. The rest had probably wandered off looking for surviving wildlife to eat.

"I found her here when I woke up five minutes ago," the pilot said.

It was Scary. Pig-mask on her head, she was propped up against the roof railing and was dead.

Scary had killed herself. Using the same knife with which she'd avenged Hogwash's death, she had almost completely cut her left hand off—it hung on her wrist by skin and tendons. In addition, as if to make sure she'd get the job done right, she had also slit her neck open; its left half gaped wide beneath her mask's lower edge. Her shirt, which was all she had on, was drenched in blood. The wet spot on the concrete between her legs looked like semen.

"Why the hell did she do it?" the pilot asked.

Has to be guilt, 'cos I fucked her so soon after Hogwash's death, Gorehound realized, now remembering that he'd heard Scary complain that, "All men are pigs," before he'd fallen asleep again. *But I didn't rape the woman—she was into it too, squirming around my cock like I was her high school sweetheart. I just didn't think she was that unhinged. Shit.*

He looked coldly at the pilot. "Gimme a hand and lets throw her over to the zombies," he said. "I'm sure they're expectin' breakfast."

The pilot gulped but complied. Mask and all, they threw Scary's body down to the zombies. Gorehound watched her corpse being torn to bits, the zombies digging their overgrown and cracked fingernails into her belly and pulling out her intestines and liver; fighting over each juicy morsel of her. Those zombies that were further away, shambled over, hoping to get a few scraps; or maybe thinking the men on the roof were about sacrificing themselves too to appease the unending hunger.

Gorehound found it amusing how the zombies tried to eat Scary's latex pig mask too, biting and tugging at it, while it stretched like a rubber band and then snapped back into shape again.

But then his thoughts drifted back to his weird dream. Just like the one he'd had yesterday, it had seemed so realistic, like a vision of some kind.

But zombies flying helicopters? Yeah right, gimme a break.

"Hey, what do we do now?" the pilot asked. Gorehound turned to the man, who was standing with his back to the railing, so he didn't have to watch the zombies eating Scary.

"I've still got Hog's sat phone," Gorehound replied. "I'll call Mr. Tricks on it and report the situation. See what he wants us to do about it."

The negro nodded. "Okay, but hurry it up, man. I'm frigging tired of hanging around this shithole."

"Yeah, yeah, only take a minute." Gorehound was tired of hanging around also, more so now that Scary had offed herself and he was stuck on the roof with this black guy. The pilot was friendly enough, but Gorehound's only true friends were now all dead and he was itching for something to do to take his mind off of the desire to mourn them.

Thankfully, he got through to Mr. Tricks on the first try. Either there were less phone users this morning or all the AFI switchboard operators had been partying with their boyfriends last night.

Gorehound told Mr. Tricks the situation here at the museum and how their quarry had escaped. He felt like laughing at how panicked the boss sounded now—Tricks sounded like he was both shitting and peeing his pants over in Springfield.

"Get over there at once and try to stop them. I'll immediately dispatch reinforcements to you, but it'll be hours before they arrive. So everything depends on you, Gore. And don't worry, you'll have a *monster* bonus if you pull this off. Just stop that Hackman idiot. Kill him and Sanderson's niece if you like, but PLEASE, try not to kill Patterson's daughter if you can manage it. I think she's innocent in all this, fooled by love, and besides, her father will never forgive me if she dies."

"Yeah, sure," Gorehound agreed. "Where's the lab situated?"

"Pass the phone to the pilot. Hey, I remember that guy used to be a soldier. Iraq, I think. I'll order him to back you up."

CHAPTER 26

Into the Green

Paula smirked as she opened up one of the helicopter's cabin doors. "You wanna know why we, the general public, can't buy pets yet? The rumor I heard is that ChoZo has a plan to implant biochips into the eyes of the new breed of household pets, which are then intended to record the activities of their owners."

Zoe, who was carrying their newfound cat, laughed and kissed Paula's cheek. "Honey, you're so paranoid it's sexually attractive."

Ethan, however, took the rumor seriously. He felt the Church of Zombie would stop at nothing to keep its current stranglehold on the souls of all Zombelievers.

And since ChoZo is merely another name for Ambrosia Flesh International, they definitely have the resources at hand to bug everyone's new pets.

"It's madness though," Paula said. "Just imagine your cute little hamster spying on you."

"Girl, just put our cat in the chopper and let's hike," Zoe said.

Once their new cat was securely shut away in the helicopter (with another opened can of zombie spam to keep it company), Ethan, Paula, and Zoe cautiously peered out through the gap in the hospital's perimeter wall.

"I'd love to know what's keeping the zombies away from this part of town," Zoe said. "Is this green stuff poisonous to them or what?"

"I don't think so. I think the rats have been eating it," Ethan said, stroking the wall's covering of greenish skin and imagining that since it was living meat, he felt the pulse of a heartbeat somewhere in the far distance; the almost imperceptible throb of the sheet of skin's purple veins seemed to back this impression up. It smelt just like normal skin; a sweaty hint of musk, but nothing unnatural.

Ethan found it sadly ironic that the AFI contingent at the museum hadn't known that setting up camp over here would have protected them from zombie attack.

"We're lucky that animals can't get eternal life from eating zombie meat," Zoe said. "Immortal rats would be a nightmare. Imagine immortal cockroaches too or immortal worms. Ugh!"

"We have to get going," Paula said. She stepped through the gap in the wall into the street outside the hospital, with a gun in one hand and a flashlight in the other, and then gestured impatiently back at Ethan and Paula. "Hey, come on, you two."

They hurried after her. The lot opposite the hospital was vacant, full of knee-high grass, which explained the break in the green flesh cover in this area, as the zombie material seemed to have a limit to the distance it could stretch over. But the green hood resumed up ahead of them, arching across the road from one rooftop to another.

Still there were no zombies anywhere in sight. And in a city overrun by the undead, that in itself was cause for concern.

"Hey, guys, hold on a moment before we set off," Zoe said.

"What's the matter?" Paula asked.

"I need to call my dad before we head down the tunnel. Or else he'll be worried when he hears about the massacre at the camp."

Zoe already had her cellphone out and was swiping its screen on. Paula gave her a narrow look and then turned to Ethan, who shrugged back at her: "That's daddy's little princess for you."

"She'll never get through," Paula said.

"She will. Just watch, she's a senator's daughter—that's top priority."

And just like Ethan predicted, Zoe was already connected to Washington D.C. "Hey, daddy . . . no, we're fine—I mean Ethan and myself. . . . A rumor? . . . yeah, we had some trouble with the zomb last night. . . . They broke into camp and killed some people, but I'm okay, no bites or anything. . . . Hey, dad, stop worrying. I'm a big girl now, I can look after myself—no need to send the cavalry to rescue me. . . . Ethan and I are okay . . . I may be back in town earlier than planned; maybe even by this evening. . . . Okay, daddy, love you too. My regards to Uncle Tricks too."

At the mention of 'Tricks' a cold shiver ran down Ethan's spine.

Zoe hung up and frowned. "Guys, they already know about the massacre. At the moment my dad is in video conference with the AFI head of intelligence."

Paula looked worried. "Mr. Tricks? Hey, won't they trace your phone?"

Zoe shook her head. "Bug a senator's line? You've gotta be kidding."

Paula again looked at Ethan. He nodded back at her. "She's right. Tricks' head would roll if he did that."

"Okay, but can we go now?" Paula asked. "Even if you're both wrong and they are tracking Zoe's phone, it won't do them any good if we've left here before they arrive."

"True," Ethan agreed.

They hurried along and stepped inside the greenish meat tunnel.

CHAPTER 27

The New Hog Family

The helicopter pilot was angered at being drafted back into combat service. Gorehound didn't give a shit about the man's feelings. He was all about getting the job done and collecting that monster bonus Mr. Tricks had promised him.

"Hey, put this one," he said before they took off, handing the pilot the spare pig-mask he always carried with him. This morning he was riding up front in the cockpit with the pilot.

The negro looked first at the mask and then at Gorehound, who was already wearing his own mask, along with a blue ChoZo tee shirt. "You kidding me, right? There ain't no way I'm wearing this thing. Makes you look creepy, like a Halloween monster, and I hate Halloween"

Gorehound had expected some resistance. "Hey, soldier, I'm in command of this mission," he growled in what he hoped sounded like a military voice. "Now, put the mask on! I ain't asking you to join the KKK, am I?"

"Fuck this shit!" the black pilot grumbled but donned the pig-head mask.

"There! Now that wasn't hard, was it?" Having the pilot wearing a mask too made Gorehound feel like the Hog Family spirit still lived on. And it would, for sure, once he got out of this current situation. He'd find some young blood, including a new woman for himself.

"Alright, put this metal hawk of yours in the air and lets go catch us some chickens for breakfast."

Three minutes later the helicopter was back up in the sky, flying north over the Hocking River. And Gorehound had once more remembered why he hated flying so much.

CHAPTER 28

Zombie Forest

Being beneath the green covering wasn't as dim as Ethan and his companions had expected. Some light filtered through gaps in the fleshy ceiling. The spacing of these overhead gaps struck Ethan as geometrical rather than random, as if the holes were actually a biological adaptation to permit sunlight reach the tunnel walls.

Even a zombie plant needs sunlight for photosynthesis, he thought.

At first glance this space seemed formed not just of stretched zombie skin but also of some melted undead bodies. Parts of people stuck from its walls at random—hands with grasping fingers, legs with kicking feet, and heads whose faces writhed in silent agony.

Once more the smell in here was that of a human body; musk with a hint of perfume, as if flowers grew nearby.

This place really was a tunnel. Here the state of the strange flesh aggregation was nothing like the sparse coating that the hospital had received. Here the zombie covering was incredibly extensive and had completely obliterated the yards between the houses and also the intervening empty lots and all the trees, though the occasional branch poked through it.

The covering wasn't entire, however; the ground—meaning the road—was still bare, although both sidewalks were draped in the greenish flesh. In this subdued lighting, the sidewalks seemed coated in melted emerald wax.

The further Ethan, Zoe, and Paula proceeded beneath the green canopy, the more constricted the space they had to traverse became—from a street two cars wide, after about a hundred yards they were walking through a corridor barely three or four feet wide. The walls never came completely together, but nor were they ever separated enough that one could feel relaxed while passing between them.

Even the light spaces overhead shrunk in size and they had to switch on their flashlights to see their way.

Now the route bore not the slightest similarity to the area of the city that Ethan had worked in. He was able to navigate their way simply because he remembered the street layouts, and also because the zombie aggregation wasn't covering the roads; although all the traffic signs and traffic lights had been subsumed in the zombie green.

Ethan wondered if maybe the zombie mass was so thick around here because it somehow 'sensed' this place as 'home'—meaning where its existence had historically begun. But then he dismissed the supposition as silly.

It has to be what Paula suggested—something in the soil.

What was really scary about this place were the bodies stuck into the wall. Hands, legs, bones; all arranged completely at random Some were frozen in place, while others jerked. Glowing zombie eyes peered at them from frozen heads with tongues that were long green flickering tentacles. Green mouths with purple veining moved silently, gnashing leaf-green teeth, but thankfully these mouths didn't drip the poisonous zombie saliva.

Still, with the tunnel so constricted, these physical projections were in the way and had to be navigated around, something that was often a creepy, icky task.

"They aren't stuck to the wall," Ethan muttered, not realizing he was speaking aloud as he shifted to prevent a projecting hand from grabbing him. "They're growing, growing like a tree will."

"Huh, baby? What was that?" Zoe asked. She'd been keeping very close to Ethan since they'd stepped beneath this living canopy.

"This is simply too fucked up for words," Paula said. "It's like an endless wall of melted people. I've never even dreamed a place like this existed."

"I'm still stunned by the size of this zombie forest," Ethan said. "Viewing it from upstairs in the museum was one thing, but to be here in person is scary. Who would have imagined a zombie aggregation could reach this size?"

"Well, here we are anyway," Paula said grimly. "And you're to blame for our being in this horrible place. Alright, man, which way do we go now? Left or right?"

They had just reached an intersection in the meat tunnel. All three corridors ahead of them looked like throats leading to a hungry stomach.

Next to Ethan, an exploded zombie torso stuck out of the wall; its rib cage was spread wide as if by retractors; the heart was still beating, the lungs still inflating and deflating. Where the body's legs should have begun, the soles of a pair of feet stuck out from the flesh. It was the most horrible sight Ethan had yet seen in here. He figured Zoe's most horrible sighting would have been the several erect male genitalia they'd seen randomly sticking out of the wall like dildos.

"Three ways to go, each of them with human limbs and heads growing from the walls," Paula said. "I'm in the middle of a freaking nightmare. Will someone please slap me and wake me up? Please?" She looked like her sanity was starting to fray at the edges.

"I feel it worse than you do," Zoe said, with a shiver that rippled through Ethan's body too like spilled ice crystals. "I keep feeling like these undead are . . . this is more than just random eyes, ears, and limbs that once belonged to people and are now fused into a single mass creature. I keep feeling like we're walking through . . . standing in the middle of a mass of suffering people. I can sense the minds . . . auras of a million tormented souls."

"Here at this crossroad, I feel the pain of the zombies," Paula said, her eyes frantic.

"Yes, I'm feeling that too, as if this zombie forest or whatever this thing is, is really alive. I think it's watching us, biding its time to feast on us."

"Ethan, which way do we go, honey? Left, right or center?"

Ethan was having a hard time too, adjusting his mind to the idea that he was traveling through a world made of living meat. Eyes were watching him from the right and left—eyes in two female heads, and eyes that were just green balls set in bulging flesh, but which nonetheless seemed to track his movements. The nearby walls throbbed as if he and the girls were standing inside a giant heart.

And yes, he felt it too, what Zoe and Paula both felt—a psychic pressure on his mind. The combined weight of trapped souls in this zombie forest was pressing on his own soul.

"We're going right!" he gasped. Grabbing both Paula and Zoe by their arms, he quickly ducked into the right-side tunnel and literally dragged both women along behind him. They went numbly, as if he was a puppeteer and they his marionettes.

Thankfully the psychic pressure lessened once they had gone a short distance. Ethan felt normal again. He pulled the two women through a solitary storefront that broke through the mess of skin.

They'd entered a one-time pharmacy. Once safe amongst dusty shelves and racks of expired and faded medicines, and with his chest heaving for breath, he stared worriedly at both Zoe and Paula. They stared back at him dazedly, like they had already lost their minds and were now searching for them amidst those trapped in the meat forest.

"That was beyond a doubt, the most fucked-up experience I've ever had," Paula said finally.

"Hey, what just happened back there?" Zoe asked.

"I think we just solved the mystery of why there aren't any zombies in this place," Ethan replied them. "I understand it now: the zomb are scared of this zombie forest."

"Scared?" Paula shook her head. "Nah, I don't think so. Everyone says the undead can't think."

Zoe nodded. "That's right, they don't think. How then can they possibly be scared?"

"Well, we all felt that crazy mental pressure back there, didn't we?" Ethan asked.

"Yeah," Zoe agreed, rubbing her throat. "It was like there were a million lost souls trapped and screaming in terror; and they were all inside my head."

Ethan nodded. "I think the zombies also sense this whole forest aggregation. They sense it . . . as an end to life in a different kind of way from that in which their lives have already ended. That crossroads was a node of some kind—I hope we don't run into any others. Do you remember how, when we drove through town yesterday, there were no zombies in either of those two tunnels we passed through?"

Zoe looked shocked. "So . . . you're saying . . . the zombies avoid the forest—this green stuff—because it eats them and makes them part of itself . . . it assimilates them."

"Something like that," Ethan agreed. "It's definitely different from the usual zombie trees that the zomb find themselves irresistibly attracted to."

Paula nodded. "And yesterday, we landed right in the middle of this thing. No wonder they didn't come looking for us."

"There's the very real chance of this sort of aggregation becoming the norm for the zomb," Ethan informed the girls. "Several biologist friends of mine have postulated that given a few decades—at the very most a century—there won't be any single zombies left at all, just forests of living meat that offer immortality to all those who've not succumbed to the zombie virus. And those forests will be self-sustaining and will continue growing."

"You know, saving the world is such depressing business," Zoe said. "I should have let you guys handle it. I wish I was back in the chopper with our cat."

Paula rolled her eyes, then waved her gun and flashlight at them. "Thanks for the lecture, Ethan, but we're wasting time here. We need to get a move on."

They left the old pharmacy. Outside, the walls still pressed in close, but they once more had enough light to permit them turn off their flashlights.

"How much further to go?" Paula asked.

"It's right around the next corner."

His use of the word 'corner' to describe their destination was a very loose one. Aside from the drugstore they had just exited from, and another similarly open storefront (this one much wider and empty of glass) a short distance ahead of them, the rest of the street was smothered in purple-lined green meat with arms and legs and heads sticking out of it. Here, even the floor was mostly meat, with random patches of blacktop peeking through like puddles or potholes. The rational past lay beneath the mass somewhere, but this present place was a surreal nightmare. The light that spilled like rain through the regular slits in the meaty ceiling only made the environment more dreamlike.

In this overall context, the 'corner' that Ethan had mentioned was a tunnel through the flesh ten yards ahead on their right.

They walked over to it. Ethan went first into the tunnel, with Paula close behind him. Once they were both inside it, Ethan looked back at Zoe. "Come on," he gestured, "the lab is just ahead on the right."

Zoe, however, was looking around out there. "Shush, I can hear something, like lots of feet—"

And then something big and green streaked past the tunnel entrance. One moment Zoe Patterson was standing there and the next she was gone, and they heard her screaming as she was carried away.

"Quick, after them!" Ethan shouted at Paula, shoving her back towards the tunnel entrance.

Together they burst out of the tunnel and looked down the road.

"Ethan! Paula! Help!" Zoe was yelling.

"Over there," Ethan said.

They saw Zoe waving her hands at them. The green thing that had snatched her was carrying her through the smashed storefront down the road. From this distance it seemed as large as an elephant and had a lot of legs.

"What the hell is that?" Paula asked.

"I've no fucking idea," Ethan replied.

Together they ran towards the storefront.

CHAPTER 29

Landing

According to the chopper's GPS, Gorehound and the pilot's destination lay somewhere beneath the green mass that covered a good portion of northern Athens.

"I hate the look of this stuff," the pilot said.

Gorehound nodded. "Me too. The tops of the buildings breaking its surface look like drowning men. But just circle over it anyway and look for somewhere to land the chopper. Then we'll proceed on foot."

"Too bad we've no explosives on board to blow a hole through its surface, 'cos the GPS says the lab is directly below us now." The black man seemed to have gotten used to the pig-head mask Gorehound had made him wear.

The helicopter was hovering in place. Gorehound looked down through the cockpit's right window. He saw no sign of a building below them. Oh yes, there was. He now made out the peaked outline of a roof, though smothered in green with thick bluish stripes.

Is this a sheet of zombie skin . . . and shee-it, are those human legs sticking out of it?

The sight was so crazy that Gorehound was relieved when the pilot's voice distracted him from it. "Okay, man, we can land over there," the pilot said. "Hey, look! There's another chopper down there."

Gorehound studied the aircraft on the ground, noting its AFI and ChoZo emblems. "That's gotta be those three damn traitors we're after. Take us down."

Their airborne helicopter descended and landed beside the stationary one.

Somewhere far off, Gorehound thought he heard gunfire.

169

CHAPTER 30

Rogue Zombie Tree

Bang, bang, bang!

The muzzle flashes from the gunshots lit up the darkened interior of the shop. Accompanying both the gun noise and flashes of light came a deep grunting sound. It wasn't exactly zombie noise, but was worryingly similar.

"Hey, keep away from me! Ethan, Paula, help!"

Once they reached the shattered storefront through which the green monster had carried Zoe, Paula restrained Ethan from charging inside with a firm hand on his arm.

"Why are we stopping out here?" Ethan angrily demanded while breathing heavily.

"So long as Zoe is shooting it means she's still alive," Paula replied him. "That thing was huge, we need to get a proper look at what it is before we take it on."

Bang!

"We need to hurry! She'll soon run out of bullets!"

"Calm down, man. Let's see what took her."

They peeked into the store, which turned out to be a coffee shop, with its tables and chairs upended and scattered like a tornado had just swept through town.

Zoe was behind the service counter, with her gun aimed at the monster, which was raging at her from its other side.

"What the . . . ?" Either Paula or Ethan made this comment, but neither of them was afterwards sure which of them had.

The giant green monster was another kind of aggregated 'zombie tree,' only in this case, one that had become uprooted from the ground. This was evident from the tentacle-like roots that projected from its rear like a tail. The creature was a twisted mess of flesh that defied reason, with arms and legs sticking out of it at random angles, although enough of its legs were on its underside to permit it to move about. Also, it had five or six heads on its front surface, all of which were gnashing at Zoe, tentacle-long tongues lashing the air in her direction.

Ethan was relieved that Zoe wasn't in any immediate danger. The creature was simply too large to reach her behind the counter, but it was also too big for her to slip past it and escape.

"How are we going to get her out of there?" he asked Paula as they stepped out of concealment.

The zombie-freak monster heard their voices and whirled to face them, which further constricted the space available for Zoe to attempt an escape through. One of the creature's six or seven heads was shattered, clearly the result of Zoe's shooting when she'd slipped from its clutches; the destroyed skull dripped a bluish ichor like plant sap to the ground. Its heads were a mixture of male and female, with one of them even seeming to be a baby's. The monster's arms all gestured threateningly at them; its eyes flashed like green light bulbs and its many mouths gnashed loudly at them with a gluttonous hunger.

Paula grimaced. "Dude, you should have stayed rooted in the ground."

For the moment the giant zombie-freak remained where it was, fixed in the coffee shop as if the building had grown a malignant tumor. Its purple-streaked form hulked and watched them. However, it seemed more concerned with not letting Zoe get away than with attacking Ethan and Paula.

"Hey, you guys, get me out of here!" Zoe screeched. "Now I've got its damn roots in my face!"

"Just hold on, we're working on it!" Paula yelled back.

Ethan considered the problem. "Bullets won't shift that thing. It'll be like shooting a tree."

Paula nodded. "I've got something for it though." She pulled one of the egg-bombs out of her pocket.

"Oh, hell no, you aren't using that," Ethan immediately protested. "You'll turn Zoe into jelly."

"No I won't," Paula said with an amused smirk. "Just watch me."

She entered a code into the egg's display screen, and then pressed both its red and green buttons simultaneously. Ethan was surprised at what happened next. The egg split into segments as if it was a tangerine. Each segment had a little blue button on one side.

Paula selected two of the egg's segments and slipped the rest of them back into her pocket. "Okay, now I need to target this right. They have to wind up right underneath its body."

"Hey, get me out of this place!" Zoe yelled.

The monster's heads growled at her scream and it swiveled around to face her again.

"Oh shit! Guys, hurry it up!"

"Hey, Zoe, make sure you don't move from where you are!" Paula called out.

"Huh? Where the hell else did you think I was planning to go!?"

"Just keep your fucking head down, and make yourself as small as possible in the corner!"

When Paula pressed the studs on each segment and flipped them beneath the monster, Ethan prayed that she knew what she was doing. Or else they'd be scraping Zoe off the wall like she was toothpaste smeared on bathroom tiles.

"Stand back!" Paula said, pulling Ethan out of the way.

Boom!

The noise was subdued, but the effect was devastating. The giant zombie-freak lifted up off the floor of the coffee shop and then seemed to dissolve and implode like it was being compressed. But then the effect reversed and the air was suddenly filled with greenish chunks of monster flying everywhere.

Despite Paula's caution, she and Ethan hadn't retreated far enough from the explosion. Both were splattered with monster gore. In addition, Paula was hit in the head by a flying zombie torso that knocked her sideways. Ethan was aware of her falling to the ground, while he stood there motionless with his eyes shut and was completely deluged by zombie guts, blood and flesh.

When the meat rain ended, he opened his eyes to find himself standing in the midst of what might have been the aftermath of a suicide bomber attack on an alien planet—ragged and disconnected parts of green people strewn everywhere.

He looked into the coffee shop. Paula's aim had been perfect. Zoe was striding through a mess of ankle-deep guts and gore. She was completely unarmed, but the front of the counter she'd been hiding behind was destroyed. A large amount of the meat forest that coated the exterior coffee shop wall had also been stripped away.

"I don't believe what just happened," Zoe said as she stepped out of the coffee shop window and hurried over to Ethan's side.

Then Ethan remembered Paula and quickly turned to look at her. She was lying on the ground with her eyes shut. There was a lot of blood around her left ear. Ethan hoped she was still alive.

But before he could kneel down to examine Paula, he felt Zoe tapping him on the shoulder. "Ethan! Ethan, we've got company," she said in an urgent voice.

He looked up and thought he was dreaming. Two men, one black and one white, but both wearing identical pig-head masks and carrying guns, were approaching them. The black pig-headed man wore a regulation AFI pilot's jumpsuit; the other man wore bloody jeans and a blue Church of Zombie tee shirt that proclaimed 'Digestion is Salvation!' in bold green letters, around a little cartoon boy eating a zombie's hand. This man's bare arms were heavily tattooed.

The men's pig masks made no sense whatsoever to Ethan. Only in nightmares could they ever have seemed logical.

"Well, well, now what've we got here?" one of the men said. Because of their masks, it was impossible to tell which of them had spoken. "If it ain't Ethan Hackman and Zoe Patterson, our two traitors who wanna cure the fucking zombies. Alright, both of you, drop your guns."

Ethan and Zoe immediately complied.

The black man pointed down at Paula. "And this lady's gotta be Paula . . . what's her surname again?"

"Doesn't matter what her surname is," his companion replied. "She's not important." And while Ethan and Zoe watched speechless, the pig-masked man aimed his gun at Paula and shot her.

CHAPTER 31

Gore & More Gore

Gorehound was relieved that they had caught the fugitives so quickly. After shooting the woman on the ground—she'd looked dead already, but he'd shot her in the belly just to make sure—he gave Hackman and the senator's daughter his full attention.

(Gorehound and his negro companion had noticed something blowing apart in the coffee shop, and a horrid gooey mess was still smeared on the road. What the hell was it? Gorehound had no interest in finding out. His mind was still reeling from that weird crossroads place they'd just passed through, where it had sounded like lots of people were screaming inside his head.)

Hackman and Zoe Patterson were both covered in gore, and both wore backpacks.

"What I wanna know first of all is one simple thing," Gorehound told the pair. "Have you two recovered the zombie cure or not?"

As he expected, Hackman looked to be a tough nut to crack. He didn't say a word. But the girl broke quickly. One extra-mean look at her was all it took.

"No, no," she immediately replied. "We've not gotten it yet. Just don't shoot us like you shot Paula."

Gorehound smirked. *Just like I thought; these rich bitches generally have no backbone at all. She's likely scared shitless that I'm gonna rape her.*

Yeah, today is a good day, he thought. True, Scary had died, but . . . his mind flitted back for a moment to the strange sight he'd seen in the fugitive's helicopter. *A cat? Where'd they find it? I thought the zomb had eaten them all.* Gorehound hadn't set his eyes on a pet in two years. *Well, that cat is mine now. I'm gonna name it Hogwash, in memory of my dead best friend.*

He returned his attention to Ethan Hackman, who was staring miserably at the dead girl on the floor as if she had been his lover.

Gorehound quickly sized the guy up. In the looks department at least, Hackman wasn't anything to write home about.

Just another geek loser with big dreams 'bout changing things, Gorehound concluded. *Weren't for the zombie apocalypse, he'd be slaving away in a lab, trying to improve suntan lotion.*

"Now listen up," he told Hackman. "We're here for serious business. We work for AFI intelligence and we're here to get those samples of ND."

He nodded to his black companion; but got no brotherly response. He sensed Marlon didn't approve of the way he'd cold-bloodedly shot the girl on the ground.

Well, fuck him; this ain't Iraq—here we don't have time for military ethics and morality about the humane treatment of prisoners.

"Now, Hackman, you listen to me real good," he went on. "What we're gonna do now is, the four of us here are all gonna walk over to that old lab of yours, and you're gonna get the vials of ND out of the vault and hand them to us. Do you get that?"

"And no tricks, man," Marlon said, then gestured at the dead girl. "You two don't wanna end up like her. You get out the vials and hand them over and we'll all fly back to Massachusetts, where you'll both have your day in court."

Gorehound almost laughed at that. This black guy was a real boy scout. *Put Hackman on trial? What trial? Once Hackman hands over those vials, I'm gonna shoot him in the head. The guy is too dangerous. What if he gets sentenced to jail and then starts making more chemicals to cure the zomb? Nah, this guy is too much of a risk. I'm gonna waste him, just like we wasted Doc Sanderson.*

Hackman asked quietly, "And if I don't cooperate with you guys?"

Gorehound laughed. "Well then, I'll simply shoot you both and afterwards AFI will fly all the lab vaults back to Springfield. Worst case scenario, they'll nuke this fucking place to destroy the cure. Either way, that zombie cure of yours won't ever see the light of day."

"Yeah, either way you lose," Marlon agreed.

"Okay, I'll do it," Hackman said. "I get the cure out of the vault and hand it over to you."

"Alright, let's go," Gorehound said. He gestured at the captives with his gun. "You two, walk in front of us. You take off running and you'll each get a bullet in your backs."

"We won't run," Zoe Patterson said in a terrified voice. "Just don't shoot us."

Gorehound laughed as they set off. "Don't worry, pretty lady. Just do like we say and daddy'll get his li'l princess back home safe and sound."

Gorehound really disliked being inside this world of greenish meat that surrounded them—it felt like they were standing inside of a zombie's digestive system. He wanted to get this over with quickly; to be done with this hellish place and away from here as soon as possible.

Hackman still seemed a little reluctant, so Gorehound cuffed him around the ears. "Keep moving, you geek sonofabitch."

But they'd only gone three steps farther when a female voice behind them said, "Hey, assholes, turn around."

Gorehound immediately spun around. It was Paula, the girl who'd been lying on the floor, the one he'd just shot.

Oh, so she ain't dead? I'll soon fix that.

But he didn't get the chance. She was too close to him for him to shoot—suddenly she was standing right in front of him and his hands were behind her. And Gorehound didn't understand what she was doing either. Paula was pulling back the waistband of his pants and slipping something inside them, something that felt like a peanut.

"Hey, what the fuck?" he gasped, a feeling of intense alarm now falling on him. What had the bitch just slipped into his trousers? And worse, it was nestled deep in his underpants, right next to his penis; it wasn't about sliding down his legs to the ground.

He grasped for her, but Paula had already slipped away from him and was doing exactly the same thing to his black companion Marlon, who'd also turned around. And alarmingly, the woman's movements were fast and fluid, those of a professional killer. With ease, she knocked away Marlon's hands and slipped inside his defenses. Gorehound watched her slip something small and shaped like a garlic clove down the front of Marlon's pants also.

Then the bitch leapt away from them both and fell back on the ground with a smile on her face and blood streaming from her side.

"See both you guys in hell," she said.

Panic spreading through him like frostbite, Gorehound flung away his gun and hurriedly began unbuckling his belt.

"Hey, Marlon, get your damn pants off!" he yelled.

CHAPTER 32

Deconstruction

Ethan and Zoe had turned too at the sound of Paula's voice.

They didn't see exactly what she'd done to the two hog-masked men, but they saw the two men hastily trying to get their pants off.

What happened next was simply a repeat of what had just happened to the zombie-freak monster in the coffee shop. The two masked men blew apart, their bodies first imploding and then exploding in a rain of flesh, bones, and blood.

"Fuck," Ethan said, covering his eyes again as he and Zoe were splattered by the mess.

When he uncovered his eyes, the remnants of their captors were scattered far and wide across the meat-cloaked street, their bones embedded in the strange zombie flesh. One man's masked head was wedged at the base of the wall near them and was already being licked by a zombie head's foot-long tongue.

"I missed the fireworks the first time," Zoe said. She looked like she'd be sick.

"Oh my God, Paula!" Ethan said and ran towards her and knelt beside her. He didn't understand how he felt. Sure, he loved Zoe, but when he'd thought Paula was dead just now, he'd felt almost as bad as he imagined losing Zoe would make him feel. In fact, he'd felt almost as bad as when he'd lost his wife and daughter.

Do I really like her that much?

Although Paula had managed to claw herself back from the dead to assist them, it didn't look like she'd be around much longer. She was drenched in blood now and was gasping for breath.

"Are you okay?" Ethan asked her, tenderly taking her left hand in his. Her hand, so deadly, seemed so delicate; the hand of a princess.

"No, I'm dying—I didn't get far enough away from the bomb blasts," Paula sadly replied. "Oh, I love you, Ethan Hackman. I love you so, so much. Take good care of Zoe for me, and save the world."

And then Paula shut her eyes and went limp.

Choking back tears, Ethan leaned forward and kissed her dead lips. Then he stood up. He felt cold, as if the life was being drained out of him. He felt that he had just lost something of vital importance; something crucial to his well-being.

Not looking back at Paula's corpse for fear that he'd burst into tears, he strode forward through the mess that had recently been the two pig-masked men and stopped in front of Zoe, who was just recovering from her shock.

Zoe gestured over at Paula. "Is she . . . ?"

Ethan nodded and walked past her. "Come on, honey, let's save the world, though I'm not even sure the world is worth it anymore."

He didn't look back, but heard Zoe hurrying after him.

CHAPTER 33

Revelations

Entering the AFI research facility was easy. Its front French doors were open, their glass destroyed during the initial zombie panic. And, as though it had been anticipating their arrival, the zombie aggregate hadn't covered the building's entrance.

The reception area boasted lots of shadows, several skeletons, and a few inquisitive rats, which scampered away once Ethan shone his flashlight on them.

"So, which way?" Zoe asked.

Ethan draped his arm around her shoulders. He felt more composed now after Paula's passing. Personal tragedy or not, their mission had to be completed.

"Downstairs," he told her, leading the way into the farther corridor that led off the reception lobby. "The vaults are all the basement. Mickey was always worried about vibrations from the highway agitating our stored content."

"How are we going to get back now that Paula is dead?" Zoe asked while they descended the basement stairs. "And . . . those guys wearing pig masks . . . they knew exactly who we were and what we were after."

Ethan had been worrying about that too; because amongst other things it meant that AFI Intelligence had arrested Mickey Sanderson. "I don't think we'll be able to return home," he told Zoe. "We may be in hiding for quite a long time. That's okay for me, but what about you? Your father will go ballistic if you suddenly go missing."

Zoe wrinkled her nose and pouted prettily. "Once we're safely away from here, I'll ask my father to send a chopper to pick me up. Mr. Tricks won't dare screw with daddy."

Ethan shook his head. "Honey, I don't think that's gonna work. Your immunity won't extend to me. We'll need to find a working car, fuel it up and . . . but most of the vehicles we're sure are working are parked back at the museum with the zombies!" He slammed his palm against the basement wall. "How the hell are we going to make it in and out of there alive again?"

"This place is giving me the creeps. Let's get the cure and get out of here. We'll figure something out afterwards."

Ethan knew exactly what she meant about the lab giving her the creeps. With most of the building completely shrouded in melded and webbed zombie flesh, there had been almost no light at all upstairs, and there was none at all down here. This place was both silent and dead, like visiting a planet where all the sentient races had long ago died off and left the scavengers in control. But for the glow of their flashlights and the startled rats and roaches that scurried away from the light and the tramp of their feet, they could have been walking on the surface of the moon.

For this too, Ethan had come prepared. In addition to his flashlight, he had a powerful rechargeable lamp in his backpack that he could suspend on the wall so he'd have both hands free while connecting the battery to the vault and opening it up.

"This room," he said, and swung its already ajar door fully open.

The vault room was quite spacious. It contained six vaults, two gleaming narrow upright metal boxes standing against each wall that didn't border the corridor. In the flashlight glow the six vaults looked like robots. The room's only furniture was a long table along its corridor wall and two chairs. The floor tiles were dusty, but maybe because the basement had no windows, were less so than those upstairs.

Ethan gestured to the chairs. "Have a seat. This shouldn't take too long."

Zoe took off her backpack and sat down. Covered in both human and creature blood like they both were, there seemed no point in her dusting off the chair first.

Ethan slipped off his backpack and got out what he needed: the battery, a large screwdriver, and finally the rechargeable lamp, which he switched on.

"Which vault is it?" Zoe asked after the room filled with light.

He pointed directly opposite them. "The one on the left." Then, leaving Zoe seated, he walked over to the vault he'd indicated and began unscrewing a panel on its right side.

He got the panel off, checked that the battery terminals weren't rusted, and then crossed back to Zoe's side.

"How can we be sure that the vials of ND haven't gotten denatured over time?" she asked him when he picked up the battery.

"It's a gamble. No way to know for sure. Back then they were vacuum-sealed so they might still be okay. . . but yeah, I get your point." He shrugged. "Even if they're no longer usable, we'll still have the formula and the chemical and biological process needed to recreate the cure, so we'll be able to start over from scratch. It'll just take longer, that's all."

Zoe nodded. Ethan crossed back to the vault and slipped the battery into place. He connected the terminals and flicked a switch.

With a beep, the vault came alive; digital numbers flickered across a display on its front and then red, blue, and yellow lights came on.

Ethan heaved a sigh of relief. Even at this point it had been possible that something could go wrong.

"Verification process one," the vault said in a metallic voice.

Zoe jerked at the unexpected noise, but quickly relaxed when she realized it was coming from the vault. "Man, that is so creepy."

Laughing, Ethan placed his thumb against the vault's fingerprint sensor.

"Verification process one successfully completed," the vault said. "Fingerprint recognized as that of personnel authorized to access vault contents. Verification process two."

On this statement a panel slid aside above the vault's fingerprint sensor to reveal a retina scanner. Ethan looked into the retina scanner with his left eye. A green light flickered left and right twice in the scanner and then the vault said:

"Verification process two successfully completed. Retina pattern and fingerprint confirm personnel identity as Ethan Levi Hackman. Access to vault contents granted."

With that, the vault locks clicked open. Ethan stepped back and pulled the metal door open. Zoe was already walking over.

"Wow," she said, as he got the door fully open. "Do you have to go through this long process every time?"

"Each and every time. You wouldn't believe some of the stuff stored in these vaults. If they ever fell into the wrong hands . . ."

Now temporarily lit by violet fluorescent lighting, the vault contained just the package of ND and a transparent plastic folder full of documents and CDs. Ethan removed both from their shelves and carried them across to the table.

The ND vials were packed in Styrofoam in a plastic box with a transparent cover that was sealed with scotch tape. Ethan peeled away the scotch tape and picked out one of the vials. He held it close to the rechargeable lamp and studied its violet liquid contents.

"Still seems okay," he told Zoe. "We'll know for sure once we get it to the lab."

"It looks so ordinary," Zoe said. "Not like a drug that can change the course of human history."

Thrilled that they'd succeeded in their quest, Ethan pulled Zoe close and kissed her. He sensed something lacking in her response.

"Are you okay, honey?" he asked when they separated.

"I hate this place," Zoe said. "It totally gives me the creeps."

"I know exactly what you mean. This is hardly the most romantic of locations."

"Yeah, that too," Zoe admitted with a slight smile.

"But looking on the bright side of things, the world is saved now."

"Yes it is, darling."

Ethan packed the vial of ND away again, resealed the package, and stowed it and the research documents in his backpack. "Okay, I'll just shut the vault again and we'll be out of here."

He touched the vault door and a bolt of lightning struck him. At first he thought the vault's inverter circuitry had malfunctioned after its long period of disuse. But then he realized that the intense electric shock wasn't coming from the vault, but from behind him.

The paralyzing electric shock lasted for endless seconds and then, his muscles seeming to have turned to jelly, Ethan slumped to the floor.

He lay on his back, staring stupidly, while Zoe slowly stepped into view and waved a stunner at him.

"Wh . . . wh . . . wh . . . ?"

She frowned down at him. "Oh, baby, you're so, so surprised now, aren't you? Well, you should be. Ethan, you're so naïve it's a wonder you survived the zombie outbreak. Did you really think that anyone . . . anyone *sane* would really go along with you and Mickey's dumbass plan to cure the zombies?"

Ethan wanted to protest; but his lips and tongue wouldn't move properly. His body felt like a stone now and he understood that this was why she had shocked him for such a long time. He had no idea when he'd be able to move again, but it seemed a long way off.

"Hey, news flash, Ethan!" Zoe said, leaning over him now and waving her stunner in his face as if trying to draw his attention. "I *love* eating the damn zombies. I *love* being young and sexy and pretty forever and ever and ever. I mean, who wouldn't? Only a fool like you, that's who."

She straightened back up, leaned against the vault door so it clicked shut, and laughed. "Oh, but there's more, honey." Then she frowned as if she'd swallowed bile and spat. "*Honey?* Calling you that is nothing but a bad joke. Ethan, I've never . . . never loved you; not for a day, not for an hour, not for a single second of the time we've been together. So why?—I'm sure you're gonna ask. Well, I'll tell you why: My father's presidential ambition, that's why. Surely you didn't honestly believe all that crap I said about him not having a hope in hell of winning the next election?"

Though Ethan listened, he hardly heard what she was saying. *She NEVER loved me? Our romance was all a lie?* He felt like long nails were being hammered into his heart.

"My reason for hooking up with you was simple," Zoe explained. "With all of the opinion polls leaning so heavily in favor of President Harper, my dad figured he needed something to irreversibly swing public opinion his way instead. And because zombies are the big topic now, it had to be something to do with them. And then daddy's spies discovered some old AFI documentation about how you and Mickey Sanderson had once sent a quantity of ND for destruction, and how it had vanished along the way. It then became a question of which of you I should seduce; with the idea being to discover if there were any more caches of ND in existence. I picked you—Mickey just seemed too weird. I honestly think he was screwing that nerdy daughter of his."

"N-n-no!" Ethan gasped. He wasn't protesting about her smear on Mickey's character, which was clearly nonsense. He was protesting the whole evil political conspiracy.

What a fool I've been. She and her father have been in cahoots all along?

"Whatever," Zoe said, with a dismissive flap of her hand. "Long story short, I began dating and hating you and that led us to the here and now. Thanks for the cure. Once I return to Washington with this, my father's political future is assured. He'll be promoted—praised and adored by everyone—as the man who destroyed the evil rebellion against eternal life. Daddy will be our next American president. I'll be

First Daughter . . . which, seeing as my father is single, more or less makes me First Lady of the USA.”

Now she began pacing agitatedly, her soles slapping the dusty floor like she was upset and needed to accuse him of something. She got out her phone from her pants pocket and checked the time. “Daddy will be here in three hours. Paula was right—*they are* tracking my cellphone. Me calling him before we walked into the tunnel was our agreed signal that we’d arrived here.”

She stopped pacing and smiled down at Ethan. “Daddy must have told Uncle Tricks the true situation of things by now. They’ll most likely be arriving together. Once I’m finished with you here, I’ll call daddy to let him know our plan succeeded.”

Ethan managed to move his lips. “Z-zoe, d-d-don’t you ha-h-have a c-c-c-conscience?” he sputtered.

“It isn’t that I lack a conscience, she replied, her smile now the temperature of liquid nitrogen, “but that I see no use for one. Definitely not in this current age, when everything mankind once believed in has been turned on its head. So, sorry, honey, you’re history . . . and I’m the future.”

“Wh-what’s g-g-g-gonna h-ha-happen t-to me?”

Zoe vanished from view for a few seconds then and he heard her rummaging through her backpack. While she was out of sight, Ethan tried to shake some feeling back into his body. *I need to get up and overpower her. My broken heart is the lesser issue here. If she manages to destroy that zombie cure . . . burn up the research papers and discs . . . it will really be over.*

But his efforts to move his limbs were useless, his muscles refused to respond to his mental commands. Even speaking felt like he was lifting a ton of cinder blocks.

The bitch must have used a souped-up stunner on me!

He managed to turn his head. Zoe was already walking back to him. Behind her, a brown rat ran past the door of the vault room.

Zoe stood beside him again. Now, instead of the stunner, she was holding up a slim hypodermic syringe filled with a green liquid.

“Wh-wh-what’s th-th-that?”

“This syringe contains concentrated zombie venom,” Zoe explained, waving the hypo at him. She nodded at the shocked look that entered his eyes. “Yes, darling, that’s correct. I’m going to turn you into one of the undead. And then, when you’re a mindless zombie,

I'm going to ship you back home . . . and then I am going to *eat you*. I'm going to eat you slowly . . . over a long period of time." She laughed. "It's my reward, you see. This is what *I* get for sleeping with you for a year. Baby, I'm going to make you last me a *long* time. I'm not going to kill you—each time I want some of you, I'll just cut off the part of your body I feel like eating."

Ethan was horrified. If she did what she said, surgically removing only the parts of his body that she desired to eat, she could keep him alive for years. Owning and eating zombies that way was legal, but most people didn't want live zombies in their homes because of the risk of catching their infection.

"Y-y-you . . . y-y-y-you're crazy!" he gasped.

She licked her lips. "No, baby, I'm hungry. Living with a jerk like you has made me work up a huge appetite."

He found the strength to speak. "J-ju-just make s-s-sure y-y-you t-ta-take care of th-that c-c-c-cat we f-fou-found," he mumbled. "D-d-don't y-y-you dare f-f-feed him to-to-to either the r-r-rats or-or-or the-the z-zombies." Now that he was clearly about to die, it seemed important to him to preserve that little feline life, insignificant though it may be.

Zoe rolled her eyes and then looked really pissed off. "Are you trying to make me out to be insensitive and heartless? I'll look after the damn cat, don't you worry about that."

"And d-d-don't y-y-you dare s-s-sell him ei-either."

"Shut up, Ethan. In barely half-an-hour from now—once you're fully transformed into a zombie—you'll want to have our damn cat for lunch."

Ethan shut up.

"Okay, goodbye, baby . . ." She scowled. "Why do I keep calling you 'baby?' I don't even *like* you. I guess old habits do die hard."

She knelt down to inject him with the syringe and then suddenly there was a flash of metal behind her and her right hand separated from her body.

Her arm spurting blood, Zoe screamed and leapt to her feet. Her hand and the deadly syringe clattered to the floor beside Ethan, who was wondering, *What the hell?*

Then a female hand with blue fingernails momentarily entered his range of vision and picked up Zoe's severed hand.

Paula?

Ethan strained to turn his head to the right so he could see what was happening. Zoe was leaning against one of the vaults, her left hand tightly gripping her right wrist to stop the bleeding. Zoe's gun hung at her hip, but she was right-handed; with no right hand anymore, she'd been literally disarmed. She was defenseless and was staring in horror at Paula, who was now advancing on her with a machete in one hand and the syringe of zombie venom in the other.

Ethan was too surprised for words.

Desperate, Zoe tried to run for the door, but Paula cut her off.

"NO, DON'T DO THIS TO ME!" Zoey screamed pathetically "DON'T INJECT ME WITH THAT! I'M NOT FOOD! I'M NOT FOOD!"

"You are now, bitch!" Paula said dispassionately. Then she stuck the hypodermic needle into the side of Zoe's neck and depressed the plunger.

Zoe screamed even louder now, an almost comical howl, and tried to get free. But Paula held her tight until the syringe was empty. Then she stepped back. Zoe staggered halfway to the door and then collapsed and began twitching.

Paula staggered over to Ethan and collapsed on top of him.

He managed to raise an arm and touch her.

She smiled tiredly at him; he gaped back at her. "But . . . b-b-but y-y-you . . . you're dead!"

Paula shook her head, then leaned up and kissed him. "Nah, I'm not dead, I'm just a fantastic actress," she said. "You've gotta admit that that was an Oscar-winning performance I just gave out there, confessing how much I loved you, and all that—Meryl Streep couldn't have played that better." Then she winced and grasped her left side. "I'm lucky that pig-headed jerk didn't double-check after he'd shot me, or shoot me again just to make sure he'd killed me. All he'd given me the first time was a flesh wound; it burns, but the bullet passed cleanly through my side."

It suddenly occurred to Ethan that he was more relieved that Paula was alive than he was bothered that Zoe was turning into a zombie just a few yards away from him. He wasn't worried about her attacking them. Even though the venom transforming her was concentrated, it would take at least a half-hour before she became dangerous to them. For his own part, he was beginning to get feeling in his legs again. Ten more minutes and he should be able to stand up.

Paula lay quietly on him, not saying anything, just breathing. She seemed close to exhausted.

For a few seconds Ethan felt himself slipping into despair again, but then the feeling of emptiness inverted into something positive.

Zoe had just admitted that she had never loved him; so what did losing her matter? He doubted that Paula loved him either, but at least she'd shown that she cared about him, and she definitely hadn't just stabbed him in the back. So the positive erased the negative.

"I-I-I can't b-believe Zoe would t-tu-turn on me like that," Ethan said, relieved that his tongue no long felt like a fish that had died in his mouth. "And y-y-you: wh-why pretend t-t-t-to be dead anyway?"

"I've never really trusted Zoe since first meeting her," Paula replied. "Just a bad vibe I kept getting. Why would a senator's daughter want to upset the status quo? You know, it just seemed odd to me?" She laughed. "Uncle Mickey didn't trust her either. That's the *real* reason he insisted that I accompany you—to be your personal bodyguard and keep an eye on Zoe."

Ethan wanted to mention that they needed to call Mickey, but Paula was still speaking:

"After our threesome last night, I went through Zoe's backpack and found her stun gun, hidden away in a secret pocket. It was a dead giveaway. Who was she going to use the stun gun on? Definitely not the zombies. Electricity doesn't really slow them down and even if it did you don't want to get close enough to them to use it."

"Why didn't y-y-you s-s-say anything?" Ethan asked. "Y-yo-you could have w-w-warned me about Z-z-zoe."

Paula shook her head, then adjusted her body so she was sitting next to him. He saw that she was still gripping her machete tightly and looked across at Zoe. Zoe lay on her back, and her mouth was opening and closing like that of a fish. Her skin was already developing green and purple stripes but her eyes were still clear.

"Relax," he told Paula. "She . . . she w-won't t-urn for a while yet." He reached out and cleared a strand of hair out of Paula's face, and then finally got back proper control of his tongue. "S-so why didn't you warn me about Zoe?"

"I couldn't do that," Paula replied. "I needed to wait for Zoe to make her move . . . just in case I was wrong." She sighed. "I knew how much you loved her, Ethan. I didn't want to ruin your relationship with Zoe on mere suspicion. I really, really like and respect you a lot, Ethan. If I wasn't your girlfriend I wanted to be a good friend. I didn't want to break your heart."

"It's broken now." And yet somehow, maybe because Paula was with him, he didn't feel like that. Either way, heartache could wait. He extended an almost nerveless hand to Paula. "Help me up. We need to leave here already."

She smiled down at him. "That's the spirit. You've a lot of work to do, Ethan. At the moment you're the most important man on Earth. And you have an incredibly daunting task ahead of you. You need to fix the world. You need to cure the zombies. You need to stop them being used as food, to make them human again. You need to make the world see that what is wrong is wrong and what is right is right. That decisions shouldn't be made for the sake of convenience."

Ethan remembered Mickey again. "What about your uncle? Fixing the world was supposed to be his job, not mine. I was just the errand boy."

Paula's expression turned sad and she said, "I don't think Uncle Mickey is still alive—those two goons with pig masks hinted as much. Anyway, Uncle Mickey's plan wasn't that you would return to Springfield anyway, but that you and Zoe would instead accompany me to a secret laboratory over in Detroit, one that is already equipped to manufacture massive quantities of ND. The location is an ex-military underground facility. Uncle Mickey said about the only thing that would destroy it would be a nuclear strike. There's food, water . . . everything we need is there."

She got up and helped Ethan to his feet. His legs wobbled but remained firm beneath him. "Detroit?"

"Uncle Mickey has been setting things up there for a year," Paula explained. "Getting you and the cure to Detroit was simply the last phase of his plan."

Beside them Zoe twitched and growled. Ethan walked over to the desk and picked up his backpack. All these revelations were disorienting. *A lab in Detroit? I already know that I can't go home again, but . . . ?*

"We need to go," Paula said. She winced, and he looked at her left side where she had been shot. She wasn't bleeding, but still looked a little pale. Once they reached Detroit, she was going to need a whole lot of rest, and he intended to dedicate quality time to helping her recuperate fully.

"Hey, are you sure you're okay enough to fly a helicopter?" he asked her. "Or do you need to rest awhile?"

He was relieved when she smiled. Even covered in blood like she was, that smile made her look more beautiful than ever. "I'll be fine," she replied. "Oh, and by the way, you won't be working alone at the Detroit lab. Professor Fernanda Rodriguez is already there waiting for you."

Ethan raised an eyebrow. "Professor Rodriguez? But I thought the zombies ate her when we evacuated this place."

Paula laughed. "They almost did, but she got away. Professor Rodriguez is fine. She and Uncle Mickey have been working undercover for ages."

Ethan nodded and turned off the rechargeable lamp. He felt better suddenly. "And we'll have our cat," he said enthusiastically

"There's a cat at the lab too. That one is female, so maybe they'll have kittens."

"Let's go," Ethan said, shouldering his backpack. Suddenly the future looked extremely bright.

They paused at the door and shone their flashlights back on Zoe. Her transformation was almost complete now; her eyes almost completely green and sparkling. She was attempting to sit up, but with just one hand it was proving difficult for her.

"What do you want to do with her?" Paula asked Ethan. "Should I put a bullet through her brain—put her out of her misery?" She laughed. "Or do you want us to take her to Detroit with us? In case we get hungry?"

"No, leave her," Ethan said. "She was right. She isn't food—not for us anyway. Also, I was in love with her until about thirty minutes ago. Maybe the cure will kill her, maybe it will cure her. Or maybe, she'll have fused with the zombie forest before we're ready. Or maybe, if she's really unlucky, she'll be harvested, processed and eaten."

Paula shook her head. "I doubt her daddy is gonna allow that last to happen, except if he's gonna eat her himself." Then she thought a moment. "We could take her along with us to Detroit. You can try out the cure on her there. I'll hood her with her backpack so she can't bite."

Ethan shook his head. "Oh no, girl, we're leaving her right here."

Zoe, her face webbed with green-and-purple blood vessels, was looking at them now, as if she understood that they were discussing her. She didn't look hungry yet, just confused. But of course the hunger would shortly arrive. And when it came, it would be insatiable. Her teeth still looked normal, but that would change in two days.

Ethan pulled Paula close to him and kissed her. She kissed him back hungrily.

"Don't worry," he said when they separated. "I'm not on the rebound. "I'm just trying to motivate you to get a move on."

She giggled. "Oh, you can rebound on me all you want, Ethan Hackman—you know I'm already incurably smitten with you."

They stepped outside of the vault room. And then Ethan shut the door on the new zombie woman inside it. Zoe had just successfully gotten up and a warning light was flashing in her green eyes. Her hunger had arrived.

"Just in case she decides to tag along," Ethan said after latching the door shut. "I can't stand the undead anymore."

***

"I really hope we're doing the right thing," Ethan said with a nervous laugh as they stepped out of the lab and into the zombie forest again. "When I'm an old man and about to die, you know, like just a few paces from death's door, I don't want to look back to this moment and regret today's actions."

"I don't think it's that bad," Paula said. "From what I've been hearing, AFI can actually make pills of zombie extract that have almost the same longevity effect. If that's really the case, then it's just human perversion that makes us keep eating one another. It's like the ultimate power trip, you know?"

Then she sighed. "But even if the rumors aren't true, and we are doomed to grow old and die as a result of what we're doing—yes, Ethan, *we are* doing the right thing. And I'll . . ." Paula's voice faltered and she suddenly grew really emotional, "I'll back you up, Ethan . . . We're in this together. I'll stay by your side every step of the way, no matter how difficult or painful the journey to the light becomes."

Ethan laughed. "The Church of Zombie are gonna hate us forever, for sure."

"Let them hate us. ChoZo are already my least favorite people ever. Personally, I'd love to be able to attend Mass knowing that 'Eat my body and drink my blood' isn't meant to be taken literally."

That said, Ethan and Paula made their cautious way back out of the zombie forest. And then, after checking that their now sleeping cat was okay, they took off in the helicopter for Detroit, Michigan . . . and a brighter future for mankind.

The End.

ABOUT THE AUTHOR

Wol-vriey is Nigerian, and quite tall.

He believes there actually are things that go bump in the night.

He writes horror fiction—for adults only, please. And also some surrealist stuff.

Wol-vriey blogs at: *http://oddityfarm.wordpress.com*

WOL-VRIEY
BIZARRO AND TRANSGRESSIVE FICTION

BOSTON POSH (BUD MALONE #1)

In 2028 AD, the USA is a nation ravaged by hungry dragons and dinosaurs. In Boston, Massachusetts, private eye Bud Malone is hired to rescue a kidnapped heiress. But nothing is as it seems.

Malone works to unravel a tangled web involving Boston Chinatown, a 200-year-old woman with a 9-year-old body, white robots, a human-liver-eating psychopath, a golem, a porcelain dragon, and a snake goddess with a crush on him. There's also a woman obsessed with chicken sex. Then Malone meets Posh Lane, a gorgeous call girl who's desperate to quit her pimp.

Romantic sparks ignite between Posh and Malone, but Posh's past suddenly catches up with her in a BIG way. To save Posh, Malone agrees to run a quest for Earth's new rulers, the Forks. But, Malone has no idea that agreeing to the Fork's odd request will send him on the weirdest trip he's ever been on in his life.

BOSTON CORPSE (BUD MALONE #2)

MAGIC CAN BE MURDER! - Drag queen Lucy Tang is back in Boston, and is hell-bent on settling her vindetta against casino owner Sookie Ling. And suddenly, Bud Malone, PI, has the case of his life to resolve.

When Boston's robot police force are baffled by a mind transfer case, they come to Malone for help. The one person who can likely help Malone out here is the witch Soledad Bathory. But Soledad seems to know a lot more than she's telling him. It's a case not made easier when Malone meets Soledad's beautiful cousin, Josephine 'Slave' Bailey. Slave has her own plans for Malone, most of which involve teaching him BDSM and making him her new Master.

Oh, and Rick Rogers owes Sookie Ling a whole lot of money, a gambling debt that's going to be literally Hell to pay!

BOSTON CORPSE - Not your average detective novel!

Burning Bulb

WOL-VRIEY
BIZARRO AND TRANSGRESSIVE FICTION

BOSTON LUST (BUD MALONE #3)
"Bless it, Father, for she has sinned."

Seven murdered gay women, all their bodies completely drained of blood. All also with large parts of their bodies dissolved away like acid has been pumped into their veins.

Bud Malone has to find the female vampire preying on Boston's lesbian population.

Then Malone meets the beautiful Trudi Carmen and the case gets even more tangled. Trudi needs Malone's help in recovering a ring that's gone missing. But how in the world is one little black ring related to either the dead women or their killer?

Resolving this case will lead Malone deep into Lucy Tang's legacy -The Abstracta. And then to the city of Genesis.

Boston Lust -Just when you thought Bean Town was safe to visit again.

HELL DANCER
Six people find themselves trapped in Detention, a nightmare realm where the demonic Schoolmaster is hell-bent on reforming them . . . until they die.

Porn superstar Venus Deluxe came to Springfield, MA to party, and next found her life hanging by a thread. One wrong answer will mean her death.

Suspended BPD detective Tanya Rockford was trying to stop one kind of violence, but found a terrifying another. With her and her companion's lives hanging in the balance, it's going to take all of her courage and resourcefulness to escape this hell she's stumbled into.

Porn stud Chad Cannon has made a career from his ten-inch penis. Here in Detention, however, it's his brains that matter. He'll soon be hoping all the pot he's smoked over the years hasn't completely messed up his memory.

The three students, Sherri, Jordan, and Mike? They were all just in the wrong place at the right time. Will anyone survive Detention?. The evil Schoolmaster doesn't plan on letting that happen . . .

Burning Bulb
PUBLISHING

WOL-VRIEY
BIZARRO AND TRANSGRESSIVE FICTION

VAGINA MUNDI

Rachel Risk is a professional thief with super-strong hair that can stretch like tentacles to manipulate objects. Ashley Status has both a digitally augmented brain, and 'muscle-purses' in her arms and legs in which she stores inflatable objects—cars, guns, rocket launchers, etc.

When Raye is framed as the fall girl in a jewel robbery, the pair flee Chicago's vengeful robot gangsters and take refuge in the Hotel Bizarre, where the gorgeous 'vagina singer,' Femina, is performing for a week.

But the Hotel Bizarre is even stranger than its name suggests, and very soon Raye and Ash are involved in an deadly adventure, a struggle for survival the likes of which they'd never imagined possible with loads of deviant sex, drugs, music, and violence at every turn. And just what is the old woman in the skin desert really doing with all those cats glued to her walls?

VAGINA MUNDI—a Bizarro Hymn in praise of WOMAN!

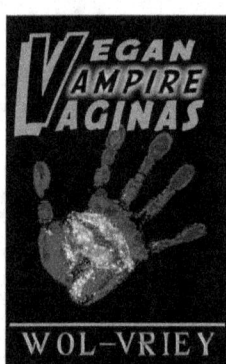

VEGAN VAMPIRE VAGINAS

The biggest bank heist in US history. And Tom Palmer can't remember pulling it off. And no, this isn't your standard case of amnesia. After a one-night-stand gone horribly wrong, Boston salesman Tom Palmer wakes up with a vagina implanted in his left hand. Then his day gets worse.

Tom is transported across space-time to a nightmare version of Boston, one where the Bizarro virus has transformed half the population into cannibals. Worst of all, Tom discovers that in this new Boston, he's the infamous gangster Pussypalm, wanted for robbing the Federal Reserve Bank of Boston a year ago. He also learns that the vagina in his hand is prophetic, i.e. it talks . . . after sex.

With 130 people left dead during his bank heist and six billion dollars missing, Tom knows he's living on borrowed time. It is in his best interests not to remember anything. Because once he does . .

Burning Bulb
PUBLISHING

WOL-VRIEY
BIZARRO AND TRANSGRESSIVE FICTION

VEGAN ZOMBIE APOCALYPSE

In the post-apocalypse worlderness, zombies rule the earth. They're allergic to meat, and brains literally make them explode. Zombies now eat blood potatoes, parasitic tubers grown in the flesh of humancows corralled in maximum security farms. Two fugitives meet in the ancient ruins of Texas. The first is Soil 15-f, a womancow who's escaped her farm a week before she's due to be killed and her blood potato crop harvested. The second fugitive is Able Kane, former head necros food technician, now sentenced to death for heresy. But Soil is no ordinary humancow.

Unknown to herself, she's the vegan zombie agricultural revolution, and the zombies desperately want her back. And the necros equally desperately want Able Kane dead. He's fled with a forbidden discovery which will reshape the world for the worse if used. And Able is just hardheaded/misguided enough to use it.

MELANIE NEMESIS CATCHPOLE

In Springfield, Massachusetts, Melanie Catchpole is hired to fetch back a magic teddy bear worth millions of dollars from a warehouse across town. Problem is, the warehouse is down in Springfield's O-Zone that totally weird sector of the city where Bizarro fell to Earth. The 'O' is a fairytale land, a place where dreams and nightmares literally live and breathe..

Worse still, the gingers—mutant cannibals—prowl the O. The gingers have already eaten everyone else Melanie's employers sent to get back the magic teddy bear.

Accompanied by the handsome but ruthless Doug Fisher (who she finds sexy but doesn't dare entrust her heart to), Melanie enters the O-Zone. Melanie and Doug are instantly caught up in an adventure they'd never have believed credible even if written as fiction . . . and Melanie's used to experiencing the very weird as the norm.

And now, additionally, there's a mystery to unravel: What does the dark, freezing-cold being called The Fixer want with Mary, the barkeep's daughter?

Burning Bulb

WOL-VRIEY
BIZARRO AND TRANSGRESSIVE FICTION

BIG TROUBLE IN LITTLE ASS

From Bizarro master storyteller Wol-vriey comes a truly weird western tale that will leave you awe-struck and on the edge of your seat...

In the town named Little Ass, tight-assed prostitute Rosa overhears a gunslinger's plans to assassinate rancher Edison Bennett. Once the badass Bennett learns of the plot, he ensures there'll be hell to pay for any attempt on his life!

Yes, it's going to take all of gunslinger Jude's shooting prowess, his eclectic collection of strange firearms, a trusty horse that requires an owners' manual, and the help of the lovely and invigorating Nell (who's EXTREMELY odd when the going gets weird), to survive the Bizarro hell that Edison Bennett unleashes in order to hold onto the land that he'd stolen from Madam Zizi.

BIZARRO 101 (A BASIC PRIMER)

Welcome to the strange place:

A collection of 37 flash fiction stories designed to introduce one to the Bizarro/New Weird Genre.

Weird, dreamy, nightmarish, absurd, sad, surreal, humorous . . . this collection of tales is all this and more.

***

"This primer is the very essence of any and all styles and types of Bizarro writing. Wol-vriey collects, distills, and bottles up these 37 tiny stories for your sensory enjoyment. This is an absolute must-read for anyone new to the genre, because it demonstrates the scope of what Bizarro is, and what it can be."
                    —Teresa Pollack, Bizarro commentator and blogger

Burning Bulb

WOL-VRIEY
BIZARRO AND TRANSGRESSIVE FICTION

Dr. Orgasm

Courtney Taylor is young, intelligent, beautiful, and successful. She also has a boyfriend who loves her deeply. The problem is, no matter what Courtney does, she can't climax during sex.

When Florence Rigid's communist forces destroy the city of Metaphor, Courtney and her friends Teresa, Highball, Miki, and Heather are cast into the midst of a quest to find the only person able to save the land of Innuendo—Dr. Carol Orgasm, wanted by the communists for developing the O-Pill, a wonder drug that grants women sexual ecstasy on demand.

The communists will do anything to get their hands on the O-Pill and prevent its reaching the millions of Innuendo's women. But Courtney desperately wants that pill too. And so it's now a race between Courtney and the communists to find Dr. Orgasm first.

And Courtney has no choice but to win this race. She must win it: For her own orgasm . . . and for the freedom of female sexuality everywhere.

PUSSY TRANSMISSION

Pussy Transmission were the most decadent Pop Art ensemble of the 90's. Led by the beautiful painter Isis Lynch, the trio revolutionized the art world. Then suddenly, without explanation, Pussy Transmission vanished into historical obscurity. Now, twenty years later, three women come to Lynch Place. Lily and Nina are journalists desperate to interview Isis Lynch. Raven, on the other hand, wants to find her boyfriend, who's gone missing inside Isis's house. Raven's worried—she's heard that Pussy Transmission broke up because Isis began dabbling in black magic . . . with devastating results. All three women will shortly wish they'd never left home. Particularly once the rats in Lynch Place start warning them that they're going to die . . . and Raven meets Betty Butcher, the bouncy supernatural psycho who's intent on chopping her into bits. Pussy Transmission, Baby! Just because . . .

Burning Bulb

WOL-VRIEY
BIZARRO AND TRANSGRESSIVE FICTION

GIRLS ARE NOT SMILING

Welcome To The Road Trip From Hell

Pagan is demon-possessed.

Lori is suicidal.

Britt is just terminally pissed off.

Meet three young Boston women on the run from the law, each with problems that will fuse into more than the sum of their individual parts, becoming a holocaust of sex and violence and terror, a literal rain of blood and horror and gore and evil.

And if that wasn't already bad enough, Pagan's pet demon is slowly transforming her into something both unspeakable and unholy. Truly, these girls aren't smiling.

BLUE NIGHTMARES

Consummate EVIL is coming.   It is relentless and unavoidable. It is Blue.

Jessica Schreiber is seeing things. Very horrible things. Since arriving in Raynham for what should have been a relaxing vacation, she's been seeing *The Big Blue*.

Jessica is smelling things too—dead and rotting things that she can't see. She is sure those dead and rotting things are dead people. Lots of dead people.

Jessica's worst nightmares will soon become her reality. Her reality will soon become a terrifying nightmare.

The tentacled residents of the House of Death have a lot that they wish to show Jessica Schreiber. They have a lot that they wish to tell her. But will she survive long enough to learn their lessons?

Burning Bulb
PUBLISHING

WOL-VRIEY
BIZARRO AND TRANSGRESSIVE FICTION

BRAINCHEW

It was supposed to be a simple jewel heist, but it went badly wrong. Chuck got shot and died.

Lance hid his friend's corpse in the Pleasant Street Cemetery. But that was a big mistake—there was something undead, something extremely hungry . . . something eXXXtremely horrible, buried in the Pleasant Street Cemetery.

And Lance had just woken it up.

They called the monster Brainchew because it ate brains. Human brains. And it preferred those brains fresh from the heads . . . of the living.

And now it was awake again, Brainchew planned on feeding big-time tonight. Oh hell yes, it did.

BRAINCHEW 2: OUT OF THEIR HEADS

After Tiff Hooper recognizes Josh Penham, the man who abducted her and kept her in his basement and abused her, she brings her three friends to Raynham for a night of well-deserved revenge on him.

Only things don't go according to plan.

It is never a good idea to leave a corpse in Raynham's Pleasant Street Cemetery. You run the very real risk of awakening what lies underground there. And that thing—Brainchew—is more horrible and more evil than anything the average mind conceives of even in its worst nightmares.

Brainchew is back! And this time the monster is extra-hungry. But there are plenty of delicious human brains about tonight, and Brainchew intends to eat them all before dawn.

Burning Bulb
PUBLISHING

WOL-VRIEY
BIZARRO AND TRANSGRESSIVE FICTION

DARIA: AN EROTIC NIGHTMARE

Even the best laid women can go wrong.

Daria Simpson is HUNGRY. She's HUNGRY for sex and bloodshed and death.

Shelly Parker just wanted to have a threesome with her boyfriend Craig and her best friend Erica. Everything was shaping up nicely for their weekend of sexual fun and games, until they stopped at the creepy Crossway Diner and met Daria.

From the moment they met Daria, EVERYTHING went wrong for them; and it went wrong in the most horrific and terrifying of ways!

Daria: Paranormal service has been resumed.

WET BONES

Greg is about learning the hard way that you don't mess with Aunt Grace.

Nine completely fleshless skeletons recovered in the Massachusetts woods. Two detectives on the trail of a horrible, hungry monster.

Broken-hearted Allie Jackson has a date with a creature from Hell.

Things are about to get well out of hand for everyone, and in horrifying, terrifying ways they don't expect.

Burning Bulb
PUBLISHING

WOL-VRIEY
BIZARRO AND TRANSGRESSIVE FICTION

MR. UGLY

When a rotting corpse appears and starts butchering Raynham's youths, there's really only one question that needs answering:

Is this faceless and rotting monster Peter Howard, or isn't it?

Problem is, Peter Howard died 15 years ago. So how can he possibly be back from the dead and murdering people with such relentless and incredible brutality?

Peter's mother Malicia, who's just been released from the lunatic asylum may have the answers to the crazy puzzle, but the two detectives investigating the deaths don't even know the right questions to ask her yet.

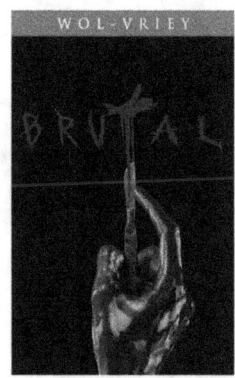

BRUTAL

Jane Winters is 28 years old.

She works as a checkout cashier in a department store. She's an attractive woman with a winning personality. She has both a photographic memory and an I.Q. of 189.

She's met the man of her dreams.

But she's also a cannibal with a unique and very scary mode of operation.

The group known as TULIP (The Urban Legend Investigation People) are out to either prove or disprove the legend of Insane Jane.

But have TULIP bitten off more than they can chew?

Burning Bulb
PUBLISHING

WOL-VRIEY
BIZARRO AND TRANSGRESSIVE FICTION

EVIL

The Evil began the week before Sylvia Stewart's 30th birthday.

Cathy Higgins died.

The Bargainer resurrected Cathy . . . for a price.

The price? Cathy's father Ronan had to plant some seeds for him.

But these were no ordinary seeds the Bargainer gave to Ronan Higgins. These were seeds from Hell: seeds which required human flesh as both soil and fertilizer.

And meanwhile, the unsuspecting Sylvia Stewart went ahead with the plans for her birthday party, which was to be held on Ronan Higgins' sunflower farm . . .

666

Ohio's State Route 666 stretches 14.7 miles between Zanesville and Dresden.

Most days, it's just a normal road with a funny name.

But for six minutes on the 6th of June each year, Route 666 becomes a gateway to somewhere else . . . a gateway to Hell.

Each year 13 unfortunates get trapped in the 666 underworld, with no way to get back home.

This year though, things are going to be very different. For one thing, there are currently a whole lot of turbulent human emotions at play in the underworld. And also . . . the psycho Al Gore is just about completing his collection of human heads.

And . . . what the hell is a church doing in Hell, of all places?

Burning Bulb

WOL-VRIEY
BIZARRO AND TRANSGRESSIVE FICTION

THE CLEAVERMAN

It began as a joke, a gag to pass the time that turned deadly. One rainy August night in Raynham, MA, nine friends jokingly invoke the evil phantom butcher called the Cleaverman.

These nine friends get a whole lot more than they ever bargained for. Because there's only one way to return the deadly Cleaverman back to the darkness he came from, and that is to solve his riddle, which starts: "Tell me the name of John Cleaverman's wife . . ."

And human beings being what we are, even with the Cleaverman out to butcher them all, our nine friends still manage to stir A WHOLE LOT of human misbehavior into the deadly mix.

At the rate they're going, it'll be a wonder if anyone survives THE CLEAVERMAN at all.

PERVERSE

When 21-year-old Heather Forrest accompanies three of her friends on a weekend trip up to Vermont, she has no idea what she's getting into.

Because, during a brief stop in the western Massachusetts woods, the girls get kidnapped and things go rapidly downhill from there. Soon Heather and her friends are fighting for their lives, fighting to survive the most perverted and impossible situation imaginable. And meanwhile, Hank Rollins is also in the woods, hunting the unholy monster that killed his wife and son . . . and he's hunting it with live human bait.

Oh yes, there will be blood. And there will be terror and buckets of gore also. And truly horrible atrocities will happen. Most definitely so.

Burning Bulb

WOL-VRIEY
BIZARRO AND TRANSGRESSIVE FICTION

THE VIRGIN

10 million dollars in prize money. 1000+ video cameras, lots of deadly weapons, 10 Suitors, 5 Virgins & 3 Hours . . . to keep your hymen intact.

Hailey Osborne wants to sell her virginity for a hundred thousand dollars. But then she's made an offer she really can't refuse: how about competing to win ten million dollars in a no-holds-barred underground game show, where all she has to do is remain a virgin?

There's just two problems:
1. Four other women also want that prize money.
2. There's ten suitors all contesting to take Hailey and the other virgins' precious hymens . . . by any means necessary . . .

But hey, it's just for 3 hours, right? How hard can it possibly be ? Hailey Osborne is about to find out.

THE BOOK OF ATROCITIES

Bestselling author Drake Melville has been missing for three years now. Drake vanished after publishing The Bleeding Oysters, an epic novel that set new standards for depictions of sleaze and depravity and human monstrosity in popular fiction. On vanishing, however, Drake Melville left a message for everyone, saying he'd 'left town' to go work on his follow-up novel The Book of Atrocities. The problem was, no one could find Drake. It seemed like he'd vanished off the face of the Earth. And now, three years later, Drake has just sent messages to his ex-wife Liz, his current (and abandoned) wife Melody; and his younger sister Chloe . . . asking them to meet him in Raynham, MA. Drake says he's now completed The Book of Atrocities and is ready to present it to the world. But there's a whole lot that Liz, Melody, and Chloe Melville don't know about Drake's Book of Atrocities. And unfortunately they're on their way to find out those excruciatingly painful truths. Because, see, Drake Melville is a VERY EVIL man with a VERY EVIL plan . . .

Burning Bulb
PUBLISHING

WOL-VRIEY
BIZARRO AND TRANSGRESSIVE FICTION

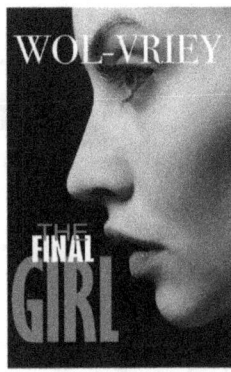

THE FINAL GIRL

Here there be monsters . . . because we made them.

At a secret location, 8 young women assemble to compete on the ultimate reality/game show—The Final Girl. The 8 contestants are: A young wife and her grown-up stepdaughter, a police detective, a prostitute, a nurse, a school teacher, and unemployed twin sisters.

The Final Girl is a no-holds-barred show beamed to an audience on the Dark Web, a show where murder is permitted and mutilation is encouraged.

The Rules:
1. Avoid being killed and eaten by the show's monsters and bogeymen.
2. Find the prize money—24 million dollars in cash.
3. Hold on to the money.

But only 1 woman can win. And to win The Final Girl reality show, that woman will need to be even more bloodthirsty and ruthless than the show's monsters.

Have a seat, everyone. The most dangerous game is about to begin!

WOMEN

John Miller must die . . . TONIGHT!

Megan Kemp initially went to the Penderson Mansion to collect a debt. But from the moment she stepped in there, getting back outside proved extremely difficult. And then what had merely been difficult for Megan suddenly turned deadly. Because something was going on in the Penderson Mansion that night. Five VERY ANGRY women had a score to settle, and no obstacle on earth would stop them. . . . And no one would get in their way and live to tell the tale either.

"John Miller must die," the women had decreed, and it looked like the forces of Hell would help them accomplish their deadly aim tonight.

But as the night progressed, Megan, who was now trapped in a deadly game of cat and mouse in the Penderson Mansion, found that despite her own troubles, her biggest question was: "What the hell did John Miller do to anger these five women this much?"

Beware, folks . . . sometimes things really do go too far!

Burning Bulb

WOL-VRIEY
BIZARRO AND TRANSGRESSIVE FICTION

RATIO OF BROOKES TO ASHLEYS

After being cursed by a dying woman, Mike Broadman's love life completely nosedives. One girlfriend cheats on him and the next one dies a very messy death.

Next, a psychic informs Mike that he's under an evil spell that will keep killing his girlfriends, and that the ONLY solution (the ONLY way that he'll ever have a happy love life again) is for him to only date women named either Brooke or Ashley from now on.

Mike tries to comply with this, but still, the deaths continue, and now they're becoming even more brutal and bloody. Mike now finds himself in a race against time. He needs to 'equalize the ratio of Brookes to Ashleys' before it's too late.

And then, just when it seems things can't get any crazier or deadlier for Mike, he meets 'Brash' — the twins Brooke and Ashley Lawrence . . .

And the body count keeps rising . . .

DELICIOUS ZOMBIE

The zombie apocalypse happened two years ago. Today, zombies are mankind's new cattle. The undead are headed like cows and killed and eaten by everyone. The reason for this atrocity? Eating zombie meat has been scientifically proven to reverse human aging. Therefore, anyone who eats the zombies will live forever. Nowadays there are no old people anywhere on Earth. Everyone is young and healthy. Even deadly diseases have regressed. "

Digestion is Salvation," the Church of Zombie preaches. But three people—scientist Ethan Hackman, ex CIA assassin Paula Neyman, and socialite Zoe Patterson—seek to change this madness that is modern life.

With a group of ruthless and sadistic bounty hunters hot on their trail as they attempt to save the world, will Ethan, Paula, and Zoe succeed in curing the zombies, or will the age of the 'Delicious Zombie' continue? One thing is for certain, however; there will be a HUGE amount of murder and mutilation, bloodshed, violence and gore before the knotty issue of the zombies' food status is resolved.

Burning Bulb
PUBLISHING

www.ingramcontent.com/pod-product-compliance
Lightning Source LLC
Chambersburg PA
CBHW070006260626
47159CB00005B/1685